Advance Praise for *Eve*

"At once tender and defiant, *Eve...* ...... sparkles with humour and warmth while probing the truths of the familial and cultural ties that define and confine us. Iryn Tushabe knowingly writes the turmoil of adolescence and the bond between siblings with wit and love. This is a big-hearted debut about the small graces we offer each other in the face of injustice."

—Janika Oza, author of *A History of Burning*

"Iryn Tushabe's debut novel, *Everything Is Fine Here*, is a bildungsroman set in contemporary Uganda, where Aine is confronted with harsh choices that will determine how she moves into adulthood. This is a gorgeous and tender portrayal of a young person for whom society offers freedom that is reliant on rules and ideas that are no longer enough. Aine seeks a world where her beloveds are possible, but she must decide between the familial, cultural, and religious mores of this beautiful country pulsating with memories of a rough history that resonate in the present."

—Otoniya J Okot Bitek, author of *We, the Kindling*

"I love this novel and the ardent young woman at its heart. Aine is a heroine for our times; a natural truth-teller with a volatile secret, she comes of age in a world shimmering with promise and pain. *What are you made of?* that world demands, and Aine rises to respond. As long as we have hearts and minds like hers—and her creator's—everything might be fine here after all."

—Alissa York, author of *Far Cry*

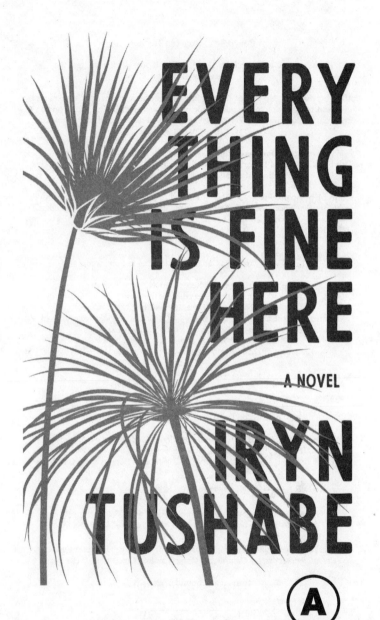

EVERY THING IS FINE HERE

A NOVEL

IRYN TUSHABE

ANANSI

Published in Canada and the USA in 2025 by House of Anansi Press Inc.
houseofanansi.com

House of Anansi Press is committed to protecting our natural environment. This book is made of material from well-managed FSC®-certified forests, recycled materials, and other controlled sources.

House of Anansi Press is a Global Certified Accessible™ (GCA by Benetech) publisher. The ebook version of this book meets stringent accessibility standards and is available to readers with print disabilities.

29 28 27 26 25   1 2 3 4 5

Library and Archives Canada Cataloguing in Publication

Title: Every thing is fine here : a novel / Iryn Tushabe.
Other titles: Everything is fine here
Names: Tushabe, Iryn, author.
Identifiers: Canadiana (print) 20240489799 | Canadiana (ebook) 20240501063 |
ISBN 9781487013134 (softcover) | ISBN 9781487013141 (EPUB)
Subjects: LCGFT: Bildungsromans. | LCGFT: Novels.
Classification: LCC PS8639.U815 E94 2025 | DDC C813/.6—dc23

Book design: Alysia Shewchuk
Cover image: zzayko / stock.adobe.com

The epigraph from *Unless* by Carol Shields on page vii is reprinted with permission from the Carol Shields Literary Trust.

House of Anansi Press is grateful for the privilege to work on and create from the Traditional Territory of many Nations, including the Anishinabeg, the Wendat, and the Haudenosaunee, as well as the Treaty Lands of the Mississaugas of the Credit.

 Canada Council Conseil des Arts
for the Arts du Canada

 ONTARIO ARTS COUNCIL
CONSEIL DES ARTS DE L'ONTARIO
an Ontario government agency
un organisme du gouvernement de l'Ontario

With the participation of the Government of Canada
Avec la participation du gouvernement du Canada | Canadä

We acknowledge for their financial support of our publishing program the Canada Council for the Arts, the Ontario Arts Council, and the Government of Canada.

Printed and bound in Canada

 MIX
Paper | Supporting
responsible forestry
FSC
www.fsc.org   FSC® C103567

To my darling sprogs, Precious and Jordan.
And to my mother, Anne, who died much too young.

"Unless you're lucky, unless you're healthy, fertile, unless you're loved and fed, unless you're clear about your sexual direction, unless you're offered what others are offered, you go down in the darkness, down to despair."
—Carol Shields, *Unless*

1

F ROM WHERE SHE SAT on the front steps of the administrative building, Aine had an unobstructed view of the wide path from the towering school gate with the white banner arching above it: "Welcome to #CareersDay at Pike Girls' Boarding School."

It had been nearly two hours since she began her stakeout. She had ignored the supper bell and now her stomach grumbled, tying a hungry knot. Each time she heard a boda boda driving alongside the wall of tall cypress trees that surrounded the campus, her pulse kicked—but so far, no one had come through the school gate.

Earlier in the school term when the headmistress, Madame Kyaligonza, had told Aine that her sister would give this year's Careers Day commencement speech, Aine had stared at her, unbelieving. "She's confirmed this, Madame?" she'd asked. She knew it wasn't the first time the headmistress had invited Mbabazi, a distinguished alumna, to Careers Day. But Mbabazi was a busy woman.

"The world shines wherever Dr. Kamara touches it," Madame said.

All Aine needed was a straight response, yes or no, but Madame frightened her. The woman always looked at her with an expression of anger, making her wonder if some other student had pissed off Madame and she mistook Aine for that student. Nonetheless, Aine gathered up all her courage for a confession. "Do you know, Madame, I haven't seen my sister in over two years."

Madame chuckled. "How do you think I managed to convince her this time?"

A joyful overture surged through Aine. "She's coming because of me!"

"And me!" Madame said in a too high voice that tickled Aine. "You're welcome to spend as much time with her as you like at my house. That was her only condition, and I was more than happy to grant it."

It was all Aine could do not to throw her arms around her headmistress, the woman whose nickname was "the Copper" on account of her perpetually sour police-woman-like demeanour. After Madame disappeared around the corner of the library, Aine squealed into her hands, tightly cupped over her mouth. Her sister was coming to see her.

Mbabazi had recently returned to Uganda from Canada after completing the Gynaecologic Reproductive Endocrinology and Infertility program at the University of Toronto. The nine-hour time difference had meant few phone calls and a ton of email. Mbabazi had sent photographs from her travels around Canada: Niagara Falls, Banff, the Badlands. But nothing had captivated Mbabazi more than the aurora borealis: curtains of light green and purple dancing over the horizon. "It goes on for hours, Kanyonyi," she had written, calling Aine by her nickname, "little bird." "The oceans have tides, and the northern skies have the aurora borealis. It's magic!"

As time passed, Aine started to perceive her sister as a guiding spirit narrating a foreign landscape enclosed in the colourful bubble of dreams. And then Mbabazi had the nerve to come back from Canada one week after Aine returned to school in Fort Portal for her second term in Senior Six.

Another boda boda zoomed by, its roar growing louder as it approached the school gate, fading as it sped past. As far as Aine knew, her sister had no car; she hated driving. She'd probably travel the five hours from Kampala by bus or commuter taxi. In downtown Fort Portal, she'd hop on a boda boda or hire a taxi to bring her the three kilometres up to Pike Girls.

The sun dipped below the horizon. The cypress trees among the tall hedge started to look more blue than green, darkness gathering in their boughs. *Soon*, she told herself. *Mbabazi will be here soon.*

Aine tried to get her head back into the novel that lay open in her lap, which she was rereading now that her A-level mock exams were less than two months away. *No Longer at Ease* was Chinua Achebe at his finest. In the fading light of evening, she read about Obi Okonkwo kissing Clara for the first time on the deck of the ship, MV *Sasa*: "Their eyes met for a second, and without another word Obi took her in his arms. She was trembling as he kissed her over and over again. 'Leave me,' she whispered. 'I love you.'"

So dramatic!

A car horn beeped. Aine looked up to see Vipsa, the askari, exiting his gatekeeper's office not much bigger than a telephone booth. Of course Mbabazi had opted for a special hire taxi. More than two years' worth of anticipation tightened Aine's chest; she could hardly bear the flood of emotions. She felt her heart pushing against the walls of her chest.

A medium-sized vehicle the colour of chocolate rolled through the gate and stopped, the out-of-view driver talking to the askari. Weren't special hire taxis usually smaller? But consider Papa's Landcruiser. A luxury suv, yet he drove tourists in it for a living.

Aine put Chinua Achebe in the kangaroo pouch of her jumper as the vehicle curved along the elbow bend in the gravel path, kicking up dust. She stood on jittery legs.

The passenger window slid down, revealing her big sister's face. "Kanyonyi!" Mbabazi shouted, giving Aine wings, the sensation that she could leap up and fly.

"Mbabazi!" Aine matched her sister's high note of excitement. She bounded to where the car was pulling up. Mbabazi slammed the passenger door and ran to meet her, her hands waving above her head as if she were rearranging the clouds. Aine threw her arms around her sister's narrow waist and squeezed. She breathed her in, resting for a while in her embrace.

Now Mbabazi tilted Aine's chin, her thumbs tracing across Aine's cheeks to her ears as though she were reminding herself of how the parts of her face fit together. "How's it possible you haven't changed at all?" she asked in Rukiga, the language of their birth.

"How is it possible you have changed so much?" Aine spoke Rukiga, too, though English was mandatory on campus. Mbabazi had trimmed her hair and permed what remained into short wet-looking curls tinted burnt yellow, like the sun rising. It had made her already fair skin look even lighter.

"Have I?" Mbabazi said doubtfully, raising her right hand to the back of her neck.

"It suits you, this look," Aine said. "The short hair. I'm not sure about the relaxer, though. The smell of cooked hair." Weren't there any salons for Black people in Toronto? People who knew how to install braids?

Mbabazi patted the air dismissively. "You get used to it."

Aine grinned. All that mattered was that her sister was here. Her sister who'd inherited every bit of Mama's Tutsi loveliness, so that by the time Aine came along more than a decade later, all that remained were Papa's indelicate Bakiga features—a large nose and skin darker than the richest loam.

"You did these yourself?" Mbabazi was running her hands over the bumps of Aine's chunky cornrows.

5

"Zai," Aine said. "My bunk mate."

"Speaking of friends." Mbabazi gestured toward the driver, who had just closed the car door and was crossing toward them on the paspalum lawn. She had the shape of a mother: big bones and soft curves. Widely spaced fawnlike eyes, a smooth complexion of the blackest black. "This is my roommate, Achen."

A name from the north, possibly Acholi. Achen flashed a brilliant smile, teeth like the sun on white paper. "Delighted to finally meet you, Aine," she said, pumping Aine's hand. "M talks about you all the time."

"She does?" Then why was this the first time Aine was hearing of this roommate who spoke English with an accent too BBC to be genuine?

"All the time," Achen confirmed.

"I'm sorry," Aine said, "but I can't say the same."

Achen massaged her massive afro: chunky tufts dyed a cola colour, black with a bit of red trapped inside. She cast a sideways glance at Mbabazi, who fixed Aine with a look.

"I could've sworn I told you about her," Mbabazi said.

"Achen?" It was not a name Aine would have forgotten easily. It conjured a very specific image and smell—the mineral scent of charcoal just doused with water. Aine stared back at her sister, shook her head. "Uh-uh."

Aine knew she'd somehow let her sister down. Mbabazi scrunched up her face, as if caught in a lie. She turned to her roommate. "I'm sorry."

Achen smiled. "It's all right, love. You know it's fine."

"I meant to," Mbabazi said. "I should've."

Achen squeezed Mbabazi's shoulder. "I promise. It's nothing. Sure, you know that."

And now Aine knew too. She understood the thing that was announcing itself to her: the strange electricity between Mbabazi and Achen. They were looking at each other in that way lovers had, communicating in a language they thought impenetrable, as if they were the ones who'd invented it. Aine suppressed a gasp. What to do with this knowledge?

"We shouldn't keep Madame waiting," Mbabazi said. "The askari called up to the house when we came in."

Fear shot up Aine's spine at the mention of Madame. Not too long ago, it was announced at an impromptu general assembly that two Senior Five girls had been discovered snogging in the bathroom they were meant to be mopping and would be expelled.

"Lesbianism offends God," Madame had said, before quoting from Scripture: "Nothing is covered up that will not be revealed, or hidden that will not be known."

"You're both staying here?" Aine heard herself ask. It had taken her all of one minute to see through their roommate ruse; how long before the Copper sniffed out the truth? "At Madame's, all weekend long?"

A hint of disappointment came over Achen's face. "Would you rather I didn't?"

Aine opened her mouth to respond, but Mbabazi shot her a threatening look, a hard glint in her eyes that said *Stop it right now.* Turning to Achen, she asked if she wouldn't mind going on ahead and parking the car. She

7

indicated the space, in the distance, between Madame's residence and the sick bay. "Little sis and I will catch up."

Achen strode purposefully to the vehicle. When the engine roared and the car lurched forward, Aine turned to her sister. "Have you forgotten this place? What it's like?"

Mbabazi reverted to her usual evasive self. She stepped into the gravel road, sudden awe widening her eyes. "Everything is just as I remember it." Her gaze swept over the sick bay to the main hall with its graffitied walls, and lingered on the laboratory block beyond the netball court to its right. Girls hung out on the rows of concrete steps that seemed to hold the brick building upright. "Except shorter somehow, you know?"

Aine exhaled, exasperated. "I mean, buildings don't shrink."

"You know those big bulldozer tractors that flatten · roads?" Mbabazi said. "It's like one of them sat on the lab and sunk it into the ground a little."

Aine chuckled. "How long exactly since you went here?"

"Fourteen—no, fifteen years. Goodness me. Has it really been that long? Am I that old?" She drew a deep breath, started walking up the road lined with flowerbeds.

Aine interlaced her fingers between her sister's. "Speaking of years," she said, tugging at Mbabazi's hand to slow her long-legged stride, "how long have you had the roommate?"

"Going on six years."

"Six?" Aine squeaked. Sadness rushed at her so real she felt it course through her stomach to her fingers. She always told Mbabazi everything. How hard could it be for her sister to reciprocate for once? To say, *Oh, by the way, Kanyonyi, your big sister has found love!* But Aine wouldn't pry. Well, most likely she would, but wouldn't she be within her rights? Mbabazi was her one and only sister.

In the near distance, Achen opened the boot of the car and heaved an oversized rucksack onto her back. Looking at her, Aine realized Mbabazi had brought Achen to a place where only Aine—not Mama or Papa—could meet her. This was an introduction. Mbabazi was finally opening the door into her very private life and saying to Aine, *Come on in if you want.*

That made Aine smile. "I love it," she said. "That you have a roommate. It's brilliant."

Mbabazi halted. "Really?"

Her eager response took Aine aback; Mbabazi had never needed Aine's approval before. "Would you care if I didn't?" She chuckled. "Too bad she's just a roommate and nothing more, right?"

Mbabazi shrugged. "That's what I said."

Aine kicked at a miniature wall of rocks that encircled a flowerbed. The marigolds shuddered, wagging their little orange tongues. Given the choice, Mbabazi would rather walk barefooted over burning embers than be straight with her. "Just..." she said. "We'll have to be careful around Madame, won't we?"

Mbabazi slung her arm around Aine's shoulder and pulled her in. "Is it fun worrying all the time?" she said. "You are going to have wrinkles before I do."

9

2

CREEPERS AND IVY CLUNG to the facade of Madame's house like a second wall. The dense foliage was masterfully coiffed to frame the windows and door, which opened as soon as Mbabazi knocked, as if someone had been standing behind it, waiting.

"I'm very happy to see you, Doctor," sang Madame's housemaid.

"Birungi?" Mbabazi looked uncertainly at the much shorter woman. "All these years and you're still as young as I remember you."

Mbabazi had spent her final Senior Six break at Madame's. Feeling insufficiently prepared for her A-level finals, she had requested to stay at school, where she could maintain her strict study routine, the library and laboratory well within reach. But rather than have her stay alone in the dormitory, Madame had welcomed Mbabazi into her home, sparking their years-long friendship.

"Eh!" Birungi exclaimed. "But Doctor! Me, I would pass you on the road and not know that it is you I am seeing."

"I would recognize you anywhere," Mbabazi replied.

But of course she would, Aine thought. Birungi was one of only a handful of albinos Aine had ever seen. Her complexion tended toward yellow, with red blotches along her eyelids as though they were prone to spontaneous bleeding.

"You are more beautiful now than when you were a teenager," Birungi continued her spirited compliments. "How can it be?"

"You're sweet to say that." Mbabazi went ahead into the foyer to make room. "This is my friend Achen."

"Welcome, Doctor," Birungi said.

"Just Achen," she corrected, pumping Birungi's proffered hand. "I'm not a doctor."

"It's a pleasure to meet you, just Achen."

"And you must know my little sister, Aine," Mbabazi said.

"I didn't know you were the sister of Doctor," Birungi said, looking at Aine. "You do not resemble at all."

Aine gave a nervous smile. This was a comment she was accustomed to hearing, but not one she appreciated; it felt much like being told she was far less beautiful. Was it possible to love someone so fully but also be jealous of the grace with which they carried themselves, the very structure of their bones?

"Oh, but I disagree," Achen said. "You've got the same forehead and eyes. A near identical laugh."

11

"Huh," Aine said. "What a keen observation." This roommate was quickly growing on her. Aine crouched to unlace her sneakers and placed them next to the others on the woven mat that said, in colourful calligraphy, "As for me and my house, we will serve the Lord—Joshua 24:15."

"Please come and sit." Birungi lifted the edge of her blue shawl and flung it around her shoulder as she led them into the sitting room. The black-and-white linoleum floor glistened cleanly. Aine stuck to the black squares in case her sweaty socks stained the white. She looked, mesmerized, at the artworks mounted on the walls like so many extra windows.

"Make yourselves at home." Birungi indicated the sofas with blue velvet cushions. "I shall tell Madame that you have come."

Aine was drawn to the paintings. A landscape with a fiery sun dipping behind some disharmonious mountain ranges; a market scene so vivid she could almost smell the oranges and pineapples, almost hear the din of people haggling; a river rushing over a boulder, the thin curtain of water cut off by the painting's wooden frame.

"Impressive, isn't it?" Achen's distinctive voice spun Aine around. Achen was standing a hair behind her, examining the same glossy oil painting. "Just beautiful."

Aine considered the word *beautiful*, an adjective people were quick to throw around when they couldn't be bothered to actually define the object in front of them.

"Classic chiaroscuro," Achen added, stepping forward so that they now stood side by side.

"I'm unfamiliar with the um…" Aine didn't want to risk butchering the word.

"It's a technique," Achen explained. "Leonardo da Vinci, Caravaggio, Rembrandt. They all used it."

Aine recognized two of those names. "What distinguishes it? This technique."

"Notice how almost unnaturally bright the water is here." Achen pointed to the pearlescent centre of the painting where the spilling water looked luminous. "It lights the whole scene. Shadows in the margins here and here. It creates the illusion of three dimensions on a flat canvas."

Aine saw the trick now, how the contrasting light and shadows directed her gaze, showing her where to look. "And that's chiaro…?"

"… scuro, yes!" Achen smiled. Clearly a person who liked to teach or otherwise share the things she knew. "Brilliant, isn't it?"

Achen's way of talking, the way her words seemed to form loving liaisons with each other, elevated everything she said.

"Yeah," Aine said. "Just beautiful."

Madame breezed into the living room, trailing a luxurious current of Imperial Leather soap. "Walalalala!" She ululated a high pitch, her tongue wagging in her mouth. "My long-lost daughter has finally returned," she sang. "Glory to the most high God. I have dreamed of this day for many years."

Mbabazi stood up and threw herself into Madame's ample bosom. After a long embrace the older woman stepped back. "Let's have a good look at you." She cupped Mbabazi's face as if measuring its weight. "Is it really you?"

"It is I, Mama K."

"But you are too slim, Doctor. The wind can pick you up and toss you around. They were not feeding you well in Canada?"

Mbabazi tightened her arms around Madame's waist and lifted her off the ground. "Slim does not mean weak, Mama K."

"Put me down." Madame laughed, making Aine and Achen explode with laughter as well.

Aine had never seen this side of Madame before, hadn't even thought her capable of such open-hearted laughing. Her short-cropped hair was sprinkled all over with grey, but happiness transformed her into a young woman. Finally freeing herself of Mbabazi, she turned to Achen.

"You must be the journalist," she said.

"Podcaster, actually." Achen swiftly crossed to shake Madame's hand. "A storyteller."

"Podcaster?" Madame repeated the word as if trying to make sense of it. She lowered herself into the loveseat, a quizzical expression on her face. "This is on television?"

"It's like a radio documentary delivered via the internet," explained Mbabazi, sitting back down on the two-seater sofa across from Madame. "She's very modest about her work, but Achen's stories have won international broadcast awards three years in a row."

Madame leaned forward in her seat. "You must tell me more about your work."

Under the glass-topped coffee table between them, the zebra hide's ears pricked as if it, too, were curious about radio documentaries delivered via the internet.

"The stories I'm most drawn to are ones that knock me sideways and wound me a little," Achen said, tugging at her copper-coloured slacks before sitting down to share Mbabazi's loveseat. Aine's heart hammered in her throat. There was plenty of space on her three-seater sofa; why was Achen practically sitting on Mbabazi's leg? Aine scrutinized Madame for anything like suspicion, but the headmistress was focused only on Achen's face as she described the nature of the stories she told. Stories, she said, about ordinary people navigating their ordinary lives.

"And it's come a long way, the podcast," she continued. "I wrestled with it in the beginning, forcing every episode into a three-act structure. But as time has gone by, nearly five years now, I'm the one who's been shaped by the podcast. It's moulded me into something of a vessel. A receptacle, if you will, for other people's stories."

Aine sensed a disquieting air about Achen, something portentous yet inexplicably endearing.

"These stories," Madame said, "they are political?"

"Not always," Achen replied, crossing her legs, a habit Madame wasn't terribly fond of. She liked to pinch the earlobes of any student who sat this way, which she considered unbecoming of a woman.

"But if they are personal stories, then surely they are political." Aine flexed her knowledge. She'd seen the slogan not too long ago in a photograph in the *Daily Monitor*. It was written on a placard someone was waving outside a gay-friendly bar as police raided it to arrest the men and women participating in a beauty pageant as part of a Pride event.

"Quite right," Achen said. "I think it was John Berger who said, 'Far from dragging politics into art, art has dragged me into politics.'"

"Indeed, indeed," Madame said.

Aine regretted that she'd never heard of John Berger. That knowledge might have saved her from nodding her head wordlessly, a version of Madame's "Indeed, indeed."

Birungi swooped into the sitting room, balancing a pitcher of juice and some glasses on a tray. Aine hastened to assist her, pushing the vase of pink carnations from the centre of the table to make room. Her mouth watered as Birungi poured the juice into drinking glasses embossed with a pineapple pattern. A steady boarding school diet— maize porridge for breakfast, posho and beans for lunch and supper—caused her to miss the simplest of home-made delights. Aine took a generous gulp of the chilled juice and grimaced. Much too sweet, it sent her heart into palpitations. She forced herself to drink some more and then sucked her teeth; the sweetness seemed to coat them with a layer of fuzz.

"You must be so hungry." Madame slapped her thighs and rose from her chair. "The journey from Kampala is a very long one."

"I'll help set the table," Mbabazi offered, following

Madame and Birungi through the arched entrance into the dining room.

Aine and Achen sat in awkward silence.

"Seems about ready to leap off the plinth and join the living," Achen finally said. She rose and crossed to a wooden carving of a dog in a far corner of the cavernous room. The puppy's eyes were beady, a pink tongue hanging limply outside its mouth.

"Check this out." Aine indicated a more interesting artwork, a medium-sized portrait to Achen's left.

"Do you think it's Madame?" Achen said. "The resemblance!"

It did look like a much younger Madame smiling at something beyond the frame, an orange kikoy wrapped many times around her head, a clay pot balanced on top. Intense colours dominated the work: fiery reds and vivid oranges. The absence of black seemed almost intentional.

"Her late husband taught fine art," Aine said, wondering if all the paintings and sculptures that filled this room were the work of the late Mr. Kyaligonza. "I never met him, but Mbabazi probably did. He died before I started going to school here."

"How terrible for Mrs. K."

Over the clanking of cutlery in the dining room, Aine could hear Mbabazi blowing Madame's mind with talk of Canada's free health care, how everyone, rich or poor, got to see a doctor free of charge.

"The ghost of Mr. Kyaligonza haunts Freedom Square,"

Aine said in a low, ominous voice. "At night he hangs out in Freedom Tree, this hundred-year-old banyan in the square where we do morning assembly."

Achen arched her brow. "You lie."

"No." Aine reeled her in. "These lumberjack guys were contracted to trim off the weaker branches. The ones that had grown dangerously heavy. Well, Mr. Kyaligonza's kapongi chased them away."

"How?"

"It threatened them through a bird." Aine embellished the old kapongi story that cruel sophomores still used to frighten new students. "A great blue turaco. It told them that if they so much as laid a finger on its home, they'd be dead before sunset. The men ditched their axes and ran."

"Sure," Achen said. She was hard to read, with those big eyes.

"It's true." Aine maintained her air of seriousness. "If you find yourself near Freedom Tree at night you must pass it looking down. Or with your eyes closed. If you lock eyes with the kapongi, you're finished, my friend. It snatches your soul and turns you into one of its night dancers."

"Night dancers?"

"You know, you go to bed, and you think the bad dreams you're having are just that. Nightmares. But they aren't, and you're not asleep. You're out there, in the black night, doing ritual dances to appease the gods of long ago."

"Okay, be honest," Achen said. "How long before you realized that whoever told you this tale was teasing?"

"Too long." Embarrassing to admit it, but Aine's entire first term at Pike was one long nightmare. Even now whenever she passed through Freedom Square, she sometimes caught herself casting her gaze downward. Terrible dreams had plagued her. Dreams in which she was running away from rapidly spreading finger-like roots that, when they caught up to her, twisted and gnarled like ropes around her body, squeezing the living daylights out of her.

Achen was listening, her face the very picture of sympathy. "That must have been horrific."

Aine shrugged. "That's boarding school."

When Achen smiled, half-circles like quotation marks appeared at the corners of her mouth.

IN THE DINING ROOM, steam rose from the generous spread of food and curled toward the chandelier, whose dangling crystals looked like dewdrops frozen mid-trickle. Aine pulled up a chair. Fried rice, beef curry, a basket of kalo, matooke, groundnut sauce, steamed vegetables. It was a feast. Her mouth watered.

"Let us pray," Madame said once they were all seated.

They closed their eyes and bowed their heads. Madame's blessing for the food stretched on and on. She prayed in that spirited Pentecostal way that had recently taken over the school. When Aine started here, Pike Girls was still relatively Protestant. But with every Scripture Union conference, Pentecostalism took hold. Evangelists came who called themselves apostles or prophets, who wore shiny shoes and brightly coloured suits, who spoke English with an African American accent, who, when they prayed in tongues, caused swaths of born-again students to fall to the ground writhing and kicking as if in a collective fit of epilepsy. This, supposedly, was how the spirit of God moved. Aine had written about it in an essay that she sent to the *Daily Monitor*. After, to her surprise, the national newspaper published it, she got into so much trouble she regretted having written it at all.

"And we thank you, dear Lord, for your journey mercies," the headmistress continued. "You took my daughter to Canada, and you brought her back safely. You have covered her with the precious blood of your son Jesus Christ. You have called her to your purpose, Father Lord. Through her, you're breaking the curse of infertility so that the barren can bear fruit…"

Why was she giving so much credit to God for the miracles of medical science? Aine worried the food would get cold before she was allowed to touch it. She opened her eyes a smidge and peered at Madame. She reminded her of Mama, who was similarly given to illustrious praying. On the night Mbabazi announced she'd received a grant from an international women's organization to study in Canada, Mama had erupted in confusing anger. "You're already a gynaecologist," she complained. "You want more certificates and diplomas for what?"

Mama had a wrong notion about doctors: that they, especially the older ones, could treat just about every ailment. She didn't understand Mbabazi's obsession with specializing when she could gain expertise through cumulative practice and experience. And although she'd never said it outright, Mama believed Mbabazi's insatiable career ambitions were partly to blame for her not bringing a suitor home.

That night, Mbabazi had seemed on the verge of tears. Mama's reaction had caught her off guard. She had expected that becoming an expert in infertility would please Mama, who had suffered many painful miscarriages before finally—and miraculously, according to her—carrying a second child, Aine, to term.

"I thought you'd be proud," Mbabazi had said, disappointment making her voice childlike.

"Proud that my daughter keeps running away overseas?" Mama hadn't been enthusiastic either when, not long before that, Mbabazi had taken a placement at a hospital in India. "This is faraway Canada we're talking about. It is where the world ends."

Papa, who always stayed out of Mama and Mbabazi's squabbles, intervened this time. "When she comes back, she will be a top doctor in her field. We want this for her, don't we?"

"*If* she comes back, you mean?" Mama had started to clear the dining table, though everyone was still eating. That night she rolled up her mat and went to stay overnight in the church. Aine pictured her asking God to bend fate, pleading with him to turn her kuchu daughter straight and find her a husband.

"In your name alone we pray," Madame finally said.

"Amen."

Aine thumbed a hole in a lump of kalo, the millet patty soft and brown, and used it to scoop up savoury curried stew. Sucking it into her mouth, she licked her fingers for every last remnant of flavour. She was determined not to let Mbabazi's detailed explanation of in vitro fertilization spoil her appetite.

"So, the egg is fully fertilized when you put it back in?" The very notion seemed so impossible to Madame she'd barely touched her food. "It's already an embryo?"

"Hmm-hmm." Mbabazi nodded, touched a white serviette to her lips. "Just yesterday I was performing an embryo transfer. A delicate procedure. But this client of mine. Funny, funny woman. I'm talking her through the process, right? I pick up the catheter and I'm ready to introduce it into her cervix and she says to me—" Mbabazi burst into fits of laughter. "She says, 'Naye, Doctor, take a girl out for supper first.'"

Achen guffawed at the joke, but Aine restrained herself when she noticed that Madame was nowhere near laughing. Was Mbabazi pushing this idea of hiding in plain sight too far?

"Anyway, you had to be there," Mbabazi said.

"No, no, I understand very well the funny woman's joke," Madame said, her face unflinching. "She wants you to court her before making her pregnant. What I can't wrap my head around is how you can inject this embryo into her womb. Is it not like jelly?"

Mbabazi explained about special catheters, thin and soft. The state-of-the-art ultrasound equipment her team had on hand for when complications arose. "Most times the transfer is quick and atraumatic. But there's the odd time when it can be difficult. When there's blood. That can muddy things up very quickly."

Aine tried to tune them out. Phrases such as *endocervical canal* and *mucous plugging* made her gag. As soon as the talk of reproduction reached a natural resting place, she quickly turned to Achen. "So, what about you?" she said. "What are the specific challenges of telling stories for a living?"

"Oh gosh," Achen said, "where to start?"

"Did you also go to university abroad?" Madame asked.

"In England, yes," she said. "At Oxford University."

Aine almost choked on her water. "Okot p'Bitek went to Oxford."

"Kanyonyi has a pedestal in her heart for p'Bitek," Mbabazi said.

"I picked up on that," Achen said, "from your essay in the *Daily Monitor*. You referenced *African Religions in Western Scholarship*. I've been looking for a copy ever since, but I can't seem to find one in any bookshop here. Surprisingly, a friend found one in London, but she's yet to mail it."

"I'd be happy to lend you mine," Aine said, glad to deflect from the subject of her essay, which had since its publication inspired bitter backlash both at school and from commenters online. "It's all marked-up, though, and heavily underlined. My grandfather was a serious annotator. It's like reading p'Bitek and my grandfather in dialogue."

"So that's who gave you your writing brain?" Achen said. "Your grandfather."

"He was a primary school English teacher," Aine said. "But when he was a little boy, back when Uganda was still a British protectorate, he worked for a white missionary doctor who treated lepers on an island in Kabale. That doctor taught him English. Taught him how to read. Bequeathed him a bunch of books."

"He would have been impressed by you, no doubt," Achen said. "Certainly, I am."

"Well, thank you, Achen," Aine said.

"When Aine was a kid," Mbabazi said, "actually not that long ago, she'd write these poems and stories and give performances in front of our mum's shop in the trading centre. Tourists gave her money. Lots of it. I took loans from her."

"That you never paid back," Aine said.

"Yes, I did," Mbabazi said.

"That's truly adorable," Achen said.

"I also recited psalms," Aine said, hoping to draw Madame back into the conversation. "My main act was Psalm 23."

"'The Lord is my shepherd, I shall not want,'" Madame said, quoting the first verse. "It's one of my favourite psalms."

"Mine too." Psalm 23 described God as a good

shepherd caring for his sheep. Back when Aine still believed in God's munificence, she'd found the psalm so comforting she sometimes recited it in lieu of prayer. She couldn't remember exactly when, but at some point, she'd stopped believing, like a child suddenly outgrowing a fairy tale.

The conversation reverted to Achen's education, Madame wondering how she'd ended up at Oxford.

"Kind benefactors," Achen said. "An old couple. They paid for everything. My undergrad and postgrad."

"My goodness," Madame said. "Angels really do walk among us."

Achen said her benefactor found her through the Watoto Children's Choir. "Have you heard of them?"

Madame's face lit up. "I have all their CDs and DVDs. Oh, those orphans are just adorable. So full of talent and energy."

"I was one of them," Achen said. "For five years we toured the world. Europe and America. Australia."

"And that's how you met your sponsors?"

"I've never met them, actually," Achen said. "They wanted to remain anonymous, and I've respected their wishes. I've wondered sometimes if they know who I am. If they've been disappointed with the path I chose."

"What are you talking about?" Mbabazi said.

"Well, such people," Achen said. "Perhaps they hope you'll read law or medicine. Discover the cure for cancer. But me, when I got to Oxford I saw books—the Bodleian Library is the second largest in the whole country. Every title you can think of. I looked at those novels and thought, 'Whatever degree program allows me to read them all, that's the one I shall take.'"

"Is there such a degree?" Aine wondered.

"A master's in world literatures in English," Mbabazi responded proudly on Achen's behalf.

"Impressive," Aine said.

Achen laughed. "Yeah, not too many people are impressed by it."

The sound of a bell eclipsed the air, calling students to mandatory prep time: two hours of pre-bedtime study. Aine looked up at the clock on the wall behind Madame. It was past eight o'clock already. If she wasn't sitting at her classroom desk or in the library reading room by a quarter past, she'd miss roll call and be marked absent, setting herself up for menial labour—an afternoon slashing overgrown paspalum with a scythe or mopping the mess hall after supper. She pushed her chair back and rose, rubbing her belly in gratitude. "Thank you for the delicious meal, Madame."

"You can thank Birungi." Madame gestured toward the maid, who'd suddenly appeared in the doorway. "She's the one who cooked."

"Thank you, Birungi," Aine said.

"You're very welcome," the maid replied. "You will take your breakfast with us in the morning?"

Aine hesitated; she didn't want to overstay her welcome.

"Breakfast is at eight," Madame said. "Unless you prefer maize porridge to Birungi's katogo."

"I will be here at eight, prompt," Aine said and thanked Madame once more.

"Let me walk you out," Mbabazi said.

"Goodnight, kidio," Achen said.

Aine chuckled. She was hardly a kid. "Goodnight, Achen."

As Aine and Mbabazi left Madame's house, the fluorescent tube above the door cast bluish light over the front steps and part of the lawn. On the wide path beyond, gaggles of students flocked noisily toward the classrooms.

"I forgot how cold it gets in Fort Portal," Mbabazi said, hugging herself against the chill.

"I really, really like her," Aine said. "Your lover."

Mbabazi shushed loudly, pulling Aine into the scant shadow cast by the plumeria tree on the front lawn. Even the wind restrained itself; the leaves whispered only. "Who even calls people *lover* anymore?"

"Okay," Aine said quietly. "Roommate. Whatever."

"Partner."

"In what line of business?"

Mbabazi placed her hands on Aine's shoulders as if knighting her. "The business of life, I suppose."

"Oh, is that like a kuchu thing?"

"Oh my god, Aine, you're exhausting." Mbabazi smiled.

Aine tried to separate her sister from the shadows, the bluish light blanching one side of her face. "You must be madly in love with each other."

"She's got this brain, Kanyonyi. It fires on all cylinders. It's ... She's so beautiful."

Aine's eyes filled. She threw her arms around her sister. "I'm so happy for you."

"I had an inkling you might be."

"Then why not tell me sooner?"

"And saddle you with this big secret?"

"I'm good at keeping secrets."

"Good," Mbabazi said. "Because our lives depend on it."

Aine had never felt as close to her sister as she did now. She wondered if Mbabazi felt it, too, this strong connection, hummingly alive. She tightened her arms around her. Stars pulsed in the impenetrable heavens.

3

AINE STARED BLANKLY AT the geography textbook laid open on her desk. As a child, her love for Mbabazi had bordered on obsession. Her entire identity was wrapped up in being Mbabazi's little sister. Because Mbabazi was never around much, when she did come home, Aine wanted to spend every second with her. She faked all manner of illnesses to skip school. At night she crawled into Mbabazi's bed instead of her own. Mbabazi was always listening to music. She'd stick one earbud into Aine's ear, and they'd listen together to Kate Bush running up that road, running up that hill.

Mbabazi was the first to tell Aine the story of her birth. On a rainy Saturday afternoon Mama had gone into labour a full month before her due date. At Virika Hospital, the doctors performed an emergency caesarean section while Papa, clutching Mbabazi's hand, paced restlessly.

"I couldn't believe how teeny you were under that heat lamp," Mbabazi said. "And you were covered in all this fuzzy hair. *Lanugo* is the medical term for it. You looked like a little hatchling."

"That's why you call me Kanyonyi."

"My little bird."

Then there was the matter of their names. Mama claimed that Aine's full name, Ainembabazi—the merciful one—was a tribute to God for his grace in granting Mama her heart's desire to have a second child. But in Mbabazi's version of the story, Aine was named for her. Aine meant *to have*, so in a way her name was *tohave*-Mbabazi. "Because you'll always have me," Mbabazi said. And Aine never doubted it for one second.

She remembered how whenever Mbabazi was home, she always hung behind after church to have private conversations with Reverend Erasmus. *The Sessions*. That's what they had all grown to call them. Aine loathed the Sessions. Loathed that Mbabazi always came back from them grumpy, reclusive. When Aine asked what Mbabazi and the reverend talked about, she said to mind her own business. Sometimes Mbabazi lay on her bed and faced the wall. She was so good at curling into a ball like an arthropod protecting its soft underparts. Mama wasn't forthcoming on the subject either. And Papa called himself a holiday Christian, which was to say he attended church on Christmas and Easter. He was the most clueless about it all.

One day when Aine was almost thirteen, Mbabazi refused to go to the vestry after Sunday service. She'd arrived home unannounced just the evening before. When church concluded, she shoved her travel-sized KJV Bible into her purse and walked home with Aine and Mama; in fact, she walked a step ahead, the breeze blowing her floral dress about her ankles.

"You're completely healed now?" Mama called to her. "Everything is fine?"

"Maybe I don't want to live my whole life suffering over something that can't be changed." Mbabazi walked faster in her chunky high heels as if to discourage any more questions.

But as soon as they got home, Mama called Mbabazi into her bedroom. Papa had fetched a group of German mountaineers from the airport and was taking them to Rwenzori. Aine tiptoed to the closed door and pressed her ear to it.

Their voices rose over each other, but Mbabazi was loudest. "Say you're sorry that I've been trying all my life to change who I am. Say I don't have to do it anymore. Say I'm not a mistake."

Aine could never forget how Mbabazi stormed out, her face glistening with tears. "You've only ever cared what other people think, but what about me? What about my happiness?"

Mbabazi packed her duffel bag, carelessly tossing her clothes and shoes inside and zipping it only halfway, a hairbrush sticking out.

Aine thought she'd never see her sister again. She ran after her, crying and begging her to stay, but Mbabazi broke into a sprint and didn't look back.

The following day, Aine and her classmate Isaac were representing Bigodi Primary School at the regional debating competition in Kamwenge. Her heart did a pirouette inside her chest when she stepped up to the podium and saw Mbabazi standing tall at the back of the Catholic social hall where the debate was taking place. She waved at her, and Mbabazi waved back. Aine's body buzzed as though filled with bees. Throughout the debate she kept looking at Mbabazi to make sure she was still there.

As soon as the debate finished she ran to find her. For someone who had stormed from home in tears the evening before, Mbabazi was in surprisingly high spirits. She swept Aine off her feet and swirled her around and round. "What kind of twelve-year-old throws around words like *zeitgeist*?"

Aine was dizzy and giddy with excitement. In the warmth of her sister's praise, she felt taller, smarter.

They crossed the road and went to sit on the front steps of the Catholic church, Mbabazi pretending to be a journalist interviewing Aine about her victory. "Ms. Kamara, where will you display this fine medal?" she asked of Aine's crested crane carved out of wood.

"The school will keep it, I'm sure," Aine spoke into Mbabazi's fist-microphone.

"Ms. Kamara," Mbabazi said, "in the current zeitgeist, what are your thoughts on your sister being gay?"

"Gay?" What sort of question was that? "What, like, happy?" Who in their right mind was opposed to joy?

"Being gay is definitely cool in the current zeitgeist."

At first, Mbabazi just looked confused. Then she was laughing her heart out. "This moment," she said. "I'll never forget it."

"Did I say something wrong?" Aine said.

"You're my hero," Mbabazi said. "My little innocent hero. Let's go find Isaac. I'm going to buy you two all the ice cream you can eat."

"Will you come home for Christmas?"

"I could never stay away from you, Kanyonyi," Mbabazi said, suddenly tearful. "Trust me, I've tried. It's just not possible."

Only after starting secondary school at Pike did Aine google *gay* and learn that although it did mean "light-hearted and carefree," it also, and more importantly, meant something else: homosexual, lesbian. Kuchu.

But by then Mbabazi had grown circumspect, unwilling to revisit the conversation. Each time Aine had raised the subject, casually bringing up news headlines—Uganda Court Annuls Anti-homosexuality Law, Bishop Tutu's Daughter Quits Priesthood after Gay Marriage, Botswana Decriminalizes Homosexuality in Landmark Ruling—Mbabazi had grown prickly. "Give it a rest, will you?" she'd bark. As the years went by, Aine had entertained the thought that perhaps Mbabazi wasn't all the way gay, or that she'd found some way to not be gay at all.

THE END-OF-PREP BELL SOUNDED at exactly ten p.m. Aine put her geography textbook inside her desk and hurried out of the classroom. Down the block, noisy Senior Fours were howling "Weekend mode!" at the moon. Friday nights always brought out the strangest behaviour in some girls. Almost everyone stayed up late on Fridays; morning prep—from six to eight a.m.—was optional on weekends.

Aine ran up to the biology lab, her best friend's home-room. Zaitun was studious, often extending her evening prep to just before eleven p.m., when the night watch-man switched off all the lights, pitching the campus into darkness.

She climbed the brick steps two at a time and opened the door. Girls sitting on tall wooden stools were still hunched over hefty textbooks, as if they hadn't heard the bell. Sciencers were model students. They didn't even require a prefect to supervise prep time; it was incon-ceivable for a sciencer to make unnecessary noise or try to bunk off early for no good reason.

"Zai," Aine hissed, crossing to her friend, who was writing what looked like a chemical equation on the blackboard.

"Did she come?" Zai asked, slapping chalk dust from her hands. "Is your sister here?"

"And she brought a friend." Aine squealed.

"Some of us are reading," snarled Maryam, an obnox-ious girl with a lanyard hanging from her thick glasses.

"Prep time is over, Maryam," Aine reminded her.

"I'm talking to Zaitun," Maryam shot back.

"Clearly, so am I," Aine said.

"Let's go to the dorm," Zai suggested, erasing the board. "I don't want to start a civil war."

They went outside but lingered on the steps, Aine going on about Achen's podcast.

"A podcast?" Zai balked at the idea that anyone, even an Oxford grad, could make a good enough living from a podcast. "They're for chicks with rich daddies or sugar daddies. All they do is sit around talking in forced American accents about self-actualization bullshit. Natural hair journeys, yoga journeys. Everything is a journey to the podcast chicks. Eating a piece of bread is a journey."

"I don't know what kind of podcasts you've been listening to," Aine said. "But Achen has won journalism awards."

"So, she's a journalist?"

"A storyteller."

"A storyteller? That's not a real job! It's the kind of nonsense title a podcaster would give themselves."

"I wish there was some way for us to listen to it tonight," Aine said with regret. The computer lab was closed on weekends, and by Monday Achen would be gone.

The lamppost by Freedom Tree made dancing shadows of the branches and leaves. A group of girls hanging out in front of the library burst into uproarious laughter and then dashed across to the tennis court.

"Does your sister talk with a Canadian accent now?" Zai asked.

"She was only gone for two years and a bit," Aine said. The only change she'd noticed in her sister's speech was the way she said *Toronto*, pronouncing it as though the last *t* were silent: *Trono*. But she wasn't about to disclose that to Zai, the self-proclaimed queen of sarcasm.

"Oh, you'd be surprised," said Zai, who had numerous relatives scattered all over Europe and the US on account of Idi Amin having expelled all Asians from Uganda in the 1970s. Her grandfather returned years later during Obote's regime, after Amin was forced into exile. "You should hear how Khadija talks now."

"But she's only been gone like six months." Zai's cousin had sat her A-levels the year before and was spending her gap year before university with an aunt in San Francisco.

"She talks through her nose like so?" Zai mocked her cousin's speech, talking like someone suffering from a cold. "She even, like, pretends not to remember her Rutooro or Gujarati?"

"Are you asking me?" Aine said.

"It's how she talks now?" Zai said. "Like a valley girl or whatever?"

"Dude, stop, you're killing me." Aine doubled over with laughter.

"She's so annoying though."

"When you go next year, you'll be talking like that too," Aine said. "I'll be on the phone saying, 'What? Is that another question?'"

"Walai." Zai cut her index finger across her throat. "I will never talk such nonsense to you."

"So dramatic!" Aine said as they sauntered down the colonnade that extended along the front of Hurditch, the A-level dormitory block named after one of the school's English founders.

Zai pushed her playfully. "Shut up."

"Honestly, some people have no shame." Aine was pointing at a student who was spitting frothy toothpaste between the gardenia and peace lily clusters in the flower garden beyond the terrace. No wonder the place stunk. Who knew how many girls peed there too? As if the bathroom wasn't only a few metres away.

They arrived at their dorm room, the very last on the block. The walls, once cerulean blue, were bruised and cratered, several spots showing an ugly skeleton of bricks and mortar. A wide corridor ran down the middle of the room, a dozen bunk beds on either side. Approaching their row by the window, Zai gave a loud groan. Her little sister, Jamila, was already there, spooning powdered milk into a steaming mug.

"Why do you never fetch your own hot water from the kitchen after supper?" Zai complained, lifting the thermos off the windowsill to gauge how much was left.

"Neither of you went to the canteen this evening?" Jamila responded with her own question. "I'm hungry, and there's nothing to eat."

"You have your own pocket money," Zai said.

A Senior One newcomer, Jamila lived in Maddox, a newer and more spacious dormitory. But she spent the bulk of her time here, testing the limits of her sister's patience.

"Why didn't you go, Aine?" Jamila asked.

"I hate to brag," Aine said, "but I had a sumptuous dinner at Madame's today. My sister is there. She's giving the Careers Day keynote tomorrow."

"That supermodel you were walking with is your sister?" said Eunice from the adjacent row. "I saw you together. I was in the sick bay."

"A supermodel?" Aine said.

"Honest to god, she's prettier than any Miss Uganda ever," Eunice said.

"Do you have photos?" Jamila said.

Aine reached under her bunk bed to pull out her trunk. She gnashed her teeth; the scratch of metal against concrete always went to her jaw. Girls congregated to see photos of the supermodel. They oohed and aahed as Aine turned the album pages. There Mbabazi was, her hands in the pockets of her white coat, a stethoscope around her neck. There she was crossing the finish line at the Toronto Marathon in nothing but a sports bra and little red shorts. And there she was leaning against a guardrail, misty Niagara Falls behind her.

"What's she doing here?" Tope indicated a photo in which Mbabazi, bundled up in a snowsuit, glided across a plane of glassy ice.

"It's called ice skating," Aine explained. "The boots have blades underneath to slice over hard ice."

"Seems dangerous," someone said, alarmed.

Jamila declared, "I want her life."

"Honestly, it's not fair," said Eunice. "How come God

gave her all the good things? Beauty, brains, and she's an athlete on top of that? Look at those legs. They're longer than forever."

"All right, let's not exaggerate!" Aine said. If she were to tell her dorm mates that Mbabazi was kuchu, would their envy immediately turn to pity or scorn? Leaving the photo album in Jamila's grabby hands, she squeezed Aquafresh onto her toothbrush and went outside to the boxy concrete bathroom. When she came back, the girls had dispersed. Jamila continued to browse the photos while Zai changed into her pyjamas.

"What's going on here?" Jamila pointed to a family photo with Papa and Mama bookending Mbabazi and Aine, garlands of morning glories decorating the church's arched entrance in the background. "Why are you dressed like a child bride?"

"My confirmation ceremony," Aine said, setting her toothbrush in the tumbler on the windowsill.

"What's that?"

Aine explained about the right of passage through which Protestant Christians became fully participating members of the church. After a four-week camp spent memorizing the Ten Commandments and reciting the creeds, the archdeacon headquartered in Kamwenge came to Bigodi and confirmed the group in a ceremony marked by their first Holy Communion.

"That's the little biscuits dipped in red wine?" Jamila said, her eyebrows raised either in mockery or surprise. Being Ismaili excused her and the few other

39

non-Christian students from attending chapel on Sunday.

"That, my friend, is the body and blood of Jesus."

"Eww, gross," Jamila said. "Cannibalism much?"

"There was this boy in my church camp," Aine told Jamila. "His name was Muhangi. The reverend wanted him to change it because *Muhangi* means creator."

"Did he change it?"

"No, but he suffered because of it," Aine said. "We all did. If you slipped up and called him Muhangi, not Simon, you got a nasty earlobe pinch. Him, too, if he responded to Muhangi. Once, the reverend sent him to shovel cow dung in the church's kraal. He told him to consider, while he worked, the third commandment: 'You shall not take the name of the Lord your God in vain.'"

Maybe it was around the time of her confirmation that Aine lost her faith. The more she understood of Christianity, the more disillusioned with God she became. "I mean, don't Muslims have stuff like this?" she asked of Zai and Jamila. "Commandments that make your God sound like a celestial dictator?"

"Not that I know of," Jamila said.

"Culturally," Zai said, "we're Ismaili. But religiously? Well, there isn't even a Jamatkhana anywhere in our district. There used to be one downtown, a long time ago. But now it's the public library."

"Yeah, we're pretty much pagans," Jamila said.

But Zai demurred. "The opposite of religious isn't pagan."

"Um, yeah it is," Jamila said. "We don't pray or anything."

"Time for you to go to your dorm," Zai said, exasperated. "And maybe look up the word *agnostic* while you're at it?"

"Pagan, agnostic, potayto, potahto," the younger sister said.

Aine couldn't help chuckling. The combative dynamic of Zai and Jamila's sisterhood was so unlike hers with Mbabazi. Perhaps it was their vast difference in age coupled with the fact that Mbabazi was always gone. Absence making the heart grow fonder.

Now Jamila flashed a peace sign and made for the door, disappearing as Zai shouted, "Come back and wash your mug!"

4

AINE WOKE UP TO the usual cacophonous din of the weavers and pied wagtails that lived in the kaba-kanjagala trees behind the dormitory. Insistent tweets and chirps brightened the morning, lending it a festive air. She listened for her favourite songs. The liquid chirruping of a black-headed oriole. The hollow notes, almost mournful, of a tambourine dove. She loved this good-morning chorus. She liked to think the chatty birds were twittering to each other about dreams they'd had in the night. In the dream she'd had, she was being pursued by something monstrous, but a veil of cobwebs or some other gauzy membrane had covered her eyes so that she clawed at them even as she ran, unable to see what was chasing her.

She opened her eyes now and saw the words *Love is not a potato* above her. Someone, likely the bunk's previous occupant, had scribbled the phrase on the white ceiling in red marker. Now she considered Mbabazi and Achen, how their love, which was not a potato, could get them incarcerated or even killed.

Pushing away her blanket, she swung her legs over the edge of the bed and climbed down the cold two-step ladder. She slipped her feet into her rubber slippers. Zai's bed was empty, perfectly made, the corners tucked in. She never skipped morning prep, not even on the weekend. Aine pictured her sitting at her desk in the biology lab or solving more chemical equations on the blackboard. She'd have taken her thermos with her and would dash to the kitchen when the bell rang.

Toothbrush between her teeth, Aine threw her oversized towel around her shoulders and reached for her soap dish under the bed. She went to the door and opened it, careful not to wake her dorm mates.

The morning was foggy, the light bluish as though filtered through milk. She turned left toward the bathroom, a boxy concrete structure without a roof. At the towering water tank by the entrance, she brushed her teeth before going inside. Three other girls bathed under shower heads that spilled cold water. Gooseflesh sprouted all over her body. Her teeth were chattering even before she gave the shower tap a twist. The chill went straight to her lungs and turned them into iron. Almost six years of this, yet every time felt like the first. Fort Portal, at the foot of the Rwenzori Mountains, never warmed up until the sun was at its highest and brightest. She washed only the essentials—her underarms, her crotch, her butt—and hurried back to the warmth of her dorm.

She rubbed lotion on her arms and legs and wore her school uniform even though it was Saturday. On Careers Day the school uniform was expected. Professionals from various fields would start arriving by nine. At ten, the bell would sound and everyone—students, teaching staff, and guests—would assemble in the main hall. After Mbabazi's keynote speech, the visiting professionals would give seminars for interested students to learn about different occupations. Would Achen be assigned a professional category, or had she come with Mbabazi for moral support only? There was often a journalist or mass communication professional of some kind. Perhaps Achen fit the bill.

Aine always went to the journalism workshops. The year before, a regional correspondent for the *Daily Monitor* had made the case that everyone was a journalist now. Bloggers, social media users—pretty much anybody with a smartphone and an internet connection. News agencies were shutting down their foreign offices and relying on footage regular people uploaded to YouTube or Twitter. The digital age and the twenty-four-hour news cycle was forcing journalism to redefine itself. Even newspaper editors, the journalist said, were increasingly soliciting content from the public. But those opinion pieces needed to be short and concise; attention spans were diminishing.

That workshop had inspired Aine to write her essay and email it to the opinions editor at the *Daily Monitor* on the off chance they would consider publishing the ramblings of a mere secondary school girl. Two weeks later, she was in phys. ed. playing doubles on the tennis court when the librarian yelled her name from the front step of the library. She had the newspaper in her hand. Aine ran up to her.

"Look!" the librarian said, pointing to the op-ed with Aine's byline.

"Holy gods!" Aine could barely contain her excitement. She took the paper down to the tennis court to show everyone. "The *Monitor* published my essay!"

But by that afternoon she was wishing she'd submitted the piece under a pen name. Mrs. Wasswa, her history teacher, singled her out. "What I don't understand is this," she said. "If you think Christianity is poisonous, why are you here?"

As if it had been up to Aine where she went to school. When she cited freedom of expression, Mrs. Wasswa sent her to the headmistress's office.

"I guess I'm just used to competitive debating where objections and points of information are inspired by logic, not hurt feelings," Aine told Madame.

"I'm not going to stop you from writing, Kamara," Madame told her, not unkindly, "but next time, try to write something that makes us proud. Something that will put your school on the map in a good way." She went on about Mbabazi's many accomplishments, both academic and athletic. She took Aine to the staff room and pointed to one of the silver medals displayed behind glass. Mbabazi had won it in a cross-country race involving every secondary school in the district.

It wasn't as if Aine wanted a medal for being the first student in the history of Pike Girls to have an essay published in a national paper, but getting lectured for it? They all acted as if she'd tarnished the school's reputation.

After making her bed, she dug *African Religions in Western Scholarship* from her suitcase to bring to Achen.

Outside, the fog had lifted. The morning sun bathed the treetops in gold. Netballers were doing drills, legs scissoring rapidly as the athletes, at the blow of a whistle, ran from one end of the court to the other and then back again.

She crossed the lawn in front of the sick bay, the soft paspalum springy under her feet, the dew wetting her black Bata uniform shoes. She climbed the steps to Madame's door, knocked, and stood back.

Madame's son opened the door. Eric? No. Elia.

"You must be Aine." He grinned.

"I must be."

Where had he materialized from overnight? Two years before, she'd seen him on the stage in the main hall. He and his drama troupe from Nyakasura, the neighbouring all-boys boarding school, had performed improv skits. Elia kept breaking into song for no reason at all, except to show off his transcendent singing voice. All the girls were enamoured.

"Please, come in." His eyes were direct and assertive like the migration of birds. He held her gaze even as he stepped off to the side to let her in, his hand still on the door.

"Thank you."

He was more attractive than she remembered. Onstage the boys had worn their kilts; the Nyakasura uniform paid homage to the school's Scottish founder, Lieutenant Commander something or other. In jeans and a wrinkled undershirt, as though he'd slept in it, he was sexy, handsome in a chaotic way.

"Doc went running," he offered as Aine scanned the empty sitting room. "You know her. Always training for this race and that marathon. Achen should be up in a minute."

He was standing so close to her that she wondered if his sense of personal space was always this off.

"You know Mbabazi and Achen well?"

"Mum introduced me to Doc before I started uni," he said. "She wanted me to know someone in the city. Turned out Doc was already in Canada. But get this: from Toronto, she made a dinner reservation for me and Achen at this upscale Japanese restaurant in Kampala. I tried to eat with chopsticks, but I have the dexterity of a toddler! It was one of the most embarrassing moments of my adult life. I could barely get anything into my mouth. Until Achen asked the server to bring me a fork."

"And then what?" Aine was impatient to know if he knew the true nature of Achen and Mbabazi's relationship.

"And the rest is history, as they say." He went toward the dining room, and she followed. "We were supposed to drive up here together yesterday. I even slept at their place, so we'd take off early. Beat the morning traffic jam. But when we were about to leave, I got a callback for a part I'd auditioned for."

"A part?" Aine found it endearing, his overly eager way of speaking.

"In a musical," he said, giving her a glass of juice she hadn't asked for, juice she wasn't eager to drink if it was anything like yesterday's.

"Did you get it? The part?"

"You are looking at Jesus." He gave a dramatic bow, a quick wave of his hand. "Of *Jesus Christ Superstar.*"

"Oh." Aine couldn't keep the disappointment out of her voice. "A Jesus musical?"

"It's a rock musical about his last days on earth," said Achen, emerging through the arched entrance from the sitting room. She was wearing an ankle-length beige kaftan, a veritable kanzu. With her voluminous hair wrapped in a satin scarf, she looked like one of the three wise men. "But get this: it is told from the perspective of Judas. He's by all accounts the star of the show."

"Judas Iscariot?" Aine sniggered. "Could there be a more unreliable narrator?"

"That's what makes it brilliant," Elia said.

He talked with exquisite enthusiasm about how he'd been busking at the corner of a crafts market at City Square, playing his guitar and singing Tracy Chapman songs, when a former cast member of the Ebonies—a theatre troupe once famous for the TV show *That's Life*

Mwattu—approached him and told him to audition for the role of Judas. But at the audition, the musical's director decided that Elia's voice, which lacked the rockstar quality necessary for Judas, was better suited to Jesus. "And the thing is, I prefer Jesus anyway. For me, he's just about the most complex character ever written."

"Oh please," Aine said.

"Jesus was a rebel, wasn't he?" Elia said. "Whatever they told him not to do, he did it anyway. Don't hang out with prostitutes, they said. Well, we know he went and did that. Don't touch the lepers. Oops, he healed a few. And let me tell you, that son of God suffered. He didn't want to be crucified for our sins. No, sir. On the cross he bawled his eyes out. 'My God, my God, why have you forsaken me?'" Elia touched a hand to his chest. "Doesn't that line just break your heart? I'm tearing up just talking about it."

And there were tears in his eyes. His compassion for Jesus was so genuine it moved Aine. She didn't want him to stop talking. His mouth—the lush, almost feminine curve of it—was so beautiful it was almost illusory. She kept reminding herself not to look at his face too much.

"Well, my darling," said Achen, raising her glass of water, "you were born for this role."

Aine and Elia raised their glasses too. But as they toasted, Aine caught a glimpse of a menacing scar snaking up the inside of Achen's left arm toward the pit of her elbow. It made eels turn in Aine's stomach. The healed incision was forceful and rough, as if someone had attempted to open Achen's arm using rudimentary tools. Achen caught Aine staring and pulled down the sleeve of her robe. Aine averted her gaze.

At that moment, Madame and Mbabazi came in through the front door. Mbabazi, her T-shirt drenched in sweat, bounded over to Aine to give her a hug.

"You're sweaty and you stink," Aine said, twisting away from her. But Mbabazi chased her around the dining table and into the sitting room. It was a ritual they'd engaged in for as long as Aine could remember. Mbabazi would return from tearing down the trail around Magombe Swamp and she'd chase Aine around the compound to get her to smell her armpits. "The sweet smell of endorphins," she called it.

"Smell my victory," she said now, pursuing Aine around the furniture, jumping over the lifelike sculpture of the dog.

"Are you children?" Madame intervened in her authoritative headmistress voice.

"Sorry, Madame," they both said, chastened.

"Doctor," Madame said, "need I remind you that the visitors are already arriving? And you haven't even taken your breakfast!"

"I'm the queen of quick showers," Mbabazi said, hurrying toward the hallway.

Aine followed her into the bedroom. Two single beds, brown carpet. "Madame put you and Achen in the same room?" she mused, noticing that both beds, a small distance apart, had been slept in. She dropped her voice. "Did you sneak into her bed and do the dirty?"

"You're rotten." Mbabazi parted the curtains and opened the window, flooding the room with light.

"Yeah, yeah," Aine said and rummaged through her sister's luggage. "What did you bring for me?" She tossed out lacy undergarments and balled-up socks. From her travels abroad, Mbabazi always brought Aine eclectic clothing: short dresses and tank tops she loved to picture herself wearing but never actually mustered the courage to put on.

"I left your stuff at home," Mbabazi said, peeling off her running tights.

"You've been home?"

"The weekend I came back," she said. "Papa met me at the airport."

"Did Achen go home to Bigodi with you?"

"Yeah, right." Mbabazi crossed to the bathroom. Her long legs like ropes, lean muscles rippling toward knobby, workhorse knees. "But you know, Papa met her recently." She stepped into the bathtub and drew the curtain so that Aine had to move closer to hear her voice over the rushing water. "He came to my new office two weeks ago, and she just happened to be there, hanging a painting."

Aine moved even closer; the shower was running at full force.

"And Papa," Mbabazi continued, "he didn't like the painting Achen was hanging in my office. He doesn't get abstract art at all. And Achen was working overtime to bring him on board. If she really likes something, she won't stop until you like it too. So she's going on about how this painting reminded her of solitude. Or was it 'vast quiet'? She's talking about how we live much of our lives, the most important moments at least, in silence. How a bell is not a bell without the space between the clapper and the cup. Because without that empty space, a bell can't make a sound. And that Papa gets. And before I know it, he's invited Achen to our lunch. Mine and his lunch."

Mbabazi opened the shower curtain.

"So Papa knows?" Aine said, passing her a towel.

"Knows what?"

"Don't play coy," Aine said, following her back into the bedroom. "We're past that now."

"Well, why would he know about us? He's had lunch with me and other friends of mine before." Mbabazi stepped into a black dress and spun around, showing Aine her back. "Zip me."

Aine obliged. "That scar on Achen's arm." The words tumbled out of her mouth and hung in the air. Something about that scar had reminded Aine of Mr. Kalangi, her Primary Five science teacher. His wife had woken up one morning to find him dangling from a branch of the jackfruit tree in front of their house. He was denied a proper burial. People said the evil spirit of okweyita, killing oneself, would linger around the village, searching for another life to claim. Aine had started taking the long way home to avoid passing by Mr. Kalangi's house. "It's not self-inflicted, is it?"

Mbabazi turned around slowly. "That's a question for her, don't you think?" she said. "Her scar, her story. Now let's go eat, shall we?"

OVER A BREAKFAST OF katogo, fingers of matooke cooked in a stew of goat offal, Mbabazi confessed she was nervous about speaking in front of eight hundred schoolgirls. "Teenagers are extremely judgmental," she said.

"Every single one of them is going to love you," Madame said, covering Mbabazi's hand with her reassuring one.

"Don't make any tired jokes or try to be hip," Aine advised.

"You're saying I'm not hip?" Mbabazi said. "You've just confirmed my fears. No matter what I say, or how I say it, I'm fresh meat. Until the next Careers Day keynote, at least."

"Being nervous is good, M," Achen said. "If you weren't nervous, I'd worry."

Elia chimed in. "Nerves mean you care, Doc."

AINE HELPED BIRUNGI CLEAR the table, ferrying the dishes to the washstand by the tap in the backyard while everyone else went to get ready. Then she slipped out the side gate and went to snag herself a front seat for her sister's keynote speech.

The main hall was a long rectangular breeze-block building with a slanted iron-sheet roof and four sets of doors, two on either end. Clusters of students congregated around the two main entrances. Except for the prefects, most students wore their white shirts untucked, their ties loose around their collars. No one wanted to wear the school uniform on a Saturday, but rules were rules.

Aine walked up the centre aisle, rows of joined benches on either side. The school crest was projected against the wall behind the stage, the motto—Fear God and Work Hard—underlining it.

"Aine!"

Jamila waved her over to where she sat on the front bench to the left of the aisle. She had stretched her blazer over a good length of it. The four rows of benches to the right were reserved for guests and staff.

"Zai said you'd wash and iron my uniform if I saved a spot for you at the front," she said, tap-tapping the seat invitingly.

Aine sat down. "Funny, I don't remember saying that."

"I mean, you were going to wash your own uniform anyway. What's one more, right?"

"I can wash, but I'm not ironing," she said. "I never iron my uniform. That's why it still looks new."

"But I like mine ironed."

"Don't let me stop you, Jam-Jam."

Jamila rolled her eyes. "Were you at the Copper's just now?"

"You know, she's actually quite nice," Aine said, suddenly reluctant to call Madame by her nickname. "Once you get to know her."

Jamila gave a dry, sarcastic laugh. "Oh, you're not kidding?" she said when Aine didn't join her.

"She's got all this amazing art in her house," Aine said. "Her late husband's work. The walls are covered with it. Every room. The entire house is like a monument to her man. It made me see her differently."

"A mean woman who loves her dead husband's art is still a mean woman," Jamila said without skipping a beat.

"No one is mean through and through," Aine said. "I'm telling you, she's got a soft side."

"That she's shown only to you!"

The bell rang and students started shuffling into the hall, filling it with noise and the kinetic energy of moving bodies and plaid skirts.

"You didn't tell me the Copper's handsome son was here," said Zai as she dashed in, scooped up Jamila's blazer, and sat down next to Aine. "He's out there with Madame and the guests."

"He arrived in the night, after I left," Aine replied. "Turns out he's good friends with my sister and Achen."

Just then Madame came through the door, followed by Mbabazi, Achen, Elia, and a stream of teachers and visiting dignitaries.

"Omusota," catcalled the rowdy backbenchers when Elia entered. *Snake.* Slang referencing the serpent who tempted Adam and Eve to eat of the Fruit of Knowledge.

"Think he's omusota too?" Aine whispered in Zai's ear.

"Meh," Zai said dismissively. "Too lanky. What, do you like him?"

"Madly," she said, looking at him dreamily. He was smiling shyly, his gaze falling to his shoes. He wore blue jeans and a white shirt, the sleeves rolled up to his elbows. She wondered if this overt attention from so many girls embarrassed him the way she always felt when men—boda boda cyclists and bricklayers—whistled and made lewd remarks about her body.

Madame went up to the stage and tap-tapped the microphone as if waking it up. "God is good," she spoke into it.

"All the time," everyone responded.

"All the time?"

"God is good!"

"And that is why?"

"We praise his name!"

And just like that, order was restored in the main hall. Madame welcomed everyone to Careers Day before inviting the entertainment prefect up to the podium to lead in the singing of the school anthem. The song, set to the tune of "What a Friend We Have in Jesus," hailed the women—members of the Church Missionary Society—for giving up their comfortable lives in England to be teachers in Toro Kingdom. It celebrated the king of Toro at the time, Omukama Kasagama, for his foresight in inviting those courageous Englishwomen to his kingdom and for helping them set up the original reading school, which inspired the founding of Pike Girls' Boarding School.

The chaplain was next, leading the Lord's Prayer. Then Madame took the microphone back and introduced, one by one, the distinguished guests, the visitors standing up to be recognized after their names were read. The surgeon from Buhinga Hospital, the ecological and behavioural research scientist from the nearby Makerere University Biological Field Station, the economist from Centenary Bank, the lawyer, the pharmacist, the vet, the computer engineer, the journalist—a former CNN correspondent. Aine resented the presence of the honourable Member of Parliament for Fort Portal Municipality. A member of the ruling party, he had voted in favour of the bill that scrapped the age limit for sitting presidents so that Museveni could, after more than three decades in power, continue to seek re-election.

Madame skipped over her son and introduced Achen Roy, calling her an award-winning storyteller whose audio documentaries, "delivered via the internet, have been featured on the BBC and Al Jazeera," she said. Achen rose to her feet and waved. She wore hoop earrings big enough to collar a cat. Her hair was wild in exactly the same way it had been the evening before, consistent like an anime character. Her smiling face reminded Aine of that Sudanese refugee who'd found success and fame as a fashion model in New York.

"And now our keynote speaker!" Madame smoothed her hand over a piece of paper on the podium and read a short biography that highlighted Mbabazi's many academic and professional achievements. "And she was once a student here just like you," she said with a wide sweep of her hand. "A God-fearing student loved by all her teachers. She worked hard in the classroom and on the field both as a netballer and a long-distance runner. Let us put our hands together for Dr. Kamara Grace Mbabazi."

Mbabazi was the very image of poise and self-possession as she went up to the stage, her high heels clicking metronomically. She gave Madame a quick hug and went to stand tall behind the podium, adjusting the microphone to her height.

Right from the start, her speech was not the traditional keynote Aine had grown used to hearing. Her sister ranted about societal expectations for women, how the standards were rigid and unattainable compared to what was expected of men. She said that for women, working hard was simply not enough. And she would know. Throughout secondary school and university, she'd done nothing but study hard. She figured she'd need an excellent CV in order to compete with her male counterparts. She got glowing letters of recommendation from her internship supervisors. But from one job interview to the next, prospective employers only gave her resumé a passing glance before proceeding to make blatant sexual advances. "Right in the middle of a job interview," she said, "this man, the manager of a reputable clinic, invited me to come around the desk and sit on his lap."

A wave of shock worked its way through the hall.

Looking back at those months interviewing for jobs in and around Kampala, Mbabazi said she was astounded by how often she had laughed at jokes that weren't funny, how she deflected, demurred, tried to change the subject but never once told those men off. "I couldn't let my anger and frustration show," she said, "because these were the same men standing between me and my dreams. They had my future in their hands, and they were dangling it in front of me. Teasing me with it."

Her big break was a chance encounter on a kamunye, a commuter taxi. A nurse squeezed in next to her and immediately got up on her soapbox. She'd had a tough day at work, needed to vent. "At least you have a job to complain about," Mbabazi told her. "I graduated top of my class in med school and all I'm getting are indecent proposals."

"Well, you can come work with me," the nurse said. The reproductive health clinic where she worked had a high doctor turnover. The salary was laughable, the hours abysmal, and the chances of getting accosted by mobs of anti-abortion protesters were very high. The clinic, though it didn't do abortions, was known for D&Cs, a medical procedure to clear the uterus after a miscarriage or an incomplete abortion. But if Mbabazi wanted the job, the nurse would put in a good word.

A week later Mbabazi had the job. "My foot found a solid ladder, and I have climbed it ever since," she said.

Though she didn't work at that clinic anymore, it led her to opportunities that advanced her career. She was still involved in a program there that empowered women to reclaim their agency, that made condoms and morning-after pills available to boys and girls to avoid unwanted pregnancies.

Aine wondered how Mbabazi's message was landing with the headmistress, who advocated for abstinence until marriage. The audience was captivated by Mbabazi, though, paying her unwavering attention.

"What I'm saying here is that it's our job, all of us women, to work against systems of oppression that force us to shrink, that want us to remain silent," Mbabazi said.

"Yes!" someone shouted, inciting a wave of enthusiastic agreement.

"Courage is the ability to look at another woman without judgment or malice," Mbabazi said. "Courage is refusing to unquestioningly conform to orthodoxy. Simply because an idea is popular doesn't necessarily make it right, does it?"

"No!" came the resounding response.

"Courage is not leaving the work of many to a few," said Mbabazi. "We must all do what we can, whenever we can, starting today."

"Yes!"

"Thank you, my little sisters," Mbabazi said and took a bow. "Thank you so much for listening."

As everyone rose to their feet, clapping and hooting, Aine wondered if all the girls were thinking the same thing: that no Careers Day keynote speech had ever been more invigorating, more honest and true.

5

MORE THAN HALF THE student body, including Zai and Jamila, stayed in the main hall for the seminar Mbabazi and the surgeon were giving on careers in the medical profession.

Aine made her way out and went right toward Freedom Square, where a couple of chairs had been set up under Freedom Tree. From a certain angle, the ancient banyan looked like a gigantic multi-limbed arthropod. Gnarled roots ribboned the surface of the square and fanned out toward its perimeter. The roots had discouraged the growth of the lawn, but small islands of paspalum persisted here and there. Colonies of moss covered even the aerial roots that grew downward from the branches. Aine's gaze travelled up the fat trunk to scan the canopy, where a yellow-crested woodpecker was drumming its little heart out. The patch of gold on the crown with little flecks of black told her the bird was male. More and more, thanks to the tour guide training she had undergone during the three months of vacation after O-level, she could identify various species of birds without consulting her birding guide. She was still interning at the wetlands sanctuary during school breaks, accumulating the field-work hours necessary for certification so that she would, in the gap year after A-level, become a proper birding guide. She was well on her way to an easy, fun job at Bigodi Wetlands Sanctuary come November.

Achen and the balding former CNN journalist arrived in the company of Mr. Zadok, Aine's literature teacher. "Come a bit closer," he shouted, calling the couple dozen students who'd gathered under Freedom Tree for the talk on journalism and mass communication. After introducing Achen and Mr. Mugisha Albert, the teacher asked the guests to say something about themselves.

Achen stood behind her chair, her hands on the backrest. "Stories," she said, "have always come to my rescue. Ever since I was a kid. Especially then. I had a childhood some might consider unusual."

She described waking up in hospital on more than one occasion, deeply disappointed that swallowing a dozen painkillers or drinking a bottle of bleach hadn't erased her from existence. She was suffering from a disease everyone around her was afraid to name or was in denial about. For the most part, her guardians thought they could pray her clinical depression away.

"It was like being stuck in a nightmare," she said. "One in which I was constantly falling down a deep dark tunnel, falling and falling, until I couldn't bear it. I just had to put an end to the falling."

Aine felt a lump in her throat.

Achen's foster mother had left heaps of books by the side of Achen's bed, hoping to draw her out of her head. Achen devoured them like meat for sustenance. "I could not believe that I was allowed this delicious pleasure." She grinned, explaining that sometimes her mother let her stay home from school, just reading books, as long as she completed the homework the teacher sent home for her. "It was magical. This ability to tunnel out into different worlds. While reading, we are in this world but also outside of it. What a gift!"

Aine thought of the many times when, after she'd read the last page of a novel, the fact of having to resume her life was almost unbearable.

"So, you see," Achen continued, "stories, quite literally, are always saving me."

Aine wondered about Achen's life, how the membrane separating it from death seemed too porous. Were stories really all that was keeping her from passing through? How devastated would Mbabazi be if her partner died by suicide? Surely there had to be a cure for this disease that made her want to end her life. Then again, Achen was here. Presumably she had a handle on things. But for how long? The tragedy of her demise, should it occur, made Aine's mind grow cold and panicky.

Mr. Mugisha, for his part, said a career in journalism had taken him to places he hadn't known existed. From war zones to deserts to underwater expeditions to look at the state of coral reefs.

"Journalism is learning something new every day," he said. "Keeps one alert to a world that is constantly changing."

When it was time for the Q&A, he gave dry responses as if disappointed by the quality of the questions. He was needlessly cynical about the world he'd just moments before seemed privileged to be travelling and exploring. So, students directed their queries at Achen, who was generous, treating each one as though it were the most important.

The difference between her kind of storytelling and journalism, she said, was that the news, though very important, turned people into statistics. "It can't be helped," she said, looking at Mr. Mugisha, who frowned as if personally attacked. "And it's not necessarily always a bad thing. But people quickly become desensitized to numbers. It's easy to forget that behind those numbers there are actual individuals with names and people who love them."

As an example, she said that the year before, heavy rains in the east had caused rivers of mud to flood off Mount Elgon, burying entire homesteads along the Uganda-Kenya boarder. The news cycles reported, "Forty people are dead and an unknown number of livestock have been lost to yet another devastating flood in eastern Uganda." And there were photographs of people unearthing their deceased loved ones from under the rivers of mud. And a local chief talking about the devastation. And that was that. The same visuals and soundbites were repeated whenever these mud floods happened.

But Achen, because she had no one enforcing a deadline, travelled east and stayed for nearly a week in the grieving community, talking to mothers, fathers, and children. "You get a fuller picture," she said. "A story that opens a window into the lives of these people. Why they are forced to stay in a place that's as fertile as it is hostile. My being there for longer than a few hours allowed a mother the opportunity to say, 'That's the body of my son. He was here. A living, breathing person. His life was much bigger than what you can put in your story.'"

Aine watched as Achen engaged the journalist in conversation. It seemed effortless, Achen's ability to coax out of him details about his work, anecdotes about reporting from the front lines. How did he cope with the violence he observed? Did it all weigh him down? And the man, finally, was effusive. All he'd needed was someone to draw him out.

"I'M NOT FEELING JOURNALISM anymore," Aine told Achen as they walked to Madame's house after the seminar. "Ornithology is more appealing, but there's never a Careers Day seminar for that."

"Birds?" Achen seemed baffled.

"There's so much to learn about them," Aine said.

"But you write so well, kidio," Achen said. "That essay. You're going to be the voice of your generation."

"It's not rewarding when you get attacked for expressing a simple logical opinion," Aine said. "And I don't want to just write news stories where I have to be objective and not say how I feel about certain things."

"'I wish desperately that the Church wasn't full of exclusionary politics, that it wasn't obsessed with this unquestioning belief in rigid ideas that are, in my opinion, quite embarrassing,'" Achen quoted from Aine's essay. "That's hardly a simple logical opinion by the standards of a country whose first lady flies in American evangelists to help 'heal our land.'"

That Achen had singled out this particular line and memorized it gave it such a satisfying heft of truth; Aine believed those words more now than when she'd first written them.

"But you can't give up when faced with a little resistance," Achen said. "Many of us feel the same way you do about religion. You've got to ignore the twats who have nothing better to do than threaten a woman for voicing an original thought. It's definitely not a reason to quit writing."

"I can write well about birds too," Aine said. "Birds are amazing creatures. Deciphering their languages, their behaviours. There's a joy there unlike anything else I know."

"You're really that into birds?" Achen said. "You're never going to please everybody with your writing. If I'd let the criticism get to me, I wouldn't have a podcast."

She knocked on the door, and Birungi opened it.

"Where are the others?" she asked, poking her head out.

"They shouldn't be long now," Achen said. "Is it ironic that the workshop on storytelling was the first to finish?"

"Personally, I blame your co-presenter," Aine said. "It was like he had been forced to come here and talk to us."

"Oh, well," Achen said dismissively. She marched toward the fridge and took out the jug of drinking water. As she came to stand beside her, Aine caught sight of the menacing scar again. A forceful healed incision. Without thinking, she reached out to touch it. She traced her fingers along the rough bumps like a blind person read-ing Braille.

"When I was young," Achen said, not retrieving her arm from Aine, "I thought I could extinguish my suicidality."

Erase myself from existence. Extinguish my suicidality. All these fancy ways Achen had of saying she wanted to kill herself.

Achen took her arm back and filled two glasses with water. She opened the fridge again to replace the pitcher and lingered there, peering into the blue light as if looking for her train of thought.

"A psychologist in Oxford," she said, closing the fridge door, which made a suctioning noise, "she scanned my brain and showed me the images. My brain looks like a tree with all its branches stripped away. She told me that when my mother left me on the front steps of the church, stress hormones flooded my brain and changed it. Physically and functionally. The children in refugee camps. The ones who have been torn away from their parents and displaced by war. My brain scan is identical to theirs."

"I'm sorry," Aine said. They crossed to the sitting room and went down the hall toward the guest bedroom. "How old were you when your mum left you?"

"Almost three years old."

"Do you have any memories of her?"

"One, but it's possibly a confabulation." Achen opened the bedroom door. "My mum's neck is craned as she looks back at me over her shoulder. But her face is a blur. She's this graceful figure without a face. And it's raining. Always, whenever I picture her, it's raining. As if mothers only abandon their children in a rainstorm."

They perched on the bed farthest from the door. Achen gulped the remainder of her water and set the empty glass down on the nightstand. "Oh, don't look at me with pity." She chuckled and turned up her arm so that Aine saw the length of the ominous scar. "This. It's just ravages of one particularly difficult night when I was about your age. I'm doing much better now. I truly am."

"Because of stories?" Aine read more than anyone she knew, but she found it hard to believe that a book, even the best book, could heal a mental disorder.

"I'm on this program," she said. "Every day, when my brain starts to feel staticky, filling with white noise like an AM radio station losing its signal, I sit."

"You just sit?"

"I meditate, yes," she said. "I try to empty my brain

to make it quiet. When it works, I'm restored to a tolerable level of unhappiness. It's like finding my way back to something I once had but lost without ever knowing what it was."

Aine hugged her. As if on cue, Mbabazi barged in. "Write about this, Kanyonyi," she said, leaning back against the door. "Write that you're embracing the woman your sister loves and that your sister is bawling her eyes out."

Aine rolled her eyes. If you could string a couple of words together, people started telling you what to write about next, as if generating ideas was the hardest part.

"I'M EXPERIENCING A VERY specific kind of thirst," Elia said after lunch when his mum went to take a siesta. "Only Nile Special lager can quench it."

"I could use one of those too," said Mbabazi. Over lunch, the air between her and Madame had seemed sullied. No one had remarked on the speech. The elephant in the room.

Elia took orders of beverages to buy, and when he asked for the car keys, Achen offered to go with him, a chance "to check out the old fort," she said.

"You can go, too, if you want," Aine told Mbabazi as Elia and Achen crossed to the door.

"Oh, please," her sister said, as they returned to the guest bedroom. "I know Fort Portal like the back of my hand. When you run long distance in any place, its geography becomes imprinted on you."

Aine closed the door and dropped her voice nearly to a whisper. "Did Madame give you hell about the contraception stuff?" she said. "About giving condoms and morning-after pills to unmarried people?"

"No," Mbabazi said. "But I'm not holding my breath for another invitation."

"That was some speech though," Aine said. "You managed to make a rallying call for feminism without ever uttering the word."

"I just spoke from my heart." Mbabazi shrugged. "There's nothing I said in there that I would take back. Not even if Madame confronts me."

"Some people are just set in their ways," Aine said before repeating a Rukiga proverb Papa was fond of, a saying about how trying to bend an old stick only broke it. "But your speech was for us, not them, Madame and the staff. And we loved it. Every part of it. I didn't want you to stop talking."

"Thank you!"

Aine threw herself on the bed and propped her torso up with stacked pillows. She reached for her sister's smartphone and scrolled through the camera roll as Mbabazi changed into a white T-shirt and kitenge trousers, the roomy unflattering pants favoured by tourists.

"Where's this?" She tilted the screen to show Mbabazi a photo of her and Achen, a bridge towering in the background over a river.

"London Bridge," Mbabazi said, joining Aine on the bed.

"It's still standing?"

"What do you mean?"

"London Bridge is falling down, falling down, falling down..." Aine sang the nursery rhyme. "How has it not fallen yet?"

Mbabazi chuckled. "You're a child."

"Why do you have a picture of a bathroom?" Aine said, showing a photo of a brightly lit bathroom that was white from top to bottom.

"I took it to send to Papa." Mbabazi laughed. "He wanted to show Mama how fancy and clean the bathroom at my workplace is. The soap dispenser. The hand dryer. Such big hits with mzee. He told Mama that the toilet was so clean he wouldn't mind eating in there, and Mama said, 'Show me, show me.'"

"That's disgusting," Aine said. "No bathroom is clean enough to eat in."

"I know!"

"I bet they're both so proud of you," Aine said. "Remember how upset Mama was when you were leaving? She's probably forgotten all that now."

"The only thing that would make the mukadde truly happy is me marrying a nice gentleman," Mbabazi said. "She wants an introduction ceremony and a big wedding for Reverend Erasmus to officiate. God, I hate that guy."

Aine put the phone down. "Can I ask you something?"

Mbabazi rolled onto her side to face her. "Shoot."

"That Sunday when you refused to go to the vestry after church," Aine said. "When you got into that big fight

71

with Mama and stormed off in tears. Was it because of Achen? Did you tell Mama about her and that's why she freaked out?"

"We didn't even get to that," Mbabazi said. "Honestly, I can't believe I allowed the sessions to go on for so long. That I allowed him for years to fill my head with garbage."

"You kept going to make Mama happy?"

"Funny thing is," Mbabazi said, "I liked going. In the beginning, at least. I even looked forward to it. It didn't matter that he asked me very intimate, intrusive questions."

"Like what?"

"Like, 'Have you been thinking about women? Have you masturbated while thinking about women? Did you climax?'"

Aine's mouth hung open. "He asked you that?"

"He'd write my responses on that little chalkboard of his in the vestry," Mbabazi continued. "And afterwards, after praying for me, after emphasizing again that the only intercourse God permitted was between a wife and her husband, blah blah blah, he'd take a duster and clean the board. And it was as if he was erasing my sins, my lesbianism. I'd feel so clean. A fresh new person."

"What a pervert," Aine said. "Did Mama know he asked you about touching yourself?"

"I told her that Sunday," Mbabazi said. "But she didn't want to hear any of it. In her eyes, that man of God can do no wrong. That's what pissed me off more than anything. I was ready to go and never, ever come back home. But then you were running after me, crying as if I had died or something. I swear, it took all my self-control not to turn back and swoop you up and run away with you. But, like, you can't be a lesbian and also kidnap your baby sister."

"I still have nightmares about that day," Aine said. "Nightmares where you just disappear, and we never hear from you again."

"That night, I couldn't sleep," Mbabazi said. "All I could see was your wet face, all that snot dripping from your nose."

"There was no snot!"

"You're a nose crier," Mbabazi said. "Do you not know that? Frankly, it's so disgusting."

"And yet you came to see me debate!"

"God, am I glad I came," Mbabazi said.

"So, if it wasn't for the debate …" Aine's voice trailed off. Had her nightmare been that close to realization?

"Thing is," Mbabazi flipped to her back, her knees pointing to the ceiling, "Achen and I had been dating for maybe a month at that point, and already we were having problems. She'd touch me, this gorgeous woman I was so into, and I'd feel myself leaving my body. The guilt. Erasmus's voice was forever in my head. I started doing this thing where I chugged a big glass of wine before she came over. I was an adult woman who didn't trust my own happiness. Can you imagine what that's like?"

Aine couldn't.

"And I thought talking to Mama would help, but boy, was I wrong," Mbabazi said.

"And now?" Aine said. "Do you trust your happiness now?"

"Completely."

Before she had gone off to Canada, Mbabazi said, she and Achen paused their relationship. Achen didn't want to be the only woman Mbabazi had ever been with. She told Mbabazi about rumspringa, a tradition among the Amish, a subsect of the Anabaptist Christians of America.

"It's a rite of passage," Mbabazi explained. "Youth are given a break from practising their religion. They leave their homes and go someplace outside their communities. And when their time away ends, they get to decide if they want to come back or leave the religion for good. If they come back, that's when they are baptized. That's when they become fully Amish."

"How many come back?"

"Enough that the religion still exists!"

As the significance of Mbabazi and Achen's rumspringa dawned on Aine, she saw the idea as preposterous and reckless. "Why would you test your relationship in this way?" she said, sitting up. "What if it had broken?"

"But it didn't. And that's the point."

"So, you were both dating other people?"

"The first rule of our break was that we wouldn't tell each other about our dalliances."

"Dalliances?!"

"You don't get to judge me, Ainembabazi Gloria Kamara," Mbabazi said. "You know nothing about romantic relationships."

"What are you middle-naming me for?" Aine said. "I'm not the one who went to Canada and shagged white women and called it *dalliances*."

"Some of them were Black." Mbabazi covered her mouth with her hands as if she hadn't intended to disclose that much.

"Oh my god," Aine said. "You did sleep with other women!"

"Will you keep your voice down?"

"What if you hadn't had a rumspringa to come back from? If there wasn't Achen to come back to?" Aine said. "You might have never come back at all."

"I could only stay in Canada if you were there with me," Mbabazi said. "You and Achen. But she loves Uganda like a problem. She says all her stories are here, and she's never leaving again."

"Thank goodness," Aine said, thinking of Achen as another anchor that would keep Mbabazi moored here. "So, now the rumspringa is over? You're a fully baptized member of the Mbabazi-Achen faith?"

"I'd marry her if I could," Mbabazi said.

THE EVENING SKY WAS low, the air calm and sweet, beer bottles sweating on the wicker table. Aine swatted at a wasp buzzing around, attempting to perch on the lip of her green bottle of Krest soda. The poor creature was seduced by the citrusy beverage both bitter and sweet. Every time Aine took a sip, the fizziness went to her eyes, almost making them water. She savoured it in tiny sips.

The dynamic between Elia, Achen, and Mbabazi fascinated her. Alcohol made Mbabazi and Elia even more chatty while Achen withdrew into herself, became increasingly reticent. And she was only on her third bottle of Nile Special while Elia and Mbabazi were each on their fourth. Achen sat with her head draped over the backrest of her wooden chair, her face turned skyward as if willing the stars to emerge and put on a show for her.

When the song "Adia" came on—Elia had hooked up his phone to a portable speaker the size of a potato—Mbabazi rose from her chair and started dancing in a way Aine considered seductive, Mbabazi's narrow hips making slow circles, her hands above her head.

"Isn't it funny?" Aine said, turning to Achen. "I don't know a single word of this song, but I feel as though I understand it completely." Back home, "Adia," an old song from the nineties, was a party favourite. Everyone found their dancing feet at the sound of "Adia."

"Something about the melody." Achen reached across the table and returned the song to its beginning. "Listen to those first notes," she said, closing her eyes. "There's a mysterious sublimity."

The sunny instrumentation that began the tune was a mix of notes both festive and tender, becoming sweeter still when Oliver N'Goma sang "Cherie …" in a honey voice that threatened to break Aine's heart.

"Oh, you must stop," Mbabazi complained when Aine restarted the song once more. "Some of us are trying to dance here."

Elia had joined Mbabazi, and he was swivelling his hips at a clip, humping the air in a way that made Aine look away.

"This number has got it all," Achen said over the music, the volume of which Aine had bumped up for Mbabazi and Elia's dancing pleasure. "It feels infinite. It contains within it both the beginning of time and the end of it."

"I think of it as a song for two people who have renounced all others," Aine said. "Who are hopelessly in love with each other."

"May I have this dance?" Elia said, standing in front of Aine, his hand stretched out to her.

Her mind, all her senses roared. "I'm a terrible dancer," she confessed even as her palms burned with the need to touch him.

"The trick of dancing is to pretend you know what you're doing," he said and demonstrated with a robotic dance, his limbs dangling as though independent from the rest of his body.

"I admire that," she said of his lack of inhibition, a useful quality, she imagined, for an actor.

"Try it," he said. "It's fun."

"Oh, why not?" She gave him her hand, and he helped her up. "But don't go crying if I step on your toes."

She danced uncertainly, conscious that they were not alone. Elia put one hand on her back, guiding her with a careful pressure, and held her hand lightly with the other. She mirrored his movements in reverse, stepping forward when he stepped back so that they moved as a unit.

"You're a natural," he encouraged, making her want to do better, to loosen her hips a little more. What would it be like to dance with him without anyone watching? Would he pull her even closer, maybe even kiss her? She wanted to wrap her arms around his neck, to drape herself onto him. And he was looking at her intently, holding her with his gaze. She searched his face, his eyes. Was he flirting? Oh, what a fool she was. A boy like him, a sophomore at the most prestigious university in the country. Of course, he had been claimed by someone. What would he want with a secondary-school girl?

"Is my son making you uncomfortable?" asked Madame, coming through the small gate in the tall brick wall that wrapped around the compound, shards of broken glass along the top shimmering in the pale dusk.

"Not at all." Aine shuffled back to her chair and sat down, embarrassed by what Madame might think of her.

"You haven't been drinking, have you?" Madame probed, looking pointedly at Aine.

"Just Krest," she said, reaching for the bottle.

Madame raised it to her nose and sniffed.

"I should go." Aine rose to her feet so quickly her chair tilted and fell behind her. "My literature study group is starting soon," she said, picking the chair up, stabilizing it on the lawn. "We're discussing *Half of a Yellow Sun*, which we wish was on the syllabus but is unfortunately not. So…" Garrgh. Why was she babbling on like a moron? Lit group wasn't even until tomorrow afternoon.

"We're driving out early tomorrow morning anyway,"

Mbabazi said, coming to her rescue. "Perhaps we should turn in early too."

"I bid you adieu," Aine said awkwardly, her throat constricting. *Oh god*, she thought, *please don't let me cry.* She summoned up all her stoicism. "It was wonderful to meet you," she said, shaking Achen's hand. "And you," she added, reaching for Elia's.

"I'll write to you," Aine promised them both. "Unless you prefer email?"

"Handwritten letters are far superior," Achen said. "I haven't received correspondence in, well, forever."

"I'm happy to fix that for you," Aine said, "if you promise to reciprocate."

"Deal."

"It was lovely spending some time with you," Elia said. "You will have a friend at Makerere when you start next year."

"If I make the points," Aine said.

"Of course, you'll make the points," he said. "You're smarter than me and I got in."

Aine, not knowing how to respond to Elia's compliment, turned to Madame. "Thank you very much for everything," she said.

"You're very welcome," Madame said.

"Don't worry about Madame," Mbabazi said after she and Aine had made their way through the house to the front lawn. "I'll swallow my pride and apologize for overstepping the boundaries of what can be said to girls in a Christian school. I can't believe she thinks I'd let you consume alcohol in her backyard! It's like suddenly she has lost every ounce of respect for me."

"I'm not worried about her," Aine said. "After next term I'm out of here forever."

"I don't want her to take it out on you in the meantime."

"She doesn't scare me."

"So tough." Mbabazi smiled.

Now Aine felt none of the sadness, none of the emptiness that always ballooned inside her at Mbabazi's many departures. She felt only the pull of their sisterhood. "At least you'll be home for Christmas this year," she said. "The last two were horrible without you."

"We'll resume our New Year's Day tradition," Mbabazi said.

Aine tried not to fixate on the exhausting part of that tradition: a hike to Top of the World viewpoint—the highest elevation in Kibale National Park—to gaze down upon the three crater lakes which, at sunset, gleamed like jewels.

"So, listen." Mbabazi pulled Aine under the fragrant plumeria on Madame's front lawn. "When you go home, you can't tell Mama or Papa about this. That I was here. Not a word."

It took Aine a moment to register what her sister was asking. "Why not?"

"Mama will throw a fit. You know her. She'll say, 'Would it have killed you to pass by and greet your poor mother?'"

"So, pass by and greet your poor mother," Aine said.

"It's only forty minutes out of your way. In fact, it's right on the way if you take the Mbarara route to Kampala!"

"Don't you understand? I can't risk her and Achen being in the same space, breathing the same air."

"Our mother has many abilities, but she cannot divine the air. Nobody can."

"I'm not kidding, Aine." Suddenly there was a sharp edge to Mbabazi's voice. "What Mama doesn't know can't hurt her. Do you understand?"

"All right, all right," Aine said.

"Promise?"

"Walai." Aine cut her index finger across her throat the way Zai always did. "I won't breathe a word."

6

PAPA WAS LATE. NO surprise there; he was always late picking up Aine from school. She had seen Zai and Jamila off; their driver, Mandevu, was always on time. Now she sat on top of her metal trunk, the mid-morning sun kissing her knees. All around her, the morning buzzed with excitement, students milling about, yelling goodbye before boarding kamunyes that pulled up one after the other. Parents parked their cars on the side of the road and stepped out to scan the crowd of uniformed students, looking for their daughters. A taxi conductor hopped out near the roundabout and sang the stops along his route—Rugombe, Kyenjojo, Kakabara, Mubende—like a bad poem repeated over and over. Another conductor yanked the door of his commuter taxi closed, the students inside packed shoulder to shoulder. Their suitcases, held together with a network of dusty ropes, were piled on the roof of the minibus. It circled the roundabout and went down the murram road before disappearing out of view. Orange dust tinted the morning.

Aine reached inside her backpack for *Lyrics Alley*, one of half a dozen novels Achen had sent her via post. Aine had started reading it during the dead period at the end of the school term when teachers were holed up in the staff room grading exams and writing report cards, the students left to their own devices. The young protagonist was sexier than any boy Aine had ever encountered between the covers of a book. A burgeoning poet, and he was only in college! When fate struck, leaving him paralyzed, his great despair became Aine's own.

"You're not converting to Islam, are you?" Papa's voice.

Aine looked up to see her father standing in front of her. She'd been so engrossed she hadn't seen him approach, hadn't noticed that the crowd of students had thinned, and that morning had given way to afternoon.

"What held you up?" she asked, rising.

"I wanted you to have the whole morning to read." He took the book out of her hands and inspected the cover, two women wearing red thobes. "This any good?"

She retrieved the book and put it back in her backpack. As far as she knew, Papa never touched fiction; he was devoted to the biographies of political revolutionaries and to science books. "You're looking well, Papa."

He was sharp as ever in his short-sleeved Kaunda suit, the buttons straining slightly against his hard round belly. Embracing him, she was comforted by the familiar smell of his cologne, an understated musk.

He kissed her on the forehead and then held her at arm's length. "Not a single phone call this month?" His expression had turned accusatory.

She frowned. Had it really been that long since she'd called him? In the past she'd called home frequently, especially toward the end of the term when her homesickness was most intense, but she hadn't needed or missed her parents so much lately. Whenever she'd gone to the call-box at the canteen, she talked to Achen about books and writing and Achen's podcast, which Aine had been listening to through headphones in the computer lab.

"It's the mocks," she lied. "They are just as intense as the real finals."

"Excuses, excuses." Her father was unconvinced. "And how were they?"

She produced her report card from an outer pocket of her backpack and presented it to him.

"A in literature," he mumbled. "B in history. A very unfortunate D in geography." He glared at her.

"Mocks are usually tougher than the actual finals," she said. "It's not my fault that geography was full of statistics and graphs and pie charts. I'm rubbish at maths, you know that."

Her father furrowed his brow as if angry or confused. "What will you do if the same questions appear on the finals?"

"This is not a bad grade," she said a little too defensively. "I have enough points to get me into Makerere."

"Not on government sponsorship," he said.

"I don't know what you want from me." She started toward the pine-green Landcruiser he'd parked on the side of the road, leaving her metal trunk for her father. It was nearly empty anyway, the grub she'd brought from home long finished. Climbing into the front passenger seat, she felt a pang of hunger. She'd skipped breakfast in anticipation of the delicious welcome-home lunch Mama always cooked.

Papa heaved the luggage into the boot and came around to the driver's seat. When he turned the key in the ignition, air hissed through the dashboard vents, at first warm, then cool. Aine removed her necktie and threw it over her shoulder to land on the back seat with her backpack. She undid the top two buttons of her shirt, offering her neck and chest to the cool current. As Papa eased the vehicle onto the road riddled with potholes, she switched the radio station from Kamwenge FM to Voice of Toro FM, which played way better foreign music.

"Mbwenu nkaabo nobagambahoki?" Papa was gesturing out his window at a group of girls walking along the side of the road. Three of them had traded in their flat school shoes for platform espadrilles, which were all the rage. The girls had knotted their white shirts under their chests, showing off their bare midriffs.

"They're just having a bit of fun, that's all," she said. People like Papa who had never gone to boarding school didn't understand the sense of freedom when the gates were finally, after three months, flung open. She wished her father didn't insist on driving her to school at the beginning of the term and picking her up when it ended. She missed out on exploring Fort Portal, like those girls enjoying their independence before returning home, yet another prison.

"A bit of fun!" He scoffed, signalling left as they approached the Fort Portal–Kamwenge highway. Vehicles on the blue-grey tarmac zoomed past, heading toward the town centre. When there was a break, he stepped on the accelerator and joined the sparse westbound traffic toward Bigodi. "On BBC the other day," he said, "I heard scientists discussing the teenage brain."

Aine rolled her eyes. *Here we go again.*

"Basically, the cables transmitting the signals across the highways of your brain are not fully developed yet," he said. "That's why young people famously make poor choices."

Aine felt accused. "What you're saying is that I have half a brain."

"It's just not fully developed yet," her father said. "There's a difference. It's a physiological fact. I'm not making this up. That's why, for example, you make promises but don't fulfill them—because you don't think about the consequences. How your choices affect other people."

"Oh my god, I said I was sorry I didn't call!"

"No, you didn't," he said. "And a person who is truly sorry does not say it in that tone."

"Maybe it's a symptom of my underdeveloped brain," she said. "I mean, if your science is correct, I'm behaving exactly as I should. Aren't I?"

He shook his head at her frustration and trained his eyes on the road. She watched his profile for a moment, his short greying beard. When she was little, she loved rubbing her face against his scratchy stubble in the evenings, laughing as it tickled her cheek.

"Okay, I'm sorry," she said. "I mean it."

When he still didn't respond, she said, "I love you, Papa."

"Where your love stops," he said, grinning, "that's where mine begins."

"It's not a competition."

He laughed, and she was glad to have smoothed things over. She looked out the window at the sprawling tea plantations, at the men and women pinching tea leaves and throwing fistfuls over their shoulders to land in the large baskets yoked to their backs. The bosomy landscape rolled greenly, rising and falling toward Kibale Forest.

"I cannot believe that the next time I pick you up from school will be the last time," he said, bringing Aine's attention back. "This time next year I will drive you to Makerere and leave you there, in the big city."

"Mbabazi is there now," she said. "I won't be alone."

"Have you heard from her since she returned?"

"We've spoken on the phone."

"You should see where she is working now."

"I hear the toilets especially blew you away."

The sound of his laughter filled the car. "I've never seen a toilet so white and clean."

Daylight was halved as the cruiser plunged them into

Kibale Forest. Papa slowed the car as chimps crossed the road at a leisurely pace, a playful baby jumping to catch a ride on its unwilling mother's back.

The rain came out of nowhere, as though a tap in the sky had suddenly been turned on. So far, August had been rainless, before it a dry July, sluggish days steeped in heat. Now rainfall pummelled the car with such force and volume the wiper blades had to work overtime to keep up. The road was barely visible through the windscreen.

"The rain gods have decided to waste a year's worth of water on a single afternoon," Papa said, gripping the steering wheel tightly, knuckles threatening to break skin.

"Just pull over and let it pass." The flashes of lightning followed by roaring thunder frightened Aine. "Isn't that what you're supposed to do in a storm?"

"Not when you are surrounded by trees everywhere," her father said, guiding the cruiser up a steep incline. "In the forest, the trick of driving in a storm is to steer into it."

"Into the storm? That's mad!"

"It means going against every single one of your instincts," he said. "But it works."

"Every time?"

"Don't you trust me? Your old man has been driving cars since before you were born."

He was clearly straining to make out the road through the deluge cascading down the windscreen. Another flash of lightning made Aine cower. She whimpered like a puppy.

"Lightning can't harm us in here," her father said. "I know you ditched physics in O-level, but surely you've heard of a Faraday cage?"

"Not the time for a science lesson."

"If lightning were to strike," he carried on, "these walls, the metal frame, would be our very own protective cage."

"I just want it to stop."

Within a few minutes the storm let up as abruptly as it had begun. They were exiting the forest, emerging into the grassland, a migratory corridor that connected Queen Elizabeth National Park to Kibale Forest. Here, a mild drizzle floated on the wind, washing the prickly acacias that dotted the fields of elephant grass. Aine released the breath she'd been unconsciously holding. She listened to her father talking calmly, as if the storm had not terrified him one bit. He was explaining about Michael Faraday's experiments with electric currents and magnetism.

That was the problem with her father's stories. They meandered, skirting the point, almost never ending. Years of long-distance driving had turned him into an unhurried storyteller. Now his voice became part of the ambience: the thrum of the car's machinery and the music playing at a volume just below hearing.

Aine's heart cracked wide open as the cruiser wound through Magombe Swamp on the edge of Bigodi Trading Centre. The palm fronds and papyruses, emerald from the rain's cleansing, waved welcomingly in the breeze.

Monkeys flitted among the branches of tall polita figs. Beyond the guardrail, olive baboons roughhoused on the banks of the creek, the water almost black. Now the car climbed the hill where the Bee Hive Bar and Bistro loomed, walls painted the eye-smacking orange-yellow of a honeycomb. Across the road, the Bigodi Wetlands visitor centre bustled with activity, tourists admiring colourful baskets at the entrance of the crafts shop.

Aine would rest today and report for duty tomorrow, accompanying the senior guides when they took tourists out on the trails. It was an unpaid apprenticeship, but every once in a while, a generous tourist tipped her even though she came along to learn and stayed quiet unless spoken to. Once, a Lebanese photographer intent on finding a green-breasted pitta gave Aine fifty dollars for waiting with her. Aine had entertained the woman with stories such as how the name Bigodi was derived from the Rutooro word *okugodya*, which means "ambling" or "walking tiredly." A very long time ago—before cars and all that—when visitors to Kibale Forest reached Bigodi on foot, they were almost always too tired to cross the swamp. Without a bridge or anything, it was so daunting that just the sight of the swamp doubled the travellers' tiredness. So they'd set up camp and rest before the crossing.

Papa pulled up under the mango tree across from Mama's duka, Lydia's Convenience written in yellow cursive above the entrance. As Aine opened her door, humid air rose around her. The sun was shooting down between dishrag clouds, warming the muddy post-rain earth. She bounded toward her mother, now emerging onto the shop's veranda.

"Kulikayo kikazi kyangye," Mama said, opening her arms. She was wearing her maroon shift dress with the flappy butterfly sleeves.

"Nalugayo." Aine fell into her embrace, the force nearly toppling her tall slender mother.

"Kusha onyiliire mwaanawe!" Mama kneaded Aine's waist, squeezed her upper arms. "What are they feeding you at school?"

"Are you saying I've gained weight?" Aine replied, touching her own round hips.

"You're the very picture of good health," Mama said, pinching Aine's cheeks, a superstitious thing women did after commenting on a child's health so as not to jinx it. "Your body is finding its perfect shape. That's all."

She said things like that and Aine adored her.

But then she said, "All the glory goes back to God," and Aine had to reach deep within herself to reply, "Amen," because that was no doubt the response her mother wanted to hear. It was a good thing Mama never read newspapers. If she had read Aine's article in which she compared the Christian God to a celestial dictator, the mood of her homecoming would have been entirely different.

"Smells good," said Papa, skirting the cash counter as if to follow the delicious aroma to its source. Aine followed him along the narrow path down the middle of the duka, overstocked with sacks of sugar, various flours, rice, and dried peas. In the spacious storage room at the back, crates of soda were stacked along the walls. Aine took the lid off a bowl at the centre of the round table Mama had set for lunch. Thin slices of avocado and steamed enshwiiga. She replaced the lid and followed Papa out through the back door. They served themselves from the pot simmering on the portable charcoal stove on the veranda. Fingers of matooke steeped in groundnut sauce. Katogo with avocado and steamed greens was Aine's favourite dish.

"Have you heard from your sister since she came back?" Mama asked as she ladled food into her own bowl.

"We've spoken on the phone a few of times," Aine said, repeating exactly the response she'd given Papa. She avoided Mama's eyes.

"Do you know," Papa said, "that people pay good money just to make an appointment to see her? Before meeting with her for a consultation, they pay an appointment fee. And then there's the consultation fees when they do get to see her. All of this before she determines what's causing their infertility. Before she recommends any treatments."

"The expensive treatment which may or may not work," said Mama. "Infertility can make you maskini. You may succeed and have your child, but you'll be too poor to feed it."

Aine thought about how Mama had blamed her many miscarriages between Mbabazi and Aine on witchcraft practised by malicious neighbours or relatives. So to her, Aine's birth signified light's triumph over darkness.

Back inside as they ate, her parents continued gushing about Mbabazi's practice. Aine pictured Mbabazi explaining it all to them the way she'd explained it to Madame and Aine over dinner. She wished she could tell them that their daughter, in addition to being a sought-after infertility expert, was also in love. And not in love with an ordinary woman. Achen had a knack for telling difficult and sad stories in such a way that the listener was not completely weighed down by the details. In one special episode, she had gone up north to a refugee settlement and distributed voice recorders to youths displaced by the civil war in South Sudan. The young boys and girls interviewed each other, and one of them, a wannabe rap artist, even took over Achen's role as the host. Some of the stories the teenagers gathered were light, others extremely heavy and harrowing. In one interview, a girl Aine's age said she wished she had a bunch of condoms to always carry around with her so that the next time rapists overpowered her, she could beg them to put on a condom and not impregnate her.

"Fertilization is fertilization whether it takes place in the body or outside it!" Papa was discouraging Mama from using the phrase *test tube babies*.

"Mbabazi doesn't mind when I say it," Mama said.

"It's just inappropriate."

"Kodi!" called a small voice from the duka.

"Turiyo, turiyo," Mama rose from the table, saved from Papa's relentless need to turn everything into a teaching moment. Aine could hear Mama talking to a child-voiced customer who spoke in an out-of-breath way as if he'd run all the way to the shop. His mother had sent him for cooking oil and curry powder. She pictured Mama measuring out Mukwano Vegetable Oil into a plastic baggy, tearing a sachet of Simba Mbili from a strip of many hanging from a hook.

"Gyenda mpora," Mama called after the boy, reminding him to slow down. "It is slippery out there. Don't fall."

Aine panicked when Mama came back and inquired about the mocks. Papa produced the report card from his breast pocket and slid it across the table to Mama.

"Ainembabazi Gloria Kamara!" Mama said in a tone of disappointment. The D in geography was the first grade to catch her eye.

"Owangye," Papa addressed Mama by their nickname for each other: *My one*. "Don't you know they make the mocks very hard so that students will study harder for the finals?"

Mama ignored the placation. "Your sister got twenty-five points in the mocks!"

"Mbabazi was taking four subjects," Aine said, pushing her plate away.

"And she got As in all four," Mama said sharply. "What is your excuse when you only have three main subjects to focus on?"

There ought to be a rule, Aine thought, *that parents couldn't openly compare their children. At least not in front of said children.*

"Aine, you're a girl," Mama said. "If you get fifteen points in the real finals and a boy also gets fifteen points, who do you think Makerere University will take? The boy or the girl?"

"The boy," Mama answered her own rhetorical question.

"Sorry I'm not as smart as Dr. Mbabazi Kamara." A mix of anger and jealousy crowded Aine's throat, making her voice pathetically squeaky.

"Did anyone say anything about that?" Mama demanded.

"Didn't have to."

Aine rose abruptly and crossed to the door, taking her almost empty bowl of katogo with her. Emptying it into the garbage sack, she dunked the bowl into the bucket of soapy water. Even as she went down the alley that ran behind the row of shops, she could hear Mama complaining urgently while Papa's voice remained calm, placating. She picked up the pace as if to outrun her parents' disappointment in her. She kicked an empty tin of margarine and sent it flying toward a heap of rubbish swarming with flies. The kaloli prancing about the trash made an annoyed guttural noise and carried on digging its long beak into the wet refuse. Legend had it that the creator, fresh out of raw materials, had created kaloli from leftover bits of carrion. That's why Marabou storks were hideous. Did God use up all his quality bits on Mbabazi and scrounge around for scraps to make Aine?

The jacarandas at the end of the alley were in full

bloom, large panicles a shock of purplish blue. A colour so dazzling it defied definition. The trees were full of birds chattering loudly though the sun was now heating up, filling the air with the smell of wet earth. She turned left and walked along the side of Mwebesa's carpentry workshop, a boxy structure constructed from rusted iron sheets. Mwebesa and Sons Co. Ltd. was written on a plank of wood nailed to the trunk of the mango tree in front of the workshop. Half the businesses in Bigodi, even more in Fort Portal, had "and Sons" in their name. Or "Brothers." Never "and Daughters" or "Sisters."

She considered crossing the street to Aunty Sheila's Beauty Salon, where her childhood friend Kemi worked as a hairdresser. But the mere thought of having to be cheerful for her was exhausting. She felt fat and stupid. She'd just go home and lie down, catch up with Kemi tomorrow.

She walked along the tarmac road toward the edge of the trading centre. A red Massey Ferguson tractor passed her, the *ta ta ta ta* roar of its engine filling every inch of available space in her head. She pressed her palms to her ears until it summitted, and then descended, the hill.

"Ainembabazi!" Someone was yelling her name through the fading tractor noise. She looked across the road and saw her godmother, Sayuni, waving. It was too late to pretend she hadn't seen her. She waved back at her, hoping that would be the end of it, but her godmother crossed the road hurriedly, her braless chest bouncing with each step.

"Watahamu ryaarishi?"

"Just now," Aine said, indicating her school uniform as evidence she'd just arrived.

Sayuni greeted her in the traditional way, which required Aine to bend one knee and rest her left hand on her right as she extended it to her godmother, who was one of her mother's best friends. "Keije, buhoro, buhoro-gye." *Peace and good peace.*

"Your studies are going well?" Sayuni asked in Rukiga. Aine shrugged. "They're going."

"You will finish soon," she said encouragingly. "Only one more term."

"Just one more."

"You will come over on Saturday and help me with the baking, yes?"

Oh, the baking! An excuse for nosey Sayuni, as if she were Aine's biological aunt, to counsel her about boys and marriage. She was always going on about how she'd kept herself pure for her husband. Their first time together was between crisp white sheets; there was nothing like a spot of blood to strengthen a marriage.

"I'm working at the sanctuary," Aine said, feigning regret. "I'm this close to receiving my certificate!"

"That's very good," Sayuni said. "A girl should have her own money."

"Exactly."

"Well, when you have a day off…"

"I'll try," Aine said and thanked her. They went their separate ways: Sayuni sloping toward the shops, Aine homeward. Near Forest Lodge, she turned left and took the shortcut through the banana plantation, wet mulch crunching beneath her shoes. Cassava and coffee plants were interspersed with tall banana trees top-heavy with bunches of matooke. She stripped a handful of shiny red coffee cherries from a drooping stalk and popped them into her mouth. The sweet pulp was soft and sticky. She spat the hard pits out at Rafiki. The family cat gave her one look only.

"I missed you, too, Rafiki," she said as the fat cat sauntered along her merry way, probably looking for mice and hatchlings to gorge herself on. An ironic name, Rafiki. The little beast hadn't a friendly bone in her body.

Aine entered the compound through the opening in the hedge of oleander. Home was exactly as she had left it. The ducks still pooped mid-waddle. The chickens clucked and pecked their beaks against the hardened earth as if they had a quota to fill. Two rainwater barrels stood at the front corners of the house with its red brick finish, a padlock on the door. It was deathly quiet. After the near-constant noise of school, the silence, vast and welcoming, was a salve. She fished the house key from where Mama always hid it under the clay planter in which leggy coleuses grew vigorously.

Inside, she flung the windows open and sank into the long sofa, her legs dangling over the edge. Her parents smiled down at her from a framed photograph on the wall. It was a studio portrait. Papa, in a three-piece suit and tie, perched on the edge of a tall stool, a peacock— surely a prop—balancing on his left shoulder. Mama stood beside him, her hand on his other shoulder, her big pregnant belly making a tent of her maxi dress. They were so young. Mama was barely twenty years old when she'd had Mbabazi. Aine liked Mama's big hair. Round and poofy like a soft cloud.

Removing her shoes and socks, she padded down the hall to her room, surprised by its daytime darkness. Here, unlike at the duka, there was no electricity. But there could be if Papa could afford it. Once, he'd requested a quote from Umeme, the power distribution company, but when the engineer told him the amount, Papa let out a prolonged whistle of disbelief. "That's Aine's school fees for a whole year!" Maybe if Aine got government sponsorship for uni, civilization would finally reach her home.

She unbolted her bedroom window. As she pushed it open, a lizard launched itself into the flowerbed below and skittered toward the yellow oleander beyond.

Something shiny and red caught Aine's eye. On her bed was a gift-wrapped box. She reached for it, lifted it carefully. It was hefty. Mbabazi had mentioned leaving something for her at home. A small card was taped to the box. "A little birdie told me you're on your way to becoming a bona fide tour guide. Congratulations!" was written in Mbabazi's careless, almost illegible handwriting.

Impatiently, Aine tore through the wrapping and saw a photograph of binoculars printed on the box. A squeal escaped her lips. She always had to borrow the one free pair of binoculars at the sanctuary, and sometimes another trainee or a tourist who didn't have their own beat her to it. She lifted her sleek new pair delicately out of the box and regarded them with wonder. They were a deep shade of green, almost black. The rubber armouring on the barrels made them secure in her grip. Her very own binoculars!

Screwing off the caps, she went to the window and raised the binoculars to her eyes. She pulled into view a pied wagtail poking his head in the hedge's undergrowth for a snack of worms. The focus was so crisp and sharp, as if the kanyamunyu were right in front of her, as if she could reach out and pull the worm from its beak. She swept her view past the bath shed toward the ramshackle poultry coop. A drake chased an unwilling female and mounted her aggressively. Duck sex was truly horrifying, yet she couldn't look away. What the hell was wrong with her?

SHE WASHED HER HAIR and suffused it with the expensive moisturizers Mbabazi always brought home by the boxful so that Mama never ran out. Using a wide-toothed comb, she brushed out every knot before embarking on the laborious process of making chunky twist braids that would, when she untwisted them in the morning, give her a voluminous twist out not unlike Achen's. She stood in front of the full-length mirror in her parents' bedroom, sectioning and brushing and twisting, swaying a little to the music on the radio. The chorus consisted of the groans of a male rapper and his woman. Mama disliked that sort of music, claiming it contained insidious messaging that could turn a good girl into "a harlot." So Aine turned off the radio quickly when she heard the car door closing outside. Emerging into the hallway, she relieved Papa of the backpack she'd forgotten at the duka when she left in haste. He rested her tin trunk at the bottom of her wardrobe.

"Look at this mess!" Mama was yelling from her bedroom down the hall.

"I was going to tidy up after," Aine called, hurrying back to her parents' room. But Mama grumbled on anyway, about the towel on the floor, the hair in her brushes. She held the tub of TCB Naturals. "Is it so hard to put the lid back on?"

"I wasn't finished!"

Later, at dinnertime, it wasn't long before Mama again brought up Aine's D in geography.

"What I want to know is this: What is your plan?" she said. "You have less than three months until the finals. How will you turn a D into an A in such a short time?"

Aine stabbed her fork into a garden egg. "Study hard, I guess."

"I'm so glad you said that," Mama said. "Your father and I were talking. We have decided that throughout the school break, you will focus only on your books. Your apprenticeship at the sanctuary can wait."

Aine inhaled sharply. How had she not seen this coming? "Can I work part-time?"

"Your sister didn't even come home for the school break before her A-levels." Mama reminded her how Mbabazi had asked Madame to let her stay at school and study, and how Papa was the one to bring supplies to her when school reopened. "You have to know that God helps those who help themselves."

"The swamp is not going anywhere, Aine," Papa said. "You can finish your training during your vacation and immediately start working there. This is not a punishment. It's a gift."

"Whatever," Aine grumbled. Their minds were made up. It was no use trying to convince them otherwise.

"You're angry that you get to sit on your buttocks and read?" Mama said, furrowing her brow. "Let me laugh at you. The rains have started. Other girls will be digging and planting from morning to evening. They will be dreaming of going back to school."

Actually, Aine thought but didn't say, *so will I.*

"You're a very smart girl," Papa said, his voice low and soft. "You've just gotten used to coasting along. You get good grades without trying too hard. But that was O-level. I'm sure you understand that A-level is different."

Aine took her plate outside to the kitchen, and without a word, she went to her room.

"I FEEL LIKE I'M being punished," she told Mbabazi on Mama's phone the following day.

"They're not wrong though," Mbabazi said. "Your final exams. They are your one shot to set yourself up for a good career. It's all that should matter to you right now. When the exams are finally out of the way, you'll have nine months to do as you please. Nine months!"

"Did Mama put you up to this?"

"Aine, I'm always on your side."

The problem with being the youngest was that everyone else got to make your decisions for you. "I wouldn't have minded working half days or even just on weekends," Aine said. "I mean, am I going to study every minute of every day? From morning to evening? Even you didn't study that hard."

"That's true," Mbabazi said. "But I didn't have any distractions either. I want that for you too."

"Fine," Aine said. "Is Achen there? Can I say hello?"

"She's in Mbarara for a story."

"When's she back?"

"Tomorrow."

"And Elia?"

"Okay, get this: he was here for dinner two days ago," Mbabazi said. "Brought this girl with him. Delassai or some such name with *sigh* in it. She's the Mary to his Jesus. Apparently, they haven't got the right chemistry or something, so the director is having them do these bizarre bonding exercises together. Elia was cutting her meat for her. Feeding her with his fork. It was so uncomfortable to watch."

Aine had no right to feel betrayed, she knew that, but fuck! "Were Jesus and Mary even that close?" She slumped onto her bed.

"Nkugambireki," Mbabazi said. "Theatre actors are such weirdos."

"Do you think they're sleeping together?"

"Who cares if they are?" Mbabazi said. "I just want him to admit the weirdness of it all, but he won't."

"A name like that," Aine said, "I bet she's pretty."

"Wait, do you fancy Elia?" Mbabazi's voice was tentative, as if the very idea were an impossibility, entirely out of the question. "Did I know this?"

"Why would you?"

"You cannot fancy him, Aine," Mbabazi commanded. "He's one of my closest friends. It would be too weird."

"Clearly, you have nothing to worry about," Aine said. "I doubt he even remembers I exist."

"That's not true."

"Oh yeah? Does he ask about me?"

"Like I said, actors are a strange breed," Mbabazi said. "We love them because they make us feel things. But when you fall for an actor, it's likely you're falling for someone who does not exist. Trust me, you've dodged a bullet."

"How lucky for me!"

7

I N THE MORNING, AINE woke to the shrill voices of poultry piercing the dawn. One rooster started, setting all the others off, an alarm clock without a snooze button. She got up; she needed the loo anyway. Yawning sleepily, she wrapped a shawl over her nightdress and stumbled down the dark hallway. No sooner had she reached the door than she heard the crisp, clear sound of a bicycle bell, one of her uncles delivering the milk. She turned back, took the milk jug from the dining table, and opened the door.

"Mwaramutse?" Nshuti, her favourite uncle, greeted her brightly.

"Mwaramutse," she replied and went to give him a hug. Uncle Nshuti always spoke to her in Kinyarwanda, and unlike Mama, he didn't make a fuss when Aine butchered the language. She held the white jug against the stainless-steel can strapped to the rear bike rack.

"Your father isn't home?" he asked, indicating the empty spot where the Landcruiser always parked.

"Kasese," she said and asked about her uncle's honey-bees, her curiosity meant to inspire him to bring her some honey already. Nshuti kept an apiary, bee boxes hanging from the trees that demarcated the boundary between the forest and his vegetable garden. The buzzing insects also discouraged elephants from crossing over to destroy the crops belonging to him and his mother, Kaaka Nyirasafari.

"I'm harvesting some honey this afternoon," he said. "Do you want to come and assist me?"

"Her books are keeping her very busy," said Mama, crossing the veranda.

"Don't worry, darling," Uncle said, securing the lid back onto the can. "I shall bring you some honey tomorrow. A full jerry can."

"Thanks, Uncle."

He disengaged the bicycle kickstand and started toward the main thoroughfare; there were at least a dozen more stops on his milk route. Late delivery was bad for business, and people often paid for a month's worth of milk at a time.

Aine took the milk across the compound to the kitchen, an ochre log cabin. Bands of orange glowed over the horizon, daylight's long fingers erasing the night's darkness, brightening the sky. She went to the latrine, which was tucked away in the banana plantation. When she came back, she loaded charcoal onto the sigiri and kindled it, fanning the embers with a plastic plate. Already she was falling into a familiar routine, making breakfast while Mama got ready for her day at the duka. She emptied the jug of milk into a saucepan, topped it up with a bit of water, and set it to boil. With a pestle, she smashed a thumb of ginger into a yellow pulp, which she added to the steaming milk along with shredded mdalasini and a handful of Golden Tea. The chai soon turned deep brown, strong and fragrant.

"Mornings are easier when you are around," said Mama as Aine put a thermos of chai in Mama's carry bag so she'd have her breakfast, as usual, at the duka.

Aine smiled self-deprecatingly. "Sure, Mama."

"I mean it," her mother said. "Will you join me later for lunch?"

The day before, after lunch, Mama had gone across the road to visit with Jovanice, the dressmaker who sat working all day behind the sewing machine on her veranda. Aine had had to tend the duka, the most boring job, for over an hour. "We'll see."

AS DAYS STRETCHED INTO weeks, Aine realized that staying home all day wasn't nearly as punishing as she'd expected. Taking her breakfast in the kibanda— the thatch gazebo in the flower garden just outside her parents' bedroom—she browsed her geography notes and even read from the textbook. She learned that the Nubian plate of the East African Rift was splitting in two, a gradual and slow process that would, in about ten million years, create a new ocean basin. She wondered what chaos would ensue were that process to occur instantaneously, like a time-lapse video, the continent suddenly ripping apart, yawning to swallow everything on its surface. What sound would it make, the skin of the Earth ripping across thousands of kilometres?

By afternoon her imagination took over, and she sought a diversion in fiction. Camara Laye, Ngũgĩ wa Thiong'o, Graham Greene. She was spoiled for choice. Sometimes she took solo walks to the swamp to test out her binoculars. But today, just like the day before, she returned to the salon to hang out with her old friend Kemi, though the chances of Mama spotting her weren't zero.

Always, she and Kemi talked about boys. Kemi had dropped out of Bigodi Secondary School after a road worker got her pregnant and then denied ever sleeping with her. Now she had a new guy she was being coy about. But it was hard to press her about who he was when the salon was busy: Kemi dyeing an older woman's grey hair black, Alban buzzing some guy's head clean so that his scalp shone like an egg. There were posters on the walls of every haircut imaginable—various fades and crewcuts— but this guy had sprung for a clean shave. Perhaps he was balding anyway? The smell of alcohol suffused the air when Alban sprayed his client's head from a bottle.

Aine made herself useful, cleaning up while Kemi moisturized and brushed her client's hair once the hair dryer timed out.

"Are you embarrassed by him?" she pressed Kemi later

as she walked her homeward. "Is it one of those boda boda guys?"

"Over my dead body!" Kemi said in Rutooro.

Good, Aine thought. Her friend could do better than those layabouts who'd just catcalled them. "Is it someone we went to school with?"

"Yes," she said.

"Aha! Now we're getting somewhere." Aine went down the list of all the boys she remembered from their primary school days. No, it wasn't Isaac or Gerald or Odong or Peter or Naboth or Dennis or Mugume or Apollo. "Dan?"

A smile played on Kemi's lips. "Please don't make fun of him."

But Aine couldn't help herself. "Jackfruit Dan?" He'd been a year ahead of them but had repeated Primary Seven after failing his leaving exams. In the end he'd graduated the same year as Aine and Kemi. Older and taller than everyone in their class, he often brought a whole jackfruit to school for lunch. He'd slice it open on a bed of banana leaves, then go around the playground hawking palm-sized sections for two hundred shillings a piece.

"He's a game ranger now in Kanyawara," Kemi bragged. "And he's really, really into me."

"And are you really, really into him?" Aine tried to take the judgment out of her voice.

"Trust me, when you're a single mother, it's rare to find someone like that," Kemi said. "A guy who still loves you more than you love him, even after meeting your kid."

"When do you even get to see him if he's way over in Kanyawara," Aine asked, "on the far side of the forest?"

"He comes every other weekend, we enjoy life, he goes back," Kemi said. "It's better this way. Gives us a chance to miss each other."

Aine didn't want a boyfriend who was always away. "Don't you want to fall asleep in his arms every night? And wake up with him beside you?"

"Those things of romance are overrated," Kemi said, sweeping the bangs of her overly shiny weave off from her forehead. The extensions were trimmed unevenly; the sides looked like a bar graph. "It's a trick nature plays on us so that we will want to keep having sex and procreate nonstop."

"Bullshit!"

"I'm not lying. Every month there is a cluster of like three or four days when sex is all that's on my mind. Day and night. And do you know why?"

"Jackfruit Dan is a good lover?"

"Please don't call him that." She laughed. "And no, it's my stupid eggs. They are the ones controlling me. Not my brain, not my heart, but my ripe ovaries. It makes me mad because I know what's happening, yet I can't help myself. Do you know last week I took a boda boda to Kanyawara and Dan and I did it in the bush? I've still got scratches on my back."

"Okay, now you're just showing off your enviable sex life."

"Sex behind a tree is hardly enviable," her friend said.

"You should be feeling sorry for me. And anyway, Bigodi is full of men who want you. Alban's whole demeanour changes the moment you walk into the salon."

"Eww, I'm not going to have sex with Alban," Aine said. "I want my first time to be beautiful and special, with someone I love. There will be candles, rose petals everywhere. And music. Marvin Gaye or Luther Vandross."

Kemi guffawed. "Oh, my dear, you're killing me." She regaled her, as she had done before, with the unsavoury details of her own first time, how awkward and lacking in pleasure the whole experience was. She didn't enjoy it one bit, but it resulted in pregnancy, a little boy, Sweezin, already in nursery school.

"But that's why I have to plan every last detail," Aine said. "If it's something to endure, not to enjoy, then it better be with someone I truly love."

"I will be here waiting for your story," Kemi said.

BEFORE SHE KNEW IT, it was Aine's last weekend at home. She was in the kibanda rereading the "Attunement," the prelude at the beginning of Kierkegaard's *Fear and Trembling*. She'd read the stand-alone piece so many times she could almost recite it from memory. Reading it now, she was the simple man, Kierkegaard's protagonist, tagging along with Abraham and Isaac on the three-day road trip to the mountain in Moriah where the father would bind his son, a gift to him and Sarah in old age, as an offering to God.

Isaac noticed his father clench his fist in anguish, and he understood that of course Abraham didn't want to kill him; he simply had no choice. He had to do as God demanded. But just as Abraham drew the knife, the ram appeared, and Isaac was saved. But alas, it was too late. Isaac had already lost his faith. This was the part that drove Aine to the brink. That the son lost his faith in order for Abraham to become the father of faith.

"You're crying instead of reading?"

It was Mama, crouching as she approached the gazebo's entrance; the slanted thatch roof hung low.

"You're home early." Aine pushed Kierkegaard under a history textbook, but it was too late. Her mother took the smaller book, turned it over in her hands.

"Is this on the syllabus?" she said, opening it to where Aine had been.

"Yup," she lied. "Literature."

"A good person dies?" Mama squinted at the small print.

"Almost," Aine said. "And at the hands of his own father."

"This is the garbage they are having you read these days?" She threw the book onto the wooden table.

"It's Biblical," Aine said, surprised by her mother's reaction. "It's based on the story of Abraham and Isaac."

The problem with the Bible, Aine thought, was that it didn't cohere. Books preaching love alongside ones filled with carnage! How did her mother reconcile these contradictions?

"Is that what's making you sad?" Mama's expression softened, as though Aine were a child with a scraped knee. "God would never have allowed it to happen. It was a test, and Father Abraham passed it. Anyway—" She produced a chit from a pocket of her dress and set it before Aine.

"What's this?" she said, unfolding it. "Matayo 4:1–11" was scribbled in pencil across the piece of paper.

"Reverend stopped by." Mama stood up straighter. "He has asked for you to take the second reading during the service on Sunday."

Aine hadn't participated in liturgy since her confirmation. And since Mbabazi told her about Reverend Erasmus's approach to counselling, she couldn't stand the man, couldn't look at him without bile rising in her throat. "You know I don't read well in Rukiga," she said.

"You have today and tomorrow to practise," Mama said. "Reverend is dedicating the service to all our children who are returning to school. Especially the candidates sitting their O-level and A-level finals this year. You will do the reading, won't you?"

Aine had a creeping suspicion Mama had already agreed on her behalf. "That's why you came home early?" she said. "To tell me this?"

"Can't a mother make a nice dinner for her daughter?"

"Who is tending the shop?"

"Your father," she said. "He bought fresh engege from a roadside vendor, and I'm going to grill it."

Aine loved grilled tilapia, but she couldn't stand the

dirty prep work: the gutting and scaling of a fish that smelled foul. "Do you need help?"

"You just read," Mama said. "I'll call if I need you."

LEAFY BANANA TREES DECORATED every corner of the church, colourful cloth streamers floating above the lively Sunday congregation. They were singing the hymn "Ira kunaabeire ngwejegyeire," in praise of Jesus for saving us from our sinful ways. The melody was joyful, almost transcendent, robust with drums and shakers, making Aine wonder if this, perhaps, wasn't the reason why going to church every Sunday was called "a service." To dress up, clap happily, and sing songs that made a person forget their sorrows. Songs that told them that Jesus was in charge, the wonderful driver who never slept at the wheel. Destination: paradise. They sung a second hymn, and then Reverend Erasmus invited everyone to resume their seats to listen to the second lesson. That was Aine's cue. She marched up to the front and stood behind the pulpit.

"Ekikweeka kyakabiri nikiruga omukitabo kya Matayo, eshura yaakana." She raised her gaze from her Bible to regard the congregants leafing through their own holy books to find Matthew chapter four. Baskets of fruits and vegetables were lined up along the chancel. Churchgoers with no cash for the offertory basket had brought produce, which would be auctioned off at the end of the service. "I'll be reading from verses one to eleven."

As she read about the Holy Spirit guiding Jesus into the desert to be tested, she noticed what seemed like a typo.

Whoever translated the Bible into Runyankole-Rukiga had rendered *desert* as *ihamba*, "a forest." Aine found that she didn't herself know the right translation. But surely there had to be one; a desert and a forest were the most opposite of landscapes.

As soon as she got back home from church, she asked Papa, "How do you say desert in Rukiga?"

"Why do you ask?" He was spraying the Landcruiser with water from a hose attached to the rain barrel.

Aine read the verse. "'Okuruga aho Yesu yaayebemberwa Omwoyo kuza omu ihamba kwohibwa Sitaane.' Everyone knows he was tempted in the Judean desert."

"You read Rukiga so beautifully." He beamed with pride. "Do you know that more than half the students in university cannot write or read in their mother tongues? All they know is the white man's language. If you ask me, our education system is broken."

"That's great," she said impatiently. "But a desert. What is it?"

Her father wrung and re-wrung a washcloth. "Have you asked your mother?" he said, hanging the small towel on the clothesline. "If there's a word for *desert* in Kinyarwanda, it will be the same in Rukiga. Or very close."

Mama was, as usual, gossiping with her friends.

"She said there are no deserts in Rwanda or Uganda, so why should we have a specific name for a landscape that doesn't exist for us?" Aine said. "Which is mental. We've never seen God either, but how many names do we have for him?"

"*Ihamba* also means wilderness," her father said after a long thoughtful pause. "If you want to go even deeper, think loneliness. Isolation. Wasn't that what the son of God was after? Solitude?"

But Aine wasn't fully convinced. English was wordy. So many names for the same thing. Why was her language seemingly poor in comparison? "You know who would know for sure? Uncle Ambrose. Let's call him."

Papa's face closed like a fist.

"Did something happen?" Aine said. Papa's younger brother had dropped out of school after O-level to serve in the UPDF. After their parents had died within a year of each other, Papa convinced Ambrose to quit the army and take over their estate—the cattle kraal and coffee plantation—in Kabale.

"The people closest to us are hardest to forgive," Papa said in Rukiga.

"But what did he do?" Aine had only the fondest memories of her uncle. A wordsmith, he was a walking encyclopedia of folktales and sayings. He would arrive unannounced and with much aplomb, bearing gifts. Eclairs and sweet biscuits for the women, a jerry can of enturire—extremely potent banana gin—for Papa. The brothers drank themselves foolish and sang folksongs late into the night, dancing ekitaguriro under the stars. But now that Aine thought about it, he hadn't visited for a long while, though it was possible he had come while she was away at school.

"Let's just say that my brother is not the man I thought

he was." Papa's expression was mournful, almost apologetic. "That's all."

ALL SUNDAY AFTERNOON, MAMA and Aine roasted groundnuts and maize. They chopped onions and kamulari peppers and singed all that in boiling ghee. The mixture would solidify in a plastic tub overnight. At school, a spoonful of the clarified butter transformed Aine's twice-a-day serving of posho and beans into something almost tolerable.

In the evening, when she started packing her luggage, Mama came and parked herself in the doorway. "Your sister keeps discovering new ways to waste money," she said, crossing her arms as she leaned against the doorpost.

Well, it is her money, Aine thought but didn't say.

"She's buying a plane ticket to South Africa, just to run in some marathon."

"That's nothing new," Aine said. Mbabazi had run marathons in Kigali, Nairobi, Dar es Salaam, and Toronto. "Do you have something against South Africa in particular?"

"Millions of people will sleep on empty stomachs tonight," Mama said. "Children are dying from kwashiorkor. But she will use her money to go and run with strangers in faraway places."

Aine sighed. "You expect her to single-handedly solve world hunger?"

As if displeased with Aine's response, as well as by the way she was packing her things, Mama used her foot to nudge Aine out of the way. She unpacked everything and redid it systematically. The wrapped bags of flour and sugar on one side of the trunk; books, clothes, and toiletries on the other.

"She is too restless," Mama complained, stacking three boxes of Always maxi-pads into a corner of the suitcase. "The woman cannot stay in one place. She's always itching to go, go, go somewhere else."

Aine leaned against her wardrobe and watched her mother pack with precision. It was like magic the way she made things fit perfectly where Aine had run out of space.

"Some of your sister's hobbies will get her killed one day."

"All right, she's an adult woman," Aine said, her tone more forceful than intended. "I think she knows what she's doing."

Mama scoffed. She closed the neatly packed trunk and reached into her brassiere, pulling out a crisp fifty-thousand-shilling note. "Since I kept you from working at the wetlands." She pressed the money into the palm of Aine's hand and closed her fingers over it. "Don't tell your father."

"Thanks, Mama."

"Shh." She touched her index finger to her mouth as she crossed to the door, where she turned and smiled. "You're very welcome."

She did things like this, and Aine simply adored her.

8

PAPA PARKED THE CRUISER as close to the school gate as possible; there were hardly any other vehicles there this early. He was always early dropping her off at school and late picking her up. Something to be said for consistency, Aine supposed. Together, they carried her trunk between them, Papa's side tilting a little higher.

"Switch sides?" she said as they neared the mutooma tree at the elbow bend in the wide path leading up to the admin building.

"What did you pack in here?" Papa said as they set the heavy luggage down to switch. "Bricks?"

"Sure," Aine said sarcastically. "I've brought bricks to sustain me through the school term."

He helped her carry it as far as he could; parents weren't allowed beyond the library. "Will you manage from here?" he asked as they rested the trunk at the end of the library's steps.

"I'll meet you back at admin," she told him and watched as he went back the way they'd come. He would have to join the short line at the bursar's window to pay Aine's tuition.

Luckily, as she neared Hurditch dorm, a classmate came to relieve her. Prossy was the daughter of Mr. Were, the O-level geography teacher nicknamed "Magama" for his consistent mispronunciation of *magma*. She lived with her father in the staff quarters just beyond the hedge. Why did she report to school so early when she could easily wait until the last minute?

"Have you seen the timetable?" Prossy said as they crossed into the colonnade.

"It's out already?" Aine said.

"I'm out of here November twenty-second," Prossy proclaimed happily. "I can't wait to get out of here forever."

Aine felt a tinge of joy at the prospect of never having to report to this place ever again. She was standing at the precipice of her last chapter of secondary school. "Do you have big plans for your vacay?"

Everyone in Senior Six had such grand plans for their gap year that Aine's plan to work at the wetlands sanctuary seemed basic, hardly an adventure.

"My auntie in Kampala is giving me a job," Prossy bragged. "She has a big supermarket in Nateete."

"I might be able to convince my mum to let me go visit my sister in Kampala," Aine said. "Maybe we'll see each other."

"That would be awesome," Prossy said.

They manoeuvred the trunk through the dormitory door and down to Aine's corridor. Except for one other girl, the dorm was still empty. Zai, like most other students, wouldn't arrive until later in the afternoon. Soon, some of the girls would drop off their luggage and then sneak back out to window-shop in Fort Portal, coming back just before the school gate closed at five thirty p.m.

PAPA STOOD WAITING BY the towering water tank, one leg bent at the knee, foot planted against the wall behind him. He was studying a broad sheet of paper: the UACE exam timetable.

"When's my last exam?" Aine asked excitedly.

"November twenty-seventh, Literature Paper Three." He drew a red circle around November 28. "This is when I shall pick you up, yes?"

"Nuh-uh. Exam ends in the morning; you pick me up in the afternoon," she said. "I'll be at the gate by two p.m. I'll pack my things the night before."

"What? One extra night here will kill you?"

"Spoken like a man who never went to boarding school." She took Papa's phone out of his trousers pocket and input the event—"AINE!!!"—in his calendar app. "I'll take a kamunye home if you don't show."

Papa sucked his teeth at her. "So stubborn."

"I am my father's daughter, after all."

He gave her seventy thousand shillings for pocket money. It was twenty thousand more than he usually

121

gave her. "Because we kept you from your internship at the sanctuary," he explained.

Aine grinned. Who knew not working could be more lucrative than working? Including Mama's fifty, it was more pocket money than she'd ever been given. Interlacing her fingers between Papa's, she walked him to his car. She waved as he circled the roundabout to join the murram road. She kept waving until the plume of red dust swallowed the cruiser and she couldn't see it anymore.

IT WAS FINALLY BRIEFING day. Deputy Headmaster Mugabi was starting to repeat himself, going on and on about proper exam etiquette as if it were the girls' first time sitting national finals. The O-level briefing two years before hadn't lasted nearly this long. Aine fanned herself against the afternoon heat, post-lunch fatigue making her eyelids heavy.

Over the past month, she'd adopted Zai's studiousness: reading until lights out, rising as soon as the electricity was back on at six a.m. Her body was still adapting to fewer hours of sleep. She favoured the library reading room—the same room where her whole year was gathered now—where she browsed stacks of past UACE papers. She'd memorized the appropriate statistics formulae so that she, too, could calculate means, medians, and standard deviations. All the equations that had stumped her in the mocks. She felt great about her odds of passing geography. History and literature would be a breeze.

"You will be patted down every time you enter the

examination room," Mr. Mugabi went on, reminding the girls that the foreign invigilators—teachers from neighbouring schools—reserved the right to "really feel you up." "So, bring with you only the writing utensils needed for each paper. Ask yourself, Do I need my mathematics set for agriculture?"

Ms. Peninnah, the school secretary, knocked tentatively on the reading room door.

"Excuse me," Mr. Mugabi said and went to talk to her.

"The man likes the sound of his own voice," Zai said and then joked that maybe Ms. Peninnah had come to save them from him.

"I'm dozing here," Aine replied.

When Mr. Mugabi stepped back into the room, he fixed his gaze on Aine. "Kamara," he said, waving her over. "Please go with Ms. Peninnah."

Aine hesitated. "What? Why?"

"Please." His manner was suddenly grave. Aine's knees knocked together as she rose. She saw, on the screen of her mind, an airplane bursting into flames, its charred occupants falling from the sky like giant black birds. Just yesterday, she'd spent nearly two thousand shillings in coins at the callbox talking to Mbabazi. She was flying to Cape Town today to run the Sanlam Marathon on Saturday morning.

"Has something happened?" she asked the secretary, who was waiting for her on the steps.

"Just a relative here to see you," said Ms. Penny, her face unreadable.

"My dad?"

She shook her head. "I know your father."

"Then who?" Aine's fear made her impatient.

The secretary shrugged.

Aine thought about the pearl-spotted owlet she'd seen earlier that morning. She'd just come from morning prep, and when she opened the dormitory window, the cute little owl stared at her from his perch on a branch of the candlenut tree. It was as if he'd been waiting for her to open that window. Looking into his bright yellow eyes, she remembered the old wives' tale: an owl visiting means death. She shouted at the bird, and when it didn't budge, she chucked at it the little piece of wood they used to hold the window open. She tried to push the memory out of her mind now; she was just not a superstitious person. That's all there was to it. She didn't believe in omens, good or bad. And in any case, wouldn't it be the job of a more ominous-looking owl, something like a Verreaux's eagle-owl, to deliver grim news? There'd been nothing intense about that cute owlet.

She entered the secretary's office and saw, through the open door leading into Madame's office, her uncle Nshuti standing by the window.

"Uncle?" Her teeth chattered with bewildered fright. *Oh god.*

Uncle hurried to meet her, his eyes rimmed red as if burned by tears. Aine wanted to turn around and run before hearing whatever it was he had come here to tell her. But her legs had grown heavy as though full of curdled blood.

"It's your father," he said in Kinyarwanda. "A lorry trying to overtake a car collided with the Landcruiser."

Aine felt her whole life collecting inside her throat, threatening to strangle her.

"I'm so sorry, Aine." Madame was on her feet behind her mahogany desk.

Aine attacked her uncle, raining blows against his hard chest. How dare he come here wearing his cheap ruga-bire, the poor man's sandals that he carved from Papa's discarded car tires, to tell her that her father was dead? Her father, who had been driving cars since before Aine was born! Papa knew the physics of driving in storms, and he certainly knew how to outmanoeuvre a lorry coming at him. But her uncle gathered her in his arms and, lock-ing her in his embrace, went on about how Papa had been alone in the car. No tourists. A good thing. The acci-dent took place in Dura, near the limestone quarry just outside Kamwenge. The cruiser rolled over several times. He would have died on the spot and not in a lot of pain.

Aine sobbed into her uncle's chest.

"Humura, humura," Uncle repeated, holding her tightly. *Take heart.*

"I was just telling your uncle," Madame said after Aine had regained control of her breathing. "You can go with him now, but if you don't want to miss your exams, you must come back on Sunday."

. . .

I WANT MY FATHER. My father is dead. The thought ran on a continuous loop in Aine's head during the drive home. As the special hire driver pulled into the compound, she saw mourners everywhere. Her father, the man best equipped to see her through a crisis such as this, was really gone.

People scrunched up their faces as they looked at her, tilted their heads at pitying angles. Her uncle put a stabilizing hand on her back. A skinned lamb rotisseried on a spit above a firepit in front of the kitchen. Tongues of fire lapped hungrily at the fat. Black smoke rose into the evening like an offering.

Emerging into the sitting room, she saw the coffin wrapped up in white cloth as if death were an all-encompassing whiteness. Papa grinned at her from a framed portrait leaning against a wreath on top of the casket.

"Can I see him?" she asked her mother, who was suddenly by her side, holding her.

"Better that you don't." Mama's words were knotted, almost incomprehensible. "You must remember him as he was."

Aine couldn't bear the thought of her father entombed in the darkness of the coffin that was nailed shut, never to be opened. She pictured him trapped inside the cruiser as it overturned, rolling into a valley with death at its bottom. Was he afraid? Or was he brave? She cried over every moment they'd shared and those they never would. From now on, everything that happened to her would not involve him. No longer a physical presence in her life, he'd become a memory. One day, if she was lucky, she'd pass him in age and become older than him.

"Honashi ruhanga wangye tukakukoraki?" Mama was asking God what they had done to deserve this tragedy. She slapped her thighs and wailed.

Aine's aunt Mutesi came and held Mama, sat her down on the floor. Aine sat beside her. The furniture had been shoved into the adjoining dining room; the women were all sitting on mats, grief writ large on their faces.

"God gives and he takes away," Aunt Mutesi said, inciting a wave of even more meaningless platitudes from the others. *He's in a better place now. Nothing can hurt him.*

As evening gave way to night, lamps were lit and placed around the room so that the soft yellow light illuminated the women's sombre faces. Whenever a new mourner arrived, they talked at length about Papa, how vibrant and full of life he'd been when they last saw him. Death was a thief.

The reverend's wife brought an armful of hymnals and distributed them among the women. As they sang songs of praise to God, Aine tried to suppress her rage. But what a bottomless pit of attention! God was the focus even here, at the funeral of a man who believed that if there was a God, then surely he had better things to do than concern himself with the goings-on of mere mortals. But she supposed, too, that mourning was for the living. All these rituals were for them. It was what they did in order to endure lost life.

"Is Mbabazi on her way back from South Africa?" she quietly asked Mama. "You called her, didn't you?"

"Her phone is switched off," Mama said. "I called and called."

"Can I borrow your phone?" Aine knew that Achen would have a phone number for the hotel where Mbabazi was staying in Cape Town.

"Bedroom."

It was dark in Mama's room. Aine felt around for the torch they always kept on the chest of drawers by the door. She flicked it on and found the box of matches. As she lit the kerosene lamp, Papa's Seiko watch glinted. It was stretched out next to Mama's lotions and the unused tubes of sunscreen Mbabazi insisted on buying for them. Aine picked up the watch, studied it. Cracks zigzagged the crystal, but the hands beneath moved smoothly, telling the correct time, same as the clock on the wall. She put it on her left wrist and snapped the closure, her arm hairs catching in the grooves. There was a crown on the side of the watch. If she were to give it a tug and a twist, she could turn back time.

She dialed Achen's number from memory and picked up the lantern. She'd wanted to seek the privacy of the kibanda, but there were men in there drinking tonto. Everywhere she looked, there were people, as if the whole village were here, in her compound. She squeezed through a small opening in the hedge.

"It's Aine," she said after Achen picked up with her characteristic, "Hello, this is Achen."

"Kidio," Achen said. "I've been going out of my mind thinking about you."

"How'd you know?" Aine crossed deeper into the banana plantation.

"Mrs. K," Achen said. "She couldn't reach M, so she tried my number."

"You've talked to her then," Aine said. "You've told Mbabazi? She's got to fly back home tonight, Achen. The burial is tomorrow. The body—" She couldn't finish. Had she just referred to her father as *the body*? She braced herself against a banana trunk. "The accident was very bad. Closed-casket bad."

"I'm so sorry, darling," Achen said. "And I tried telling her, but..."

Aine waited for the rest of the sentence, but it didn't come. "But what?"

"I just couldn't," Achen said. "She's really pumped up for this race. She was talking about achieving her personal best record. The woman has over a dozen marathons under her belt, but she's convinced this will be her best one yet. I just couldn't bring myself to tell her that her father has died."

"Okay, well, give me the number you reached her on," Aine said, slightly annoyed. "Mama will tell her."

"But listen," Achen said, "if the funeral is tomorrow, she'll never make it anyway. It's just not possible."

"So, what are we going to do?" Panic flooded Aine so bad her hands shook.

"I can call again now and tell her," Achen said. "If you want me to, I'll do it."

Aine pictured her sister alone in her hotel room,

crippled by the news of her father's death, unable to run the race she'd travelled so far to run. If she couldn't in fact make the burial, why deprive her of the marathon too? Suffering over Papa was now the only way left to love him, and Mbabazi would have her whole life to do that. Seeing his coffin lowered into the ground changed nothing.

"I envy her, in a way," Aine said. "In her world, Papa is still alive."

Did Mbabazi, she wondered, feel any strangeness this morning? Chuck a rock at an owl? Did her world suddenly, however slightly, tilt off balance?

Achen was sobbing. Her tears caught Aine off guard. "Take heart," she said, feeling a little furious that she had to do the consoling.

"He was such a kind man," Achen said in a muffled voice. "There was a point when I was certain he'd put two and two together. That he knew about M and me. That he accepted us."

"I highly doubt that. He'd have said something."

"No, really," Achen said emphatically. "He invited me to lunch. He said that a good friend of his daughter's was his daughter too."

"Come for the burial." The words shot out of Aine's mouth like a sneeze she couldn't suppress. "Mbabazi can't be here, but you can. Right?"

"I'll be with you by dawn," Achen said.

Aine rattled off the directions. "If you get lost, call this number. It's my mum's. Say you're my friend. Say we met on the competitive debating circuit."

"Debating circuit?" Achen said. "What was I doing at a secondary school debate?"

"Adjudicating."

"All right."

After she hung up the phone, Aine sat down among the sweet potato mounds scattered across the plantation. Maybe she could stay there until Achen arrived. Maybe Achen would pick up the lamp and show her the way back.

It was the mournful sound of a trough zither that drew Aine out of the banana plantation. She emerged into the compound and listened, from the warm chiaroscuro of firelight, to the men singing an old funeral dirge. Twelve of them sat around the bonfire on low stools, the yellowish light seeming to amplify their grief. Uncle Nshuti played the inanga with his eyes closed, his voice soaring and circling with sorrow: "Sleep well, sleep well, my mother's son."

The words of the dirge, a lullaby really, travelled through her like a blue current. She hugged herself as the loneliness grew inside her. Her father's death was a mountain she didn't want to climb.

9

AINE WOKE UP WITH a start. Knocking on the door. Her head felt heavy as if her brain had calcified, turned into a rock. It seemed to move around when she sat up, bludgeoning her cranium from within.

"Ahhh." She winced as she sat up, pressing her fingers to her temples. Her feet found the cold cement.

Another knock, this one louder. "Aine." Mama's voice. "Achen is here. Are you dressed?"

Aine gasped. Achen was here! She scrambled to her feet and then sat back down, bolts of lightning going off in her head. "Yes, come in."

Mama opened the door and stepped inside, Achen a hair behind her. Aine rubbed her sleep-swollen eyes. Holy gods. What had she done? Mbabazi would kill her. She'd begged her not to breathe a word of Achen's existence to Mama, but here they were, the two of them rubbing shoulders in Mbabazi's childhood bedroom.

"You look unwell." Mama pressed the back of her hand to Aine's forehead. "At least you don't have a fever."

"Just this pounding headache," Aine said.

"I have Aspirin." Achen shrugged off her rucksack and began unzipping it.

"She does not take Aspirin," Mama said, stopping Achen. "It hurts her stomach."

It had happened only once a few years ago, but Mama still acted as though Aine were now forever allergic to Aspirin. But then again, any ailment was an opportunity for Mama to flex her herbalist muscle, brewing concoctions that tasted bitter, smelled horrible, but ultimately worked wonders.

"I will go and prepare the herbs," Mama said, opening the window to assault Aine with shards of morning light. Though she'd grown to prefer her mother's ebishaka to the pills and injections from the school nurse, Aine now felt a tinge of embarrassment. What would Achen think? That her lover's family were banyakyaaro, backwoods people who still looked to the bushes for healing? "I won't be long," Mama promised as she crossed to the door. She was, unlike the night before, the very image of composure. The grief was still there in her eyes, but she was stoic and tall, almost regal, ekitengye wrapper girding her waist.

The voices of people outside floated in, reminding Aine of why those people were here, why Achen was here.

"Sometimes I forget that he's gone." Aine closed her eyes the way she always did when she was about to cry but didn't want to. "A full minute will go by without me thinking about him. And then I will remember, and it's as if I've just heard the news."

"I know, I know," Achen said, wrapping her arms around Aine. "I'm terribly sorry, kidio."

They sat together quietly, and the silence was restful, not at all suffocating. Aine knew that it was human nature to try to surround death with a web of words, to try to make sense of it, but she much preferred this silence.

"When will we know if it was the right call?" Aine finally said, unable to stop thinking about Mbabazi. "Not telling her about Papa."

"I don't know." Achen slashed at her teary eyes with the back of her hand. "I don't regret it though. Not yet, at least. How's your head?"

"It's not so bad if I sit absolutely still."

"Can you really not take Aspirin?"

Aine gave a wan smile. "Isn't Aspirin really just willow bark in disguise?"

"Is it really?"

"I think so?" Aine said uncertainly.

"Is your mum about to feed you some willow bark?"

"Among other things," Aine said. "Don't worry. It works."

Achen squeezed her shoulder. "Okay."

MAMA SEEMED TO FLOAT into the room. She was carrying a lidded pail by its thin metallic handle. As she rested the bucket on the floor in front of Aine, Achen moved away to

134

sit on the opposite bed. Mama took a spare blanket from the top of Aine's wardrobe and threw it over Aine's head and shoulders, entombing her over the hot bucket. Aine knew the drill. She removed the lid and the medicinal steam rising into her face saturated her lungs, forcing her to open her mouth wide. Cooked herbs sloshed at the bottom of the bucket. It smelled like the swamp on a very hot day.

"It's like a sauna, is it?" Achen said.

"What is a sauna?" Mama replied.

The mattress shifted as Mama sat down beside Aine. She tensed in her cocoon. Why couldn't Mama just go?

"It's a room where you go to sweat," Achen explained. "There are hot stones in there. You throw water on them, and steam fills the room. It's meant to be cleansing."

"I see," said Mama. "May I ask: Where do you come from? Who are your people?"

Aine felt hot. A river of her sweat puddled on the floor.

"My people?" The tone of Achen's voice was curious, as though the question were a photo negative she was holding up to the light. It hung in the air, making Aine anxious. By the time she was five years old, she'd memorized the names of her ancestors on both sides going back to four generations. Papa said the purpose of the exercise was twofold. It ensured Aine would never marry someone from her own bloodline. And speaking the names of the dead was one way to keep them alive.

"Your father's father," Mama explained. "Who was his father?"

"My biological mother left me on the doorstep of a Pentecostal church when I was a toddler," Achen said. "I grew up in the church's orphanage and then a group home. So I suppose those are my people. Wonderful people, I might add."

"I'm so sorry," Mama said softly.

"My mother at the group home," Achen said, "she brings me chicken soup when I'm down in the dumps. I'm a grown woman, but she still treats me like a little girl."

"That's a good mother."

"She is," Achen said and, without a moment in between, added, "Is there anything I can do, Mrs. Kamara? Anything at all? Everyone out there is so busy. I'd like to be useful if I can."

Mama was quiet for a moment, and Aine wished she could see the expression on her face.

"My brother is using his bicycle to transport some benches from the church," Mama said. "If he were to use your car…"

"Absolutely," Achen offered with much enthusiasm. "I'll go with him to the church. Help him with the loading."

"Let me take you to him." Mama touched Aine's shoulder and said, "You're okay in there?"

Aine mopped her face. Already her head felt much lighter. "Yup."

"Give it another minute, then remove the blanket," Mama instructed. "Put on something nice and come outside and have some breakfast, okay?"

"Yup."

. . .

AS SHE EMERGED INTO the sitting room, Aine noticed that her father's coffin was no longer there. She crossed to the doorway and saw it under a canopy tent in the front yard. The dais from church stood in front of the tent: a mobile pulpit dressed in purple, vines of morning glory wound around its base. Benches were arranged in a semicircle facing the tent.

She knew that once a coffin had left the house, it couldn't, under any circumstances, be brought back in. It was bad luck. Her father's destination could now only be the grave. Men were digging in the banana plantation. She saw them, shirtless men throwing out shovelfuls of dirt. Digging a ditch six feet deep and putting someone you loved inside it suddenly struck her as the cruellest thing you could do to them. She turned and went back into the house. She was not ready to face this day. She never would be. Sobs heaved up her throat, one at a time, like abrading rocks.

Later, she washed her face once more and rubbed some lotion on her cheeks. She ventured back outside; she needed to find Achen, to stay with her. It would be easy for Achen to slip up and say something suspicious to Uncle Nshuti or Mama. At least there was a language barrier between Achen and Uncle. He spoke primary school–level English, and Achen wasn't fluent in Rukiga or Kinyarwanda.

A quick scan of the compound showed neither of them, though there were clearly enough benches now.

Aine went to ask Aunt Mutesi. She, along with half a dozen other women, was peeling a mountain of matooke to fill a saucepan big enough to feed an army barracks.

"Water," her aunt said. "They went to fetch water from the naikondo."

"Did Mama go to the pump with them?"

"Just your uncle and the visitor."

Everywhere Aine turned people were busy. Washing potatoes, winnowing rice, dicing tomatoes. Oblivious children ran around playing and laughing, hiding behind their mothers' long skirts.

"Go sit with your kaaka," Aunt Mutesi said, now regarding Aine with heartbreaking sympathy. She used her knife to point to Aine's grandmother, sitting in the boxy shade cast by the kitchen.

"You look just like him, you know," Kaaka Nyirasafari said as Aine approached. The old woman's voice was scratchy, scored by time. The skin over her face was leathery and creased, puddling under her eyes and chin. "Okuzaara nokuzooka!" *Procreation is resurrection.*

Aine lowered herself to the mat and rested her head in her grandmother's lap. Kaaka told her a story, the one that Aine, when she was little, had always begged her grandmother to tell her. It was a story about two siblings—Munguma and Nyangira—and their unnamed mother.

One day, Nyabingi, the goddess of plenty, was passing through the girls' village. Wearing the disguise of a dirty, drunk old woman, she went to the girls' house begging for food and a place to rest her head for the night. It was the goddess's favourite thing: travelling far and wide and testing the capacity of people's kindness, their hospitality. She rewarded with cattle, poultry, and bountiful harvests all those who welcomed and fed her. And punished bitterly anyone who turned her away. The girls' mother turned Nyabingi away, and so the goddess cursed her. She put a hex on her that suspended the mother in a liminal state between life and death: her eyes open but unseeing, her pulse like a memory.

Munguma and Nyangira set out on a journey to where the goddess lived in the heart of the forest. They would beg the deity to give them their mother back. When they arrived, Nyabingi held them captive for a long, long time, testing the bonds of their sisterhood. She separated them, each sister locked up in her own dark, decrepit, windowless cave. She loved testing people, Nyabingi. It brought her great joy when they failed her tests because then she could try out more creative ways to break their spirits. And she was persistent. She conjured fearsome phantasmagoric illusions meant to turn the girls against each other. But every morning and night, without fail, the sisters sang to each other, even though they weren't sure the other heard or even still lived. Nyangira, the elder sister, would start:

Munguma, Munguma, eeh
Munguma, eeh
Oreirota, Munguma?

Akatima, Munguma?
Karikata, Munguma, eeh?
How is your heart? Is it still beating?

And Munguma would respond:

Nyangira, Nyangira, eeh
Nyangira, eeh.
Oreirota, Nyangira?
Akatima, Nyangira?
Karikata, Nyangira, eeh?

After many years of trying and failing to break the sisters, to diminish their will to survive and save their mother, Nyabingi grew bored. She released the sisters and gave them a potion in the form of a candle they'd burn to awaken their sleeping mother.

When they got back home the girls were surprised to find that they had surpassed their mother in age; she was frozen in time, as young as the day the goddess had put a hex on her. Was a woman still a mother if her daughters were older than her? What title was there for a girl older than her own mother? The siblings sat waiting for the candle to burn out, at which point their mother would awaken.

"Did she wake up?" Aine asked now as she always did when her grandmother told her this tale.

"Maybe yes, maybe no," Kaaka said. The same answer she always gave.

The not knowing. It made Aine want to scream with frustration. Could a magic candle burn forever? In which case the sisters were suspended in waiting, just like their mother. Gods could be cruel indeed.

REVEREND ERASMUS READ FROM the Book of Psalms: the Lord was close to the broken-hearted. He saved those who were crushed in spirit. Afterwards, six men, with Uncle Nshuti and Uncle Kaliisa at the front, shouldered the coffin and led the slow funeral procession toward the plantation. Mama keened the whole long way. When she wasn't calling her husband's name over and over, she questioned God: *Why have you deserted me?*

Aine stayed close to her, holding her mother's hand when it was possible to do so, when Mama wasn't smacking her thighs or wailing with her hands on both sides of her face. The expression of grief was an ugly affair, a bodily spectacle, and Mama seemed to want hers imprinted on the fabric of time itself. Aine cried for both her father and her mother, whose wailing reached a climax at the lip of the grave as the coffin was lowered. Mama thrashed about as if to prevent the men from putting her husband into that hole. Her sisters restrained her, their own grief only a little quieter than hers. And then Mama quieted down as though finally accepting her fate. Time stood still. The late afternoon sun hid behind dark clouds, turning them purplish: the colour of a bruise.

. . .

AINE WAS THIRSTY. She'd been hanging around outside, graciously accepting the sympathies of friends and relations. It was exhausting. She'd much rather be asleep, or just alone with her grief. Soon, she managed to escape into the house to get herself a drink of water. Mama kept a clay pot full of boiled water in the pantry, but Aine worried there might not be any left, what with all the mourners. In the darkened pantry, she removed the plastic lid over the mouth of the bulbous clay pot, which sat on a pad of dried banana leaves. Relieved to see that it was still half-full, she ladled a cupful and drank it in one long gulp. The water was smoky with an aftertaste of burnt clay. She stood there in the restful darkness a while longer, considering how it had all gone well, Achen being here at Papa's funeral. Yet now that she was thinking about it, she hadn't glimpsed Achen in quite some time. She'd seen her earlier heaving jerry cans full of water out of her car. She'd be extremely tired by now, having driven all night to get here, only to be put to work all day. Had she even had lunch?

Achen's car was parked north of the compound, near the road, but there was no one inside it. Perhaps Achen was catching a nap? The door to Aine's bedroom was wide open, Achen's rucksack at the foot of the bed. Her pulse kicked when she heard muffled voices coming from her mother's bedroom down the hall. She tiptoed closer and pressed her ear to the door.

"You're making it sound as if I seduced her." Achen's voice, those crisp English consonants. "You cannot turn a straight person into a lesbian, Mrs. Kamara. It doesn't work like that."

"Explain to me how it works then." Mama spoke in her low angry voice, which was scarier than her loud angry one.

Aine placed a shaky hand on the doorknob, testing if it was locked. When it opened, Mama came for her, fire in her eyes. The vein snaking her temple pulsed madly.

"Today of all days, you lie to me?" she said in Rukiga. "You bring *her* in my house and tell me that she came because of you?"

"I called her." Aine swallowed to alleviate the sudden dryness in her throat. "She's here because of me."

"Look me in the eyes and lie to me again." Mama stood frighteningly close, her eyes big white saucers daubed with brown.

Aine's lips pressed together as though stitched shut. She didn't want to say anything that would make the situation worse.

"Are you holding some precious oil in your mouth?" Mama jabbed her index finger into Aine's cheek. "If you open it and speak, it will pour out and go to waste?"

Achen moved quickly, making for the door, but Mama was faster, blocking her. The women stood staring at each other. And then Mama changed tactics.

"Please," she begged, falling to her knees before Achen. She brought her hands palm to palm under her chin as if in prayerful supplication. "I'm begging you, please. Leave me and my children alone."

"I'm sorry." Achen side-stepped Mama and went out the door.

Mama lay down on her side and pulled her knees up to her chest. She was making a noise that seemed to come from deep within her, a sound like an engine trying to turn over. Aine started to go to her, but there was a bang down the hall, her bedroom door slamming.

"I'll be right back, Mama," she said and ran to the door. She emerged into the hallway in time to see Achen crossing the sitting room, her backpack in her hands.

"Wait," she called, but Achen paid her no attention. She hurried up the compound and got into her car. Aine followed semi-casually; people were looking, confusion on their faces. Achen drove off, tearing down the murram road with a theatrical squeal of the tires.

Aine sprinted after the car as fast as her legs could carry her, onlookers be damned. A flurry of debris and shredded leaves flew into her face, but she persisted. Achen couldn't leave like this. No way in hell. Aine was running fast and waving her hands above her head, but the car was getting farther and farther away. Surely Achen could see her in the side mirror. How long did she think Aine could maintain this pace? She was running so fast it felt as though she were standing still and the trees lining the road were speeding in the opposite direction.

Suddenly the car stopped and started reversing toward Aine. She jumped to the side of the road and bent forward, gasping for air, her hands planted into her knees. Her heart was trying to slam an escape route through her rib cage. She blinked against the explosion of red dots suddenly appearing in her vision.

"Get in then," Achen said, reaching across the passenger seat to open the door.

Aine had barely sat down when Achen stepped on the accelerator, the sudden velocity pushing Aine back against the seat. Soon they were joining the tarmac road, the dukas one brown smear.

"Oh god," Aine said, covering her mouth. "Oh god, I'm going to vomit."

"Don't you dare!"

"Pull over."

Just past the Bee Hive Bar and Bistro, Achen slowed down and eased the car onto the shoulder. Aine stepped over the guardrail and went to heave into the bushes. But nothing came up. Her mouth tasted like metal, but her throat was dry as if lined with cotton.

"Here."

She looked up to see Achen holding out a reusable water bottle.

"Drink."

Aine guzzled the water, its coolness healing the arid landscape of her throat.

"Better?" Achen asked.

"What the fuck possessed you, huh?" Aine exploded, her voice coarse, ravaged by anger. "What were you thinking? That you were going to be buddy-buddy with Mama now? Ask for her daughter's hand in marriage?"

"I swear to God, kidio," Achen said, fishing her empty

water bottle from a thicket of sword grasses where Aine had chucked it. "She cornered me. It's like she already knew something."

"Knew what?"

"I don't know. She's got that face," Achen said. "It's exactly like M's face, only older. I couldn't lie to her."

"Why were you talking to her about Mbabazi at all?"

"She brought her up."

"Ruhanga wangye." *Dear God.* Aine beat a path toward the trailhead. As long as she kept moving, she wouldn't think about things that had been done that couldn't be undone. But she couldn't rid herself of the image of Mama folding in on herself like a walnut. It was the shape of a person in agony. Yet Aine felt some relief, too, as if a weight had been lifted from her shoulders. Mama knew everything now. Not only was her daughter still gay, but she was also in love. Mama was not a monster. She had all the information now. Let her process it. Maybe some good would come of it.

Two baboons stood their ground in the middle of the trail. As she approached, they bared their teeth.

"Assholes," she sneered as she went around, giving them a wide berth.

"Could you slow down a little?" Achen called from a distance behind, fear tempering her voice.

Aine spun around to see her looking with terror upon the inelegant beasts. "They're just bullies," she called, retracing her steps. "Go around them. They won't hurt you."

"Shhh," Achen placated as she went around the annoying creatures. She broke into a near-jog after passing them.

"I'm sorry," she said, catching up to Aine. "I shouldn't have come here. I know that now."

"Well," Aine said and let the thought dangle. She was the one who'd invited Achen, but she was in no mood to share blame. She sat down on a hillock, her feet in the trail. Achen sat beside her, and they looked across to the swamp, at papyruses leaning sideways as if listening to the babbling marsh. A long boardwalk snaked across the muddy slough, ferns growing between the wooden slats. A red-tailed monkey leaped from one branch of a polita fig to another and stared at them as if waiting for applause. The barbets and black bishops engaged in a jazz improv of tweets and trills.

"I had a dream yesterday," Achen said, pulling Aine back into the world.

"A good dream?" Aine couldn't think of a single time when she'd listened with interest to someone's dream. It was simply impossible to capture in words the experience of one's dreams; it was a waste of the listener's time, but people, including herself, never stopped trying.

"So, I'm guiding my mother through a grassland," Achen recounted. "There's this wall of elephant grass, thick and tall. I'm cutting through it with a panga, clearing a path for us. We arrive at a waterfall, and I realize it's the sound we've been following. The powerful roar of water crashing down below. I stand on the edge of the waterfall to look down. It's a really sharp drop. So deep I can't see all the way to the bottom. Just a white cloud of mist. And in that moment, I know without a doubt why I've brought my mother there."

"This is beginning to sound a bit like a nightmare."

"I push her off the cliff," Achen continued. "No warning, no negotiations. I just shove her and watch her plummet. A black object falling through all that white. And she's getting smaller and smaller. Disappearing. But get this."

Aine was getting into it.

"At exactly the point where I should lose sight of her, this tiny little dot sprouts wings." Achen opened her arms and flapped them like a bird. "This huge pterodactyl thing. And it's rising toward me, then above me, powerful wings thumping the air, turning it syrupy. I'm watching her soar. My mother the bird. And then she's one with the skies and I can't see her anymore. Gone."

"Huh." Aine raised her brows. Sometimes she had no idea how to respond to the bizarre things Achen told her. Like how her Christmas tradition was going away to a retreat in Jinja where she didn't speak for two weeks.

"I think it symbolizes a major breakthrough for me," Achen said. "I've been struggling for years to forgive my mother, to let go of this overpowering fantasy I have of her. But killing that fantasy, even if it was only in a dream, has opened something in me. I feel lighter somehow."

"Right."

Aine looked at her and Achen shrugged, her eyes shifting as though she was suddenly nervous to have revealed this private struggle with a mother she never knew. They were quiet then, both of them. A silence pregnant with the sounds of the swamp.

"Do you reckon Mbabazi will kill us both?" Aine eventually said. "Or just me?" She was the one who'd invited Achen to Bigodi and then left her to her own devices all day until Mama cornered her.

"We shall cross that bridge when we get to it," Achen said.

Aine had survived her father's burial; what could be harder than that?

"Take me to school," she said, turning to Achen.

A look of alarm came over Achen's face. "Your mother will think I've kidnapped you. She'll send the police after me."

"Give me your phone," Aine said. "I'll explain it to her. She knows I've got exams on Monday. And trust me, if I go back home now, I'll only make a bad situation worse." There would be questions she didn't want to answer. Questions best answered by Mbabazi. Yes, it had come to that.

"Phone is in the car."

As they rose, slapping bits of grass from their clothes, there was a rustling in the middle distance. Aine crossed onto the boardwalk for a closer look. Among the petioles of a yellowing date palm perched a grey-cheeked mangabey, melancholy eyes like an old sage. "It's Owen!"

"Do they all have human names?" Achen said, coming to stand beside her.

"Only Owen," Aine said. "He's named after one of the senior guides at the sanctuary. They look alike."

"This man resembles a monkey?"

"It's mostly the facial hair." The resemblance was a well-known tidbit the guides liked sharing with tourists, but it required spotting Owen the Mangabey first. But Owen the Mangabey, as if aware of his stardom, made himself ever so scarce. His last known location was highly sought after. A guide could even charge another guide good money for this information. On the very rare occasion when Aine spotted him, she felt special, as if Owen had chosen to grace her with his presence. And for him to come to her now, on the hardest day of her entire existence! The feeling of kinship wanted to break her heart.

RATHER THAN CALL MAMA, she texted her. A cowardly move, she knew, but she didn't trust herself not to make matters worse for Mbabazi. "Dear Mama," she wrote, "I'm on my way back to school. Achen's giving me a lift. I'm so sorry to leave this way. Please be kind to Mbabazi when she comes home. I remain your loving daughter, Aine."

"Does it read okay?" she said, turning the screen toward Achen.

"Why does it read like a letter?" Achen said, turning the key in the ignition. "Do you not know how to write text messages?"

"What's wrong with it?"

"Actually, nothing," Achen said. "It's quite perfect."

Aine sent the text and set the phone down in the cup holder. Mama was not much of a texter, but Aine knew she'd see the message. If not right away, then hopefully soon, before she did anything drastic.

The car sailed down the tarmac through Magombe Swamp. The darkness thickened, solidifying as they hit Nkingo, the small trading centre on the edge of the forest. Achen turned up the music.

"To keep from nodding off," she said.

"I'll stay awake in solidarity," Aine promised, though she was fading.

Suddenly Achen slammed on the brakes, propelling Aine forward. "What?" She'd fallen asleep despite trying hard not to.

"Will you look at that?" Achen said in awe and reached for her phone. In the headlights, four elephants—two adults and two calves—were crossing the road. Gigantic creatures even though they were clearly forest elephants, supposedly smaller, their straight tusks almost grazing the road. Aine was so used to seeing their migratory tracks, heaps of their excrement larger than car tires, but she'd never been this close to one, let alone four. The matriarch leading the group seemed pissed. She stared directly at the car as if she might charge.

"Go on then," Aine quietly willed her to, but the cow seemed to think better of it and moseyed on, leading her family to the relative safety of the jungle.

"Did you see those eyes?" Achen said with way too much reverence, in Aine's opinion. She was still recording on her phone as the last of the group disappeared into the roadside bushes. "Such tenuous beauty! I've never experienced anything quite like it."

"Can we go now?" Aine said, not sure how she'd get into her school this late; the askari would have long retired for the day by now. "We may have to call Madame."

"I'm sorry if the elephants scared you," Achen said, driving on.

"How's that your fault?" Aine said a little angrily. Achen was always apologizing for every little thing. It meant that Aine had to be equally polite all the damn time. It was exhausting.

"I'll slow down a bit anyway," she said as they plunged into the forest proper. "I've never driven this road before. But my god, what a sight! Those creatures! I read somewhere that elephants have got the most impeccable long-term memory of any land mammal. Like, they never forget anything. Do you reckon that's true?"

"Where'd you hear that?" Aine said. She really didn't care much for elephants, those ginormous destroyers of crops.

"I might have read it in a novel."

"Fiction?"

"There are things you make up, and things you don't."

They listened to the rise and fall of Youssou N'Dour's arresting tenor on the stereo. The forest enveloped them in darkness, big dark to get lost in.

10

"Pens down!" bellowed the invigilator, a stocky fellow in wire-rimmed glasses, his protuberant belly threatening to pop the buttons right off his pale blue shirt.

Aine had finished more than fifteen minutes earlier but remained in her seat, trying not to doze off. During History Paper One earlier in the morning, she'd handed in her answer booklet half an hour before pens down and the invigilator had made her stand in front of him while he studied her answers, ascertaining that she'd attempted all the questions she was supposed to. Looking at the inscrutable expression on his face, she worried that perhaps she'd got some of them wrong and that he pitied her, thought her stupid for not making use of every allotted minute.

Now she stuffed her pens and pencils into her pencil case as Mr. Wire-Rims came around gathering everyone's answer booklets. She couldn't wait to climb into her bed and pull the covers over her head. In all her remembered life, she'd never needed such an abundance of sleep. It was like a raft she only had to climb onto, and off she went. Her body's way, perhaps, of protecting her from the sorrows of waking life. All day yesterday she'd slept, and still she felt tired, an all-consuming lethargy. This morning, it had taken every ounce of her willpower to get out of bed and show up to chapel, the makeshift examination hall.

As she crossed the veranda, someone called her name. She turned to see Madame leaning against a pillar. Something dreary bloomed in her chest. "Good afternoon, Madame."

"I came to see you yesterday, but you were sleeping," Madame said in that voice of hers that always made Aine feel as if she was in trouble. "I did not want to disturb you."

"Thank you, Madame," she said and willed herself not to burst into tears. If she started to cry now, she might never stop.

The headmistress reached into the pocket of her grey cardigan and retrieved her mobile phone. It was Kabiriti, the cheap burner ones telecommunication companies gave away for free during promotional blitzes. "Your sister wants to talk to you."

Aine's heart leaped into her throat. Mbabazi would have landed the evening before. By now she'd be in Bigodi. She knew everything that had happened.

"Just redial the last call," Madame said, giving Aine the

mobile only slightly bigger than a matchbox. "When you are finished, bring it to me at my place. Birungi is frying up a storm. You like chapati, no so?"

"Uh-huh." Aine could barely think straight. Her thumb hovered over the redial button. Was Mbabazi furious? Furious and sad and disappointed? The late afternoon sky had charcoaled, black clouds fomenting a storm.

She walked to generate courage and wound up under Freedom Tree. Four girls were playing doubles on the tennis court in the near distance, the orange clay of the court ominous under the greying sky. She leaned against the large trunk and called her sister.

"Madame?" Mbabazi said in lieu of a greeting.

"It's me." Aine's voice was timorous, almost a whisper. "Aine."

Silence.

Then, "Mama gave me an ultimatum, Aine," Mbabazi said, her voice breaking.

"An ultimatum?" The word pulled Aine's centre right out of her. She lowered herself to sit in the C of a twisting buttress root. Freedom Tree cradled her.

"I mean, what the fuck did you think would happen?" Suddenly, her sister's voice acquired a sharp edge. "You promised me. Not a word, you said. And then what do you do? You bring Achen to Papa's burial. And you leave me in the dark to run a marathon like some fucking moron. I've always known you could be selfish, Aine, but this? Leaving me to go on as though my father hadn't died. It's a whole new level of treachery."

Aine was crying so hard she could barely get a word out.

"Was it Achen's idea not to tell me?"

"What?"

"Not to tell me that my father was dead." Mbabazi enunciated every word as if Aine were new to the English language. "Whose brilliant idea was that?"

"Mine," Aine said.

"Liar."

"I swear it," Aine maintained, intent on covering for Achen. "Achen wanted to tell you, but I said it was too late. You were never going to make it home in time. An airplane is not like a taxi. You can't just dash to the airport and jump on one, right?"

"What do you know about the workings of air travel? Have you ever been on a plane?"

Aine ignored the question. "The ultimatum. What are the conditions?"

"I'm going to ask you one more time, and I want you to think long and hard before responding," Mbabazi said sternly. "You or Achen. Who was it?"

It was growing so loud in Aine's brain she couldn't think straight. But one thing was clear: a fracture had appeared between her and Mbabazi, and it was progressing toward a chasm. An abyss. What could she do to slow the escalation? She came up short. It was too late to redeem herself; she'd done too much damage. But if she shifted all the blame onto herself, then Mbabazi could easily forgive Achen and things would be good between them at least. Mbabazi would have Achen's shoulder to cry on through this nightmarish time. "I'm not lying to you," she said with as much conviction as she could muster. Tears blurred her vision.

Mbabazi sucked her teeth, a hurricane in Aine's ear. "Fucking little liar."

"Are you still at home?" Aine said, rising to her feet. "Please tell me what's happened. What Mama is asking of you."

"Goodbye, Aine," Mbabazi said.

The phone beeped. Mbabazi had hung up. Whatever it was that had held things together within Aine crumbled. *Liar, liar, liar* was all she could hear, a relentless echo. The phone fell to the ground. Suddenly she was having a hard time breathing. She was taking in air, but not much of it came back out. Her chest threatened to expand beyond her rib cage. She felt a sudden stabbing in her heart. Her eyes glazed over, and she lost her balance. Either she was falling, or the ground was rising to meet her face.

SHE OPENED HER EYES to see that she was being led into the sick bay. The smell of sweat filled her nostrils; her head was leaning against someone's sweaty shoulder. Sister Margret opened the security screen around a bed. Aine's helpers sat her down on it.

"What happened?" the nurse asked as the girls in short tennis outfits laid her down, the bedsprings complaining.

"She passed out," said the girl Aine recognized as the tennis captain, muscles like Serena Williams. "One minute she was speaking on the phone, the next she was falling to the ground. She hit her head real hard, Sister."

"Am I having a heart attack?" Aine asked as the nurse tightened the cuffs of a blood pressure monitor around her upper arm.

"More like a panic attack." The nurse asked the three girls to leave. "I need some space in here."

"It hurts so bad." Aine rested her free hand on her chest.

"Deep breaths." The nurse demonstrated by sucking air into her lungs, holding it for some time, and releasing it through her mouth. "Four counts. Your turn."

Aine tried to breathe, but the air wheezed as though pushed through a straw.

Was she dying?

"Just breathe, Kamara," the nurse stated calmly and directed her once more. "In … Out. In … Out. Like that. It's psychological, the pain. Try and relax, then your brain will know you're not in danger. And your heart will stop racing. In … out. There, that's a darling girl."

Aine kept sucking in air, holding it in her lungs, releasing it. In and out. Eventually, the wheezing in her throat died, and she was encouraged by the absence of that horrid noise. Someone, possibly the tennis players, had removed her necktie and opened the buttons on her shirt, leaving her chest exposed. Her bra hung loose too; it had been unclasped. Extreme attempts at first aid, she guessed.

"Whose mobile phone is this?" Sister Margret asked after a minute, holding it up for Aine to see.

"Madame's," she said, remembering Mbabazi's words. They hit her with the force of a hurricane. Hints of wheezing in her throat. In ... out. "She gave it to me to speak with my sister."

"Doctor?" the nurse said. "Shall I call her for you again?"

"No," Aine snapped.

The nurse tilted her head, as though Aine were a wounded bird. Aine suspected she knew about Papa. Everyone knew. The staff, too, had been tilting their heads like that when Aine passed them.

"Your mum, then?" the nurse said, nodding encouragingly.

Aine shook her head. She closed her eyes and felt the tears trickling into her ears. She raised her hand to her face and felt a stab of pain. There was a bruise on her forehead, soft and palpable.

"Do you want something for the pain?"

"No."

"Rest a bit, eh?" She closed the screen around Aine's bed and left.

Aine turned on her side. The rain started then, pummelling the iron-sheet roof, a robust sound like rice being tossed into a cooking pot. As the downpour increased, its roar stabilized to a sustained whirr: a different kind of silence.

When Aine was a child, rainstorms had terrified her more than any monster her brain could conjure. They evoked the Genesis flood where water rose to flow over the tops of the highest mountains, drowning all life except

159

the few animals and birds God had instructed Noah to bring onto his ark. Whenever it rained in the night, she'd crawl into Mbabazi's bed—if Mbabazi was home—and Mbabazi would hold her, teasing her about being such a stereotypical last-born. "Is there anything you don't fear?"

Now Aine slept fitfully through a dream in which she was drowning. She was floating among pieces of furniture, books, and brooms in a room quickly filling with rainwater. She woke up kicking and gasping, drenched in sweat. She took in her surroundings in the dim light. It was nighttime. She remembered she was in the sick bay. The conversation with her sister set her heart racing again. She forced herself to breathe slowly, holding the air in her lungs for a while before sighing it out.

She sat up. According to Papa's watch on her wrist, it was only a few minutes past midnight. She pushed an opening through the privacy screen around her bed. The nurse wasn't at her desk. She put on her shoes and made for the door.

The rain had abated, but the air seemed laden. It was pitch-black. She walked along the veranda and then hurried out into the night, determined to be unbothered by the bleak drizzle. Making her way toward her dormitory, she stepped into puddles she couldn't avoid in the darkness. Trying to escape one, she fell flat on her back. *Great*, she thought, lying in the mud. She was thoroughly drenched, the muck seeping into all the bad places. *Just great.*

The dormitory door was never locked. Madame— and sometimes other female teachers—needed to be able to carry out impromptu inspections, ensuring every student was accounted for in their bed. Bed-sharing was not allowed.

She let herself in and picked her way quietly toward her row. She reached under her pillow for the torch she kept there for nighttime trips to the loo. By the torchlight, she fished her wallet from where she kept it wedged in a tear she'd ripped in the mattress. She wrapped her over-sized towel over her shoulders and retraced her steps back to the door. She wiped the mud from the back of her neck, picked dead leaves out of her hair.

The wind gusting through the trees increased the volume of raindrops falling on her head. She covered it with the towel; the torchlight helped to keep her from falling once again. She ran up to the canteen and fed a five-hundred-shilling coin into the phone slot. She dialed Achen's number.

"Hello, this is Achen," she said after the second ring.

"The conditions of the ultimatum," Aine said. "Do you know them?"

"Kidio?" Achen said. "What are you talking about?"

"Mama gave Mbabazi some kind of ultimatum," Aine said. "She hasn't told you?"

"I've been calling and texting her for hours. She won't respond."

"What did you do now?"

"When I picked her up in Entebbe, she already knew about your dad." Achen explained how Mbabazi had come out of the airport with her eyes glued to her phone. People had been sending condolences. As she approached Achen in the waiting area, she told her, with a mix of shock and disbelief, "My father has died."

"That's when it truly dawned on me that I had royally fucked up," she said. "The gravity of it all sunk in there and then. I just hadn't counted on others getting to her before I did. I wanted to break the news gently. I brought flowers."

An automated voice warned Aine she had fifteen seconds left on the call. She fed the machine several coins.

"I should have listened to you," Achen said.

"I didn't exactly insist, did I?"

"I'm not sure we'll survive this, if I'm being honest," Achen said. "I have this creeping feeling she's finished with me. She's going to come back here and kick me out. Or she'll leave me and go back to Canada. They offered her a job there, you know. A fabulous salaried full-time job in Toronto."

"Slow down!" Aine could feel her breath growing quicker. "What exactly did you tell her?"

"Everything," Achen said. "She cried, of course. She was inconsolable. She said, 'Take me to Bigodi now,' but when we pulled onto the highway from Entebbe, she was suddenly furious. She said, 'Pull over right now.' And I did. And she said, 'Get out. Get the fuck out of my car.' She was yelling. That was the last time I saw her. She sped off and left me in the dust. At least now I know she made it there. That she didn't perish in the same way your mzee did."

"So you told her it was your call to keep her in the dark about Papa?"

"Of course, I did."

"Fuck," Aine said. "I told her it was my decision."

"What did you do that for?" Achen said explosively.

"I told you—the ultimatum." Aine's voice rose. "I figured if Mama had threatened to disown her or whatever, at least she'd have you."

"Fuck," Achen said.

"She called me a liar and hung up on me." Aine couldn't believe they'd both fucked up so monumentally, that they'd possibly broken their relationships with Mbabazi so irreparably. "What are we going to do?"

"You're going to call her right now and tell her the truth," Achen said. "You understand?"

"I'm not sure it will matter now."

"Just do it," Achen urged, her voice rising. "Do it right now."

"Okay. All right."

Aine hung up and called Mbabazi, but it went straight to that annoying message: "The telephone number you have called is not available at the moment..." She dialed the number again and again like a maniac, and then shouted a string of obscenities at the cold metallic recording. "...Please try again later." A sort of motion sickness came over her. She replaced the receiver, and the machine spat the coin back into her waiting hand. Where was Mbabazi now? Was she still in Bigodi or driving back to Kampala?

Anger fisted in Aine's throat as she slotted the coin back into the callbox and dialed Mama's number.

"Hello?" Mama picked up immediately.

"How could you do it, Mama?" Aine asked severely, the full force of the confrontation almost making her scream. "How could you make such an impossible demand of Mbabazi?"

"Listen to me, Aine," Mama said in Rukiga. "In this world we must do what is hard to show that we love what is good." Her speech was slow and measured, like she was teaching Aine a deep and profound lesson. "I love my daughter. No one on this earth loves her more than me. Am I not the one who carried her in my womb for nine months? The one who almost bled to death bringing her into this world? She is my flesh. My own blood. So, you listen to me and listen well. This is what we must do. I know this the way I know that the sun is the sun and the moon is the moon. If we don't show your sister that we hate her sin, she will stay in it, and she will rot in it."

"We're all sinners," Aine said, confident there was a verse in the Bible that said those exact words. "In any case, Mbabazi is an adult, capable of managing her own affairs. Why don't you worry about your own soul?"

"Our God will bring her back to us."

"Why do you keep saying *us* and *we*?" Aine asked, though she felt certain her mother was as usual not listening to her at all. "Did you include me in this ultimatum of yours? I'm not some plastic pawn for you to push around on your chessboard of evil moves."

"I've prayed about it," Mama went on as if nothing Aine said was of consequence. "I've seen her in the desert. Jesus is working on her as we speak. He's our redeemer, and he will bring her back to us changed. Can you trust me on this?"

"No, I cannot!" Aine shouted, incredulous. "Where is she? What time did you show her the door?"

"I gave her a choice! She made her decision."

Finally a real response. "And what choice would you have made if Shwenkuru had forced you to pick between your family and Papa?" Aine asked. "Would you have walked away from him?"

"If you can't see the difference—" Mama stopped and started again. "Have they been turning you into someone who does not condemn their lifestyle?"

"You're assuming I condemned it to begin with!"

Mama made some whiney noises as though wounded. "Answer me this." She sounded calm but serious. "What is the fifth commandment?"

"Do the honourable thing, and I will honour you as long as I live," Aine pleaded. "Be a good person. Call her now and tell her you love her." Just then the automated voice cut in with a warning. Fifteen seconds was all they had left.

"We must trust in his goodness, do you understand?" her mother said before the phone cut off.

Aine sat down on the little bench next to the callbox. *Goodness. I don't know what that word really means, though words are my business.* Who said that? A character from a

165

novel. A novel Achen had sent Aine not that long ago. It was one of those slow narratives that wants you to read them equally slowly, but Aine had devoured it in one long gulp. She'd read it during prep time and then in her bed, by torchlight, late into the night. The narrator was a successful Toronto writer suffering over her nineteen-year-old daughter who had become a beggar. The girl dropped out of university and sat on a street corner from morning to evening with a sign that said Goodness hanging down her chest. Her mother, the writer, was so heartbroken that she was barely functional. But Aine could see how a girl could be driven to do something like that. To sit on the street, mute and powerless, asking the world to be good to her.

She leaned back against the wall of the canteen. The rain started coming down in hard slants. The air grew bitingly cold; tiny drops of mist silvered her arms. She wrapped the towel around herself, tucked her pressed-together hands into her lap. Was there a way to transform her own hopelessness, her powerlessness, into goodness?

11

AINE SAT ON HER luggage outside the school gate. The askari had called down to the taxi park in downtown Fort Portal. He'd assured her there was a commuter taxi on its way to pick her up. She was restless, full of nervous energy. Today should have been momentous, the occasion of her final release from this jail where she'd lived out six years of her life. Maybe she'd have convinced Papa to take her out for a celebratory lunch. When he'd picked her up after her O-levels, he'd taken her out to Garden's Restaurant and said she could have anything on the menu. It had taken Aine forever to decide, but eventually she had picked spaghetti bolognese.

"The *g* is silent," Papa had whispered after the waiter had taken their orders.

"Now you tell me, after I've made a fool of myself in front of the waiter?" Aine had said before taking her frustration out on English. "Such a weird language. It's so uppity it resists mastering."

"To be fair, spaghetti bolognese is Italian in origin."

"Whatever, I still loathe English sometimes," she said, drawing out the *loathe*.

They agreed that it was too precise, yes, a language of sharp lines that cut through the bones of things, flattened nuance. "If I think of something in Rukiga," Aine said, "saying it in English almost always makes the sentence much shorter and, like, too clean."

"It's a sanitary language," Papa had said. "Hygienic."

"Sterile, more like," Aine had said. "But if you have a good command of it, people think you know stuff. That you're smart or clever. It's the language of knowledge."

Papa told her a story: As a new tour driver back in the day without much work coming his way, he'd phoned a safari magazine to advertise his services. The receptionist had put him on hold for the marketing manager. When he'd come on the line, he'd asked Papa, "Sir, you wish to take out an ad in our next issue?"

"I want to put an ad in your next issue," Papa had said.

"Take out an ad, you mean, sir?"

Papa had maintained he wanted to put one in, not take one out, and he'd grown increasingly frustrated with the man for not understanding something so basic. Then the manager had said that these things were one and the same, except that "take out an ad" was the correct expression. Papa had been embarrassed.

"So, he knew what you meant from the start," Aine said. "He was being a show-off."

"People who know English well can't resist showing off," Papa had surmised. "They are such peacocks."

Now, soft sobs engulfed Aine like a mudslide. There had always been a kind of intellectual rigour to her conversations with Papa. He was interested in poking at ideas, interrogating them even, and she did her best to be his equal. How was she supposed to live out the rest of her life without him? The picture of her future without him in it looked blurry, completely out of focus.

For now, every memory of her father and her sister was still fresh in her mind, sharper even, unchanged by the passage of time. They'd both—individually and together—nurtured her over her lifetime, touched her indelibly. Her love for them would never pass away.

Aine's love for Mbabazi had grown fierce, morphing into something like a sorrow that contained every past and present loss, plus the ones to come, which would harden her from the inside out. After Geography Paper One, she had dashed to the computer lab eager to email her and found herself instead googling race results from the Cape Town Marathon. Mbabazi's name was fifth in women. She had finished with a gun time of 02:29:45. Aine had marvelled at the feat. What sort of determination and strength, both physical and mental, was required to keep a steady, fast pace well past the point when every cell of one's brain screamed *STOP*?

Aine had written a long email, apologizing. "Grief

makes us strangers to ourselves," she had written. "It's the only explanation I can offer you for my catastrophic errors in judgment. If you can't forgive me, then please just drop me one line to let me know you're alive."

When she'd checked her email the next day, there was a one-line reply from Mbabazi: "I'm alive."

Aine had replied, "I miss you beyond any means I have of coping with missing you this much."

When she had found no response from Mbabazi the following day, she restrained herself from writing another note. Perhaps that was a way to be good. Perhaps what Mbabazi needed was for Aine to shut up and let her be. Perhaps the accumulation of time would create space for things to change, for perspectives to shift, for rifts to close or new bridges to form.

THE KAMUNYE RATTLED EFFORTFULLY up an incline as it edged toward the end of Kibale Forest. It was hot inside the overly full minibus. Aine sat squeezed between a mother breastfeeding her infant to her right and an extremely skinny man to her left. Everything about the man was sharp; he was all hip bones and elbows. They poked Aine in her ribs. Yet she had no choice but to angle her body ever so slightly in his direction. A foul smell had been emanating from the breastfeeding baby since before they had reached the forest. The newborn had clearly soiled its nappy. The mother had tried to contain the smell under a double wrapping of her shawl, but it was no use.

As the kamunye entered Magombe Swamp, eels turned in Aine's stomach. She dreaded seeing her mother, having to finally, after two weeks, talk to her in person. Aine had rehearsed her spiel about the ineffectiveness of disinheritance and shunning. She'd done some research. She'd read articles and first-person accounts of people who had been excommunicated from their religious communities or kicked out by their families. Most of the stories were from former Jehovah's Witnesses. Disfellowshipping, disinheritance, shunning. The psychological toll of isolation, of being pulled up by the roots and tossed out to dry. Some didn't survive it; there were stories of people who had taken their own lives. Yet those who practised shunning sincerely believed they had scriptural backing and were therefore doing right. It made Aine resent all gods, those supreme beings who imposed moralities that served only themselves. Yet she also thought that perhaps religious fanaticism magnified in people what had existed inside them all along. All Aine could do was relay this information to Mama calmly and without judgment. Ultimatums almost always made things worse for everyone involved, including family members, who in effect became the grass that got trampled when elephants fought.

It was six p.m. when the taxi poked its head into Bigodi. Aine craned her neck to look through the dust-coated window over the stinky baby. Lydia's Convenience was closed. Mama always kept the duka open until at least eight p.m., not wanting to lose out on the business of those who waited until late to make their evening meals.

Aine entertained a wildly impossible scenario: Mama and Mbabazi had reconciled, and they were both at home right now, waiting for Aine so that they could all, finally, mourn Papa properly as a family.

The taxi stopped at the stage and Aine alighted. Apollo, a boda boda cyclist, helped the conductor heave Aine's luggage down from the rooftop carrier rack. Dust covered the palm frond mat inside of which Aine's mattress was rolled. She'd have to wash the mattress cover and hope the dust hadn't crept into the foam as well. Her luggage, previously blue, was entirely brown.

She paid the conductor as Apollo strapped the luggage and the mattress onto the back of his motorcycle.

"You can fit also," he said, scootching forward on his seat to create a narrow space between himself and the luggage.

"You go on ahead." She paid him with the change the conductor had returned to her. "I'll walk. If there's no one home, just leave it on the veranda."

She swung her backpack over her shoulders and walked slowly, buying herself time. The evening was warm and humid. She removed her necktie, rolled it into a tight ball, and pocketed it. Turning left after Forest Lodge, she saw a flurry of activity in the maize shamba beyond the sweet potato garden. Women and children were spread out across the field. As she got closer, she saw they were collecting ensenene, teasing the longhorn grasshoppers from where they liked to burrow under the leaf sheaths of maize plants. Women reprimanded the children, threatening to send them back home if they didn't take care not to destroy the maize plants. Too excited about filling their containers with their catches, the children didn't listen.

Aine, too, had been such a child once. She'd so looked forward to grasshopper season. There was an air of celebration whenever the insects arrived unannounced, as if they'd fallen from the sky. Everyone paused their plans and took to the fields to collect as many ensenene as they could catch. Papa devised a system that involved the Landcruiser's headlights at full brightness and panels of iron sheeting that led into a large barrel full of water. The silly nocturnal insects were drawn to the bright light, slamming into the iron sheet, which tunnelled them toward the water. Death by drowning. But what a delicious treat. Aine and Papa would pluck off the wings while Mama fried the insects golden and crispy. They'd sit late into the night, plucking and roasting and eating. And still there was plenty left over for Mama to sell by the cupful at the duka. Squeamish tourists often recorded themselves on their phones as they attempted their first bite.

She stood off to the side as some cows passed her.

"Agandi," greeted Caleb, the young boy herding the cattle.

"Ndyaho," she replied. "Nogambaki?"

"Ndyaho."

She continued homeward. She was so lost in thought she didn't see Zakayo coming toward her. And now it was too late to hurry along and evade him, Papa's waragi supplier. He was shirtless, had likely been working in his banana planation, which wrapped around his compound.

"Kurikayo," he said, welcoming her back home.

"Narugayo," she said and accepted his hand for the traditional greeting.

"Keije, buhoro, buhorogye." *Peace. Good peace.*

Aine instinctively crossed her arms in front of her bosom as his eyes lingered lower, as they always did whenever he talked to Aine.

"Honashi mazima sho akazaara omwana aheru?" he asked, his hand reaching out to brace against the trunk of the jambula tree.

It took Aine a minute to wrap her head around the question. Was this weasel accusing Papa of having sired an illegitimate daughter?

"What outside child?" Was he talking about Achen?

"Don't you know she came to the funeral to demand her inheritance?" How quickly a piece of gossip was accepted as fact in this village. "She cornered your poor mother in the house. On the day of her husband's burial, moreover!"

"Who told you that?"

"You are the one who ran after her." Zakayo looked at her accusingly. "I was there. I saw you with my own eyes."

Did he think that now that Papa was dead, he could discipline her?

"I better get going," she said and walked away with determination.

The sun was setting as she arrived home. She entered

the empty compound timidly and went straight toward her father's tomb in the banana plantation, drawn to it as if by a force outside herself. Where there had been a mound of dirt, there was now a menacing slab of cement, bluish in the fading light. Rather than sadness, terror engulfed her. He was here, her father, trapped under the concrete, already dry and hard. Her hands trembled as she felt around the smooth edges of the tombstone. The epitaph read "Yesu yaamugira ati. Niinye kuzooka namagara; orikuunyikiriza, nobu yaakufa, aryaba ohuri-ire." Words Jesus spoke as he raised Lazarus from the dead. Papa had never openly criticized religion, but he'd once told Aine that God and his son were metaphors. Aine hadn't asked what the metaphor represented. She sat down at the foot of the concrete slab and cried unre-strainedly. A breeze rustled the banana leaves, making them susurrate.

The sound of crunching mulch startled her. She lifted her gaze and saw Mama approaching, her hands held behind her back. Aine's heart squeezed for one extra beat. She dried her eyes with the back of her hand, but the tears flowed harder and faster. Mama looked about a decade older. She was gaunt and had the sunken eyes of someone recovering from a terrible illness. Aine stood and put her arms around Mama. She rested her chin over her thin shoulder.

"Now that you are home," Mama said after a moment, "we can start planning the last funeral rites."

Aine stepped back to look at her.

"You will write the invitations. Your handwriting is good, much better than mine. I will hand them out discreetly at the shop. We shall invite few, few people. Close friends only and our relatives. Feeding too many people is costly."

She continued, hardly a breath in between. "Of course, we have some money coming to us now." Had she always spoken in this way that welcomed no interruptions, left no room for a response? Or was this something new, like the crow's feet that ribboned the corners of her eyes? "The man who caused the accident, the company he was working for is giving us some money. Nshuti is taking care of everything. He wanted to sue them. You know how hotheaded my brother can be. But I told him, for me, there is nothing more to be gained by taking these people to court. Even if he goes to jail, will this bring your father back?"

"No, but it will ensure the bastard isn't out there driving another lorry," Aine finally interjected. "What if he kills someone else?"

"What if they put him in jail and the money offer goes away? What then?" Mama said. "Who will pay your university fees? Do you think I can manage it myself? We have to pick our battles now. Anyway, back to the last funeral rites. We shall—"

"Why are you so keen to throw a party for people who are busy gossiping about us?" Aine was shaking with rage. "They are saying Achen is Papa's outside child. That she cornered you in your bedroom to demand her inheritance."

Mama pressed her lips together, not the slightest hint of surprise on her face.

"This isn't news to you, is it?" Aine talked around the horrified pit in her stomach.

"If people want to talk, you can't stop them."

"You can correct them." It was all Aine could do not to scream. Mama was willing to let people believe this terrible rumour that tarnished Papa's name. "And while you're at it, you can treat Mbabazi like an adult capable of making her own decisions. Do you really think banishing her will make her straight? This is madness, Mama. You're making Papa turn in his grave."

Her mother's expression suddenly sharpened, and she smacked Aine hard across the face. *Thwack*. It happened so quickly Aine almost doubted it had happened at all. She must have been five years old when her mother last smacked her, and Mama never did it ever again. Aine's face was ablaze. Mama stared at her wildly. She started to walk away but turned back.

"Okyari omwana," she spat, calling her a child. "You know nothing about what makes a father turn in his grave."

Aine was stunned. She watched as her mother hurried toward the compound. Aine perceived her as a small part of herself that was drifting away, without a chance of ever reattaching.

But when she went into the house and lit the kerosene lamp in her bedroom, she kept the door wide open. Sitting on the bed, she wished that Mama would come in with an excuse to fetch something: a box of matches, say.

"Mine's empty," she'd say, and Aine would reply, "Here, mine is full," and she'd give it to her, and they'd look at each other and know the real reason she'd come.

She sat and waited, her eyes trained on the open door, but Mama didn't come. Aine felt strangely cold and heavy, as though the air in the room had acquired weight and thickness that pressed down on her. Then a fresh wave of anger rolled through her. Suddenly she wanted to be anywhere else in the world but here, in this house with Mama's hostility, her violence.

She emptied the contents of her backpack onto the bed and crossed to her wardrobe. Without any sense of where she'd go, she packed feverishly, as though in a trance. Her hands shook. She could go to Kabale and find Uncle Ambrose. Someone with whom she could talk about Papa. It didn't matter if their relationship had soured; Papa and Ambrose were brothers. And he was Aine's only paternal uncle. Did he even know that his brother was dead? Why was there no word, the equivalent of *orphan* or *widow*, for when you lost a sibling?

As she undressed, she caught a whiff of her armpits. She smelled like the kamunye she'd travelled in; its mustiness had burrowed into her clothes, curled into her skin. She needed a good scrubbing.

Outside, she filled a basin with water and carried it into the bath shed. Mercifully, the water was lukewarm after a day in the sun. As she washed herself, she excavated memories, now distant, of when the whole family went to visit Papa's ancestral home in Kabale. Her

grandfather suffered from elephantiasis, which disfig-
ured his legs, swelling them up to the size of tree trunks.
His feet were equally misshapen and grotesque. Kaaka
Mary was always fussing over him. She rubbed on his
legs and knees mineral clay she scooped from a nearby
hot springs. It was supposed to soothe his aches, but it left
his clay-encrusted legs looking like those of an elephant.
Aine had been afraid of him. He was always reclining in
his chair under the trees, always reading, unapproach-
able. But eventually she warmed up to him. He was the
one who taught her how to read—"How to make words
reveal their secrets," he said—by sounding out the sylla-
bles he scratched into the ground with his cane. By the
end of their visit, Aine was able to read and write some
simple words—*fox*, *box*, *socks*—and she was only in nursery school. But her shwenkuru died before she could visit
him again, and now all she had left of him were boxes of
his books. Sometimes when she was reading them, she
felt his presence. She read the notes he scribbled in the
margins and understood he'd been sharp-witted, a careful
thinker. Conservative, sure, but a man of ideas.

She towelled herself dry and hurried into the house.
In her room, she pulled on her grey leggings and wore
over them a striped shirt-dress with a braided faux leather
belt. The ensemble was a gift from Mbabazi. The shirt-
dress was asymmetrical, longer at the back. She put on
her hiking boots. She'd take a boda boda to Kamwenge
and sleep on the bus that set off for Mbarara at dawn.
From Mbarara she'd take a taxi, or maybe another bus,

to Kabale. Then all she'd have to do was make her way to the market on the shores of Lake Bunyonyi, which was a short leisurely walk from her grandfather's house. There she would ask around. Someone was bound to remember old man Kamara, who had for many years taught English and history at the primary school on an island across the lake. A school accessible only by boat or canoe. For sure someone would remember him. They'd know his son Ambrose.

She tiptoed out of the house, closed the door quietly behind her. The night was bright, a giant full moon threatening to crash down behind Magombe Swamp. She hurried up the compound and, reaching the murram road, ran like a bush rat escaping a wildfire. Faster than when she'd run after Achen's car. She only slowed down as she neared Forest Lodge, catching her breath as she came to the main road. Sweat pricked her armpits. The tarmac radiated all the heat it had absorbed throughout the day. She sloped toward the trading centre to hail a boda boda.

12

BEEP, BEEP. A DOUBLE-CABIN Hilux pickup truck honked, slowing as it neared her. She braced for the inevitable catcall or cheap pickup line men driving trucks vomited at women. But when the driver's window lowered, she heard him call her name.

"Dan?" she said, surprised to see Kemi's boyfriend, Jackfruit Dan, behind the wheel.

"Where to?" he said.

"Kamwenge," she said, approaching the vehicle. There was a young guy she didn't recognize next to Dan in the front cabin.

"Then you're going in the wrong direction, my friend." He smiled, bending his arm out the open window.

She gave a dry laugh. "I'm going to catch a boda boda, smarty pants. Did you see any still at the stage?"

"We can give you a lift." He indicated the empty back cabin and said he and his buddy Paulo were headed for a country resort in Kamwenge where Paulo's uncle and aunt were celebrating their twenty-fifth wedding anniversary. "Free food. Free booze."

"I'm Paulo," the passenger said, giving Aine a little wave. His bushy eyebrows met in the middle, giving him a kind of primitive look that wasn't at all unattractive. Aine shook his hand, a big hand that felt like it could easily deal with the oilier parts of a big engine. "I work with Dan at Kanyawara."

"Nice to meet you."

She climbed into the back cabin of the white truck. It had to be a sign, she thought. A lift to Kamwenge: the universe's way of signalling to her that bigoted mothers could use a little abandonment themselves.

"Sorry about your mzee," Dan said as he eased the truck back on the road out of Bigodi.

"Thanks, Dan," she replied and was grateful that he was driving and couldn't make eye contact. She still didn't know how to respond. There were others who, after saying sorry, stood looking at her with a kind of hunger in their eyes as if expecting more than a thank you. Those were the ones who made her most uncomfortable. What more did they want her to say? Yet she preferred even them to the ones who said nothing at all. There were girls at school who'd kept mum about it all, just interacted with her same as before, as if nothing had happened. As if she were the same person they'd always known.

"Why are you going to Kamwenge this late anyway?" Dan asked.

"I'm taking the morning bus to Mbarara, and from there to Kabale. My father's ancestral home."

She immediately regretted divulging this much information. If Dan told Kemi, she might tell her mother, and then it would be just as if Aine had left Mama a note. The mothers in Bigodi were a gang. But Kemi could be close-mouthed, a good friend. Aine would call her from Kabale. She hoped she could stay there, far away from this place, for a good long while.

"I see," Dan said.

"So, Paulo," she said, eager to change the subject, "are you named for the apostle who wrote all those letters?"

Paulo fixed her with a look, as if trying to bring her into focus.

"Sorry," she said. "I've offended you."

"Not at all," he replied. "But are you a savedee?"

"Me? No. Now, my mum, on the other hand. Queen of the savedees. She alone knows what's good for everybody. But anyway, I've always been curious about Paul. The way he dropped his Hebrew name, Saul, and adopted the Roman version, Paul, so that the Romans would think he was one of them and welcome his proselytizing. A little disingenuous, don't you think? A would-be saint taking a less-than-honest approach to things. The end justifies the means and all that."

Paulo seemed to take in her ranting with a degree of interest. "Proselytizing? Disingenuous?" he repeated the words as though he'd never heard them spoken before, drawing out each syllable. "Why are you speaking English like a white person?"

"Do you mean that as a compliment?"

Dan gave a barking laugh. "In primary," he told Paulo, "Aine used to walk around with a dictionary. A big, big one. At break time when the rest of us were playing, she'd be sitting in the doorway of the classroom reading the big dictionary."

"I didn't *read* the dictionary," Aine protested. "I kept it nearby in case I needed it."

"You'd ask her a simple question and she'd reply with big English words you'd never heard," Dan continued. "Even the teachers were always telling her, 'Ainembabazi, please, speak normal English.'"

Aine held her face in embarrassment. She'd indeed been one of those flamboyant people Papa called peacocks. She'd flaunted her English vocabulary like it was the best thing about her. Maybe she was still guilty of a little peacockery.

"This one time—" Dan went on.

"Oh, great, you're not finished," Aine said.

"We are in class, and it starts to rain, yeah?" Dan picked up. "Our Aine here, she goes to the blackboard and writes a word: *petrichor*."

The memory rushed at Aine so vivid it was as though it had happened only yesterday.

"Petri who?" Paulo said.

"Petrichor." Dan slowed the truck through Kahunge, a trading centre smaller than Bigodi. "I have never forgotten it. To this day, when it rains after a long time, I go to the door and smell it. That perfume! I wish they sold a body spray that smells like petrichor. I would buy many boxes so that I never ran out."

"That's so lovely," Aine said. "At least one good thing came of my being obnoxious."

"What do you mean obnoxious?" Dan said. "You were the most interesting kid in our year. You seemed to enjoy the company of your books more than people, but you would close the book when someone came to talk to you. Or if the ball landed in front of you, you picked it up and kicked it back to us on the field."

"I thought everyone hated me." All Aine remembered of primary school was that she was lonely. Apart from Kemi, all the girls ignored her, never picked her for their netball games. They left her out of their kwepena and jumping rope so that she was always bored, watching from the sidelines. She was only included during PE when there was a teacher making sure everyone participated.

"All the teachers worshipped you," Dan said. "Remember when you and Isaac won that debating competition? They treated you like gods. It was as if you had walked on water."

"So, what secondary school do you go to?" asked Paulo, perhaps feeling excluded from the conversation.

"Pike Girls in Fort Portal," Aine said. "I wrote my final UACE exam just this morning."

"Then we must celebrate," Paulo said, smacking his hands together for emphasis. "It's your first day of vacay!"

"Yes, well." Celebrating was the furthest thing from

her mind, but she didn't want to burden the boys with her melancholy.

"The bus for Mbarara doesn't set off until six a.m.," Paulo went on. "You want to tell me that you'd rather sit in an empty bus by yourself all night long when you could be having fun with us?"

Now that he'd said it, sitting alone on the bus all night sounded unnerving. She'd packed books to fill the hours and a blanket to sleep, but would she be safe?

"We shall take you to the bus station well before six," Dan promised.

"Okay, all right." She even managed a chuckle. "Thank you."

"Did I tell you Paulo's uncle is the town clerk?" Dan said. "So you know it is a no-nonsense party, this one. The man is loaded with wanainchi dough."

"A bureaucrat who isn't pocketing your money is rare as hen's teeth," Paulo said.

"Are you defending the man or accusing him?" Aine said.

"Maybe both?"

Something told Aine that she and Paulo would get along just fine.

THEY REACHED THE OUTER limits of Kamwenge Town and Dan turned left at Padre Pio Road. Soon Igogora Country Resort emerged, a beacon in the moonlight. A privacy wall surrounded the sprawling complex of hotel rooms, restaurants, and bars. Dan pulled through the gate and into the gravel parking lot. Aine was suddenly reluctant to leave the truck, its warmth. But Paulo opened the door, and she gave him her hand, the other gripping her backpack. She'd eat the free food and then she'd leave. She knew where the bus station was, through the town toward the old railway station.

They crossed to the crowded gardens on a paved path through manicured box hedges, strings of lights blinking purple and white. Soft music floated over the patrons, some sitting, others standing, the tea lights on each table casting everyone in lovely forgiving colours. She felt out of place in tights and hiking boots, with a ratty and overfull backpack.

A server wearing a crown of flowers around her bunched-up braids showed Aine and the boys to an empty table on the edge of the gardens. The table was set against a large bird of paradise plant whose leaves fanned long and wide like green tongues.

"Drinks?" she asked and went on to list the brands of beer on offer. She upturned the glasses already at the table and filled them from a bottle of Rwenzori mineral water.

"Bell for me," Dan said promptly.

"Is there wine?" Paulo inquired.

"Four Cousins," said the lady, scratching her pencil across a page in her little notepad.

"We shall take a bottle of that," Paulo said. "And a Tusker Lite."

She praised the boys on their choices and left.

Aine was shocked and confused. "Is it odd?" she

wondered out loud, gesturing at the departing woman. "Am I invisible to her?"

Dan and Paulo looked at each other across the table.

"I'm sorry," Paulo said. "Do you not drink red wine? Many girls like it."

Aine didn't want to make a scene at a party she was crashing. "I'll try the wine," she said.

"Kemi likes it when I order for her," Dan said. "Chicks dig that, not so? When your man orders for you?"

"They do?" Aine truly had no idea; she'd never been out on a date. But she'd read enough novels to suspect when patriarchy was disguising itself as romance. She turned to Paulo. "Do you also order for your girlfriend?"

"I don't have a girlfriend."

"It's romantic," Dan explained with the confidence of a teacher. "It shows that you know your woman well. That you pay attention when she tells you things she likes."

"If you want to order something else …" Paulo raised his hand to get the attention of another waitress passing by.

"It's all right." Aine touched his elbow and lowered it gently.

The only problem was, of course, that she'd never tasted wine before. She and Kemi had tried alcohol on several occasions, adding a splash of Papa's banana gin to a bottle of Coke. A few sips made Aine woozy, an unpleasant light-headedness she was never keen to replicate.

Two men wearing chef's jackets brought food over and served it in a steamy onrush of skewered meats, deep-fried potatoes, and grilled plantain. As they finished serving, the pretty waitress returned with the two beers and a bottle of red wine. She poured some into a glass with a long stem and smiled as she set it in front of Aine. "Enjoy, please."

Aine took one sip and knew right away she'd made a mistake. Could she spit the foul beverage back into the glass without attracting any attention? The boys were looking at her expectantly. She swallowed. The lingering sweetness reminded her of accidentally biting into an overripe mango that had crossed over to rottenness. "God, this is vile," she said, trying not to gag. She took several cleansing sips of water. The boys laughed raucously.

"I'm putting an end to this." Paulo flagged down a waitress and Aine ordered a bottle of Krest bitter lemon soda.

"When I get a girlfriend," Paulo declared, "I will never order for her."

"Unless she wants you to," Dan said.

"Then I will ask her if she wants me to order for her."

"And who doesn't like being asked, right?" Aine said. "I would even say it's romantic."

As the evening wore on, she allowed some lightness to enter her spirit, permitted herself to enjoy the boys' company. Paulo's behaviour toward her was warm and a little restrained. She found herself breaking off pieces from her life and turning them into little stories for his enjoyment. He listened with interest and asked questions.

He knew many people at the party, and whenever someone stopped to say hello, he introduced Aine as a friend who was celebrating her first day of A-level vacation before starting university.

"Congratulations," they said and wished her good luck.

"Were they very hard?" Paulo asked. "People say that UACES are the toughest exams."

"You study hard and hope for the best." Aine was disappointed by his level of education, that he, like Dan, hadn't pursued his A-level certificate.

"When I finished O-level my father found my job for me," he said. "He's also a game ranger."

"What exactly do game rangers do?" Because they often carried AK-47s, Aine put game rangers in the same category as soldiers.

"We patrol the forest and remove the snares poachers set to catch wild animals," he said. "We remove hundreds every year."

A cousin of Paulo's pulled up a chair and started to talk to Paulo and Dan about football. It seemed strange, the boys' unwavering commitment to European football teams. Paulo was a red devil, which he explained meant that he supported Manchester United. Dan was a gunner.

"Gunner?"

Dan leaned in and paused as if to give a lengthy explanation but said only, "Arsenal for life." The combination of beer and Four Cousins had slowed Dan's tongue. There was a wetness to his words as if he suddenly had an excess of spit in his mouth.

"The problem with Arsenal supporters," Paulo said, "is that they worship their club more than the game."

"Sounds cultish," Aine said.

"Don't mix football with religion," Dan argued.

"There's a difference?" Aine joked, but only Paulo laughed, and perhaps only to humour her. But the boys were united when they talked about African matches, agreeing that this year, too, the Uganda Cranes would be victorious.

"Mark my words," Paulo said. "We shall lift the CECAFA Cup once more."

"What's CECAFA?" Aine dared to ask.

CECAFA, Paulo explained, stood for the Council for East and Central Africa Football Associations. "They will all be competing in Kampala in a matter of days."

"You'll watch it on TV?" Aine said. Even in Bigodi there were a couple of pubs with television sets hooked up to satellite dishes. Men passed entire evenings there drinking beer and screaming at the soccer players on the screens.

"In the forest there's no TV," he said. "We shall follow the live coverage on the radio."

"From those announcers who speak so rapidly it's almost as if they are speaking a different language?"

"It is a language we understand very well."

IT WAS WELL PAST midnight when the master of ceremonies announced that the town clerk and his wife would now officially open the dance floor. Tables and chairs were pushed back to make room. The couple wore matching outfits tailored from yards upon yards of purple ankara like wealthy Nigerian chiefs wore in Nollywood films. Swaying like maize plants in the wind, they danced unremarkably—perhaps the billowing fabric was restricting—to a pop song, a honey-voiced male singer.

People cheered and clapped for the couple, who now beckoned everyone to join them. Dan shot to his feet and was soon gyrating against a woman in a tight-fitting red dress, its sweetheart neckline pushing the swells of her breasts almost up to her chin.

"Who's she?" Aine shouted over the music, wondering if she'd have to tell Kemi.

"Dan likes to have a good time."

"I don't think Kemi will like the sound of that."

"He's very much in love with Kemigabo," Paulo said. "He wants to marry her."

"He told you this?"

"He's already saving money for the bride price," he said. "Her father wants ten million shilling and two cows."

"Ten million?" Aine could hardly believe it. Kemi's dad had kicked her out the day he learned she was pregnant. She'd had to move in with her maternal grandmother while relatives and friends intervened, pleading with him to forgive his daughter. It wasn't until Sweezin was born that Kemi was allowed back home. "Does Kemi know anything, or are these negotiations happening behind her back?"

"She must know," Paulo said.

Aine had last seen Kemi at the funeral. Not exactly the atmosphere most conducive to sharing the news she was getting married to Jackfruit Dan. Suddenly Aine felt that familiar fragility working its way through her body. Her father was dead, her sister hated her, and she was running away in search of an uncle she hadn't seen in five years.

"Would you like to dance?" Paulo was on his feet, his arm stretched out toward her.

She shook her head, trying to infuse the gesture with as much apology and regret as she could. What reason was there to dance?

"Can you walk with me to the bus station?" She reached for her backpack under the table.

Paulo glanced at his watch as if to say, *So soon?*

"Please?" she said, rising to her feet.

"Let me get Dan."

She could see Dan slow-dancing with the red-dressed woman, their foreheads touching. "Just you," she said.

THE NOISE OF THE party receded, fading gradually as Aine and Paulo neared the main road. It was deserted, not a single car or person in sight. The road sloped gently and rose, giving a view in the nearby distance of Kamwenge Primary School, where Aine had debated many times. The moonlight refracted off the iron-sheet roofing.

"I had a deviated septum when I was young," Paulo confessed, probably uncomfortable with the silence.

"What's a deviated septum?" Aine asked, though she'd

have much preferred to continue considering the eerie light that was falling around them.

"The wall between my nose holes," he said. "It was bent to one side. My nose was crooked."

"Did someone punch you really hard?"

He chuckled. "It was like that when I was born. I'd get these nosebleeds out of nowhere. I couldn't do PE, any exercise really. They operated on my nose to make it straight, but if I drink more than one beer, the bleeding comes back. The doctor said alcohol makes the blood thin or something like that."

"Then why do you drink at all?"

"Pardon?"

"If alcohol makes your nose bleed, why not stay away from it altogether?"

He shrugged. "The spirit is willing, but the flesh is weak."

A small, citrusy *ha* escaped her lips. All that fizzy Krest she'd drunk. "I don't understand why anyone drinks beer," she said. To her, beer looked like pee and smelled just as bad.

"You get used to it," he said.

They were passing the primary school now, and she looked for the social hall, the building on the right side of the road where the debates had taken place.

"Where is it?" In its place was a new modern-looking commercial building painted white and blue. A bank.

"When did you last come to Kamwenge?"

"Six, actually, seven years ago."

Paulo explained that the social hall had been demolished maybe three years before. "This bank has been in operation for at least two years."

Aine could not explain her attachment to the building that had even then been in a state of disrepair. Its absence now signified something that had been, that no longer was. Once, when a travelling theatre troupe from Kabale came through Kamwenge, Papa brought Mama and Aine to the social hall to see the play *Omwana Wabandi*, about an orphan whose fortune changes when a prince asks for her hand in marriage. Mama raved about the play for weeks, singing lines from songs the orphan had sung while slaving for her evil stepmother.

"Did they build another social hall somewhere else?" she asked, but she knew the answer before Paulo said no. People loved to destroy a good thing.

"It was owned by the Catholic parish," Paulo said. "Maybe they're using the money from the sale to build the new church."

Across the road, the skeleton of the bigger cathedral under construction dwarfed the old one next to it. The building was already at the roofing stage, the naked beams latticing and rising to a precise point as if to pierce the starry night. Aine looked at the steps of the old kelezia, where she'd sat with Mbabazi. Where Mbabazi had come out to her. A conversation that still stood out as the most embarrassing in Aine's life. Her breath was picking up speed, her chest starting to convulse with pain. These days she measured her success by the number of minutes it took to stave off a flare of her deep-seated gnawing anxiety.

"Are you all right?" Paulo asked as she engaged in elaborate controlled breathing, inhaling deeply through her nose, exhaling loudly out her mouth.

"I'm fine," she said. "Do you have a mobile phone?"

He produced it swiftly from the back pocket of his blue jeans. Dialing Mbabazi's number, Aine dashed across to the forecourt of the old kelezia to sit in the same spot where Mbabazi had asked her, "Ms. Kamara, in the current zeitgeist, what are your thoughts on your sister being gay?"

"Hello?" Mbabazi picked up after the fifth ring.

"They tore down the social hall and replaced it with a hideous bank," Aine said in a burst of tears.

"Aine?"

She expected Mbabazi to hang up right away.

"Whose phone are you calling from?" Mbabazi said.

Aine took a deep stabilizing breath. "So, get this," she said. "The rumour around the village is that Achen is Papa's omwana waheru. And Mama is letting everyone believe it."

"Are you at home?" While her voice had been groggy before, now Mbabazi sounded sharp, alert.

"Kamwenge." Aine told Mbabazi about the events that had led up to her surreptitious departure.

"She did what?" Mbabazi said when Aine mentioned Mama's slap by Papa's grave.

"I said some things," Aine said and remembered again that it wasn't the first time Mama had hit her. When

Aine was four or five, she'd snuck into her aunt Mutesi's bedroom and picked up her sleeping newborn cousin to cradle him in her arms since no one was allowing her the privilege. As she lifted the baby from the bed, he squirmed and fell from Aine's arms. On the floor, the baby's eyes widened in shock. A moment passed before he screamed so loud Aine jumped in fright even as Mama and Aunt Mutesi burst into the room. Mama had slapped Aine so hard her vision blurred. The slap, she remembered, sounded like a bare belly striking river water.

"She hit you for standing up for me?"

"I really can't get into the details of all that," Aine said. Paulo was lingering at the bottom of the steps, within hearing distance. "There are things you just can't sift through the colander of a friend's mobile phone."

"Who's this friend, again?"

"Paulo, he's a game ranger," she said. "He's walking me to the bus station. I'm going to Kabale to find Uncle Ambrose. He probably doesn't even know about Papa."

"Fucking hell, Aine, you can't run to that man," she said as though she were describing vermin.

"Why not?" Aine rose to her feet. "Mama is planning last funeral rites. Our uncle has a right to be there."

"He's not even allowed to set foot in our compound," Mbabazi said.

"Since when?" Aine's voice squeaked. "What is with our family and banishing people?"

"He assaulted Mama," Mbabazi said. "You don't think that's worth a restraining order?"

Aine's stomach lurched. "Assaulted? When?"

"Are you telling me you don't know this?"

"No one ever tells me anything."

"Don't you remember he was always making passes at Mama?" Mbabazi said.

"And that constitutes assault?" Aine didn't even recall such passes. She did, however, remember the excitement that accompanied Uncle Ambrose's visits and the sadness when he departed, how she often cried because she didn't want him to leave. He'd been such a consummate teller of fables and folk stories. But now she listened, dumb-founded, as Mbabazi talked about him showing up at their home one day to find Mama all alone, Papa away on a safari job. Mama let him stay in the guest room, but then in the morning when she went out to the loo, she came back to find him in her bedroom. He shut the door and lunged at her, pinning her to the bed.

"Uncle Nshuti is the one who saved her," Mbabazi said. "He was ringing the kengele, but Mama wasn't coming out to bring the milk jug. Yet the front door was open. When he entered the house, he could hear muffled screams. He took a panga and kicked in the bedroom door. He almost cut Ambrose's head off."

"Jesus Christ!" Aine couldn't believe her uncle was capable of something so egregious. Once when he was visiting, the radio stations forecasted a solar eclipse. He filled a basin with water and let it settle in the middle of the compound. Aine crouched at one end of the basin, her uncle at the opposite side, and together they watched as the moon, reflected in the still water, took bites out of the sun until it gradually swallowed it and everywhere became dark in the middle of the day.

"They chased him away," Mbabazi said. "Police were involved."

"So, even the police know this big thing about my family, but I don't? Does everyone believe I'm so fragile?"

"Maybe it's that you can't be trusted."

"You know I'm sorry," Aine said. "What do I have to do to prove it? Tell me. I'll do it. I'll do anything."

"Listen," Mbabazi said after a minute, "why don't you just come here instead?"

"To Kampala?"

"We'll discuss this properly, face to face," she said. "Come up with a plan."

Before Aine could express her gratitude, Mbabazi was rattling off orders like an army commander. Aine was to take the bus headed straight for Kampala. In Mbarara, the bus would stop to allow passengers out and to let more on board who were going to the capital. Aine was to zip out and call Mbabazi to give her an idea of when her bus would be arriving in the city.

"I'll be waiting for you at the terminal," she said. "Aine, you are not to leave that terminal unless it is with me holding your hand."

"Should we have known, do you think?" Aine's mind was reeling from the stark revelation about her uncle. "The way he rolled his own tobacco into cigars and smoked them with the burning end inside his mouth?

Was that a clue that he was evil? I don't know anyone else who does that. Who smokes the burning end of a cigar."

"Did you hear what I said?"

"Yes."

"And this boy?" Mbabazi said. "The one whose phone you're calling me from. How well do you know him?"

Aine made a noise like *I don't know* and shrugged. Paulo was standing with his back to her, a silhouette in the blueish night.

"Are you there, or am I talking to myself?" Mbabazi couldn't seem to keep her frustration out of her voice.

"I'm here." Aine said, chastened. If Mbabazi forgave her, she'd do everything she could to earn back her trust.

"Promise me you're safe?" Mbabazi said. "People are never who you think they are."

"I know."

"Okay, repeat the plan to me because I'm not sure you were listening."

She did as her sister asked, and then she said, "I love you."

"I love you too," Mbabazi replied but in a wretched voice.

"Was that a relative of yours?" Paulo asked as Aine returned his phone.

She nodded. "Slight change of plans. I'm going to Kampala instead."

"Who is there?"

"My sister," Aine said. "She's very bossy, but she's the person I love most in the whole world."

"Then it's good that you're going to see her," he said.

"You have no idea." She had an urge to tell him everything that had led up to this moment. She pursed her lips, and the urge passed. "Thank you for lending me your phone. I hope I didn't use up all your airtime."

"It's no problem."

They walked toward the market square southwest of the church. The dukas were gruesome structures banged together out of bricks and concrete, facing each other across a courtyard riddled with potholes. A padlocked metal gate with spikes along the top closed off the strip of the market that during the day bustled with stall-holders selling fruits and vegetables. Tarps in green, blue, and white covered the stalls.

"That used to be my mum's spot over there." Paulo was pointing through the gate to a nearby stall. "When I went to Kamwenge Primary, I would come here for lunch."

"Does she not work here anymore?"

"She passed away thirteen months ago," he said. "A heart attack. One minute she was planting sweet potato vines in the garden behind the house, the next she was face down in the soil. Kwisha." *Gone*.

He gently wrapped his arms around Aine, drawing her into his chest. She tilted her face and touched her lips to his mouth as if it was the most natural response to his news. His kiss, gentle at first, quickly became urgent. It wasn't at all how she'd pictured her first kiss. Could he sense her inexperience? At intervals, he held her face in his hands and looked into her eyes before kissing her again, their heads turning to meet the sliding pressure of their tongues. His hands slid up her waist, but when he touched her breasts, she slapped his hand away.

"I'm so sorry," he said.

"My bad," she said. "I didn't mean to slap you."

He moved in for another go, and for a second, she wanted to touch him again, to put her arms around him and kiss him some more, but she couldn't help thinking it would all lead somewhere she wasn't prepared to go with him. He held her as she rested her head against his chest a while, her body stretched with desire. Then she said, "Let's walk."

They held hands as they exited the market. Outside, smaller dukas lined the dirt road. It was narrow with many twists and turns. As they walked hand in hand, she searched herself for signs of change, but she felt no different from moments before, except a little heady from the excitement of it all. Where exactly, she wondered, was the threshold between girlhood and womanhood? Was the crossing slow and gradual, or did a girl wake up one day and realize she'd been an adult woman for some time already?

THE CONDUCTOR SAT ON a plastic chair in the headlights of an idling bus. He wore a colourful kanga wrapped around his shoulders, a receipt book on his lap.

"Kampala, please," Aine said, fishing her purse out of her backpack.

"We're stopping in Mbarara today," the man said.

"There will be many buses going to Kampala from Mbarara. Even minibuses," Paulo said when Aine turned to him for guidance on how to proceed.

"Twenty thousand," the conductor said. "Do not lose this," he warned, handing her the pink receipt he tore from the book when she handed over the cash. "It is your ticket."

Aine pocketed it and stepped away to make room for a woman who had arrived on a boda boda. While the cyclist released the ropes around the sack of produce strapped to the carrier, she cradled a rooster, its wings and legs tied together with a strip of fabric.

"How long will you stay in Kampala?" Paulo asked, walking Aine to the bus's entrance.

"I honestly don't know," she said.

There was some commotion behind them. The woman with the rooster was refusing to relinquish it to the cargo hold under the bus, arguing it would surely suffocate to death in there.

"The cock will live," the conductor said impatiently, taking the bird from her arms.

"Will you call me?" Paulo asked.

"Sure." Aine produced a spiral-bound notebook from her backpack. He looked over her shoulder as she wrote down his phone number.

"Aliganyira Paulo," he said his full name, and she wrote that too. *Aliganyira*, a Rutooro name, meant "he will forgive." She thought it suited him.

"Thank you for everything tonight," she said, zipping up her backpack.

"If you don't call me, I will die," he said.

"Nonsense." She chuckled.

But he suddenly looked serious, his expression almost grave. He held her hands, drew her to him. "Have a good trip, Petrichor," he said and kissed her tenderly.

"Be well, Aliganyira."

She let go of his hands and climbed the narrow metal steps into the bus, turned to give him a wave before proceeding inside.

The seats at the front of the bus were occupied by snoozing passengers. A few others were scattered across the bus, most of them fast asleep, some even snoring loudly. She found a seat by a window and parted the tiny curtain to peek outside. A creamy mist like thick white smoke hung in the night air.

Paulo was slightly hunched, hands in his pockets, as he walked toward the murram road that had brought them to the bus station. In a couple of hours, it would be morning, and they'd both be a little older. Supposing, Aine wondered, he discovered some hours later that he didn't miss her as much, or even at all? People were compositions of endless change. The thought of him being beyond her made her want him more.

13

SHE FELL ASLEEP AND dreamed that it was the night before Christmas. They were all at home. She, Papa, Mama, and Mbabazi were sitting on the veranda, waiting for the carollers. Papa was tipsy; he'd been sneaking sips of waragi all evening. And now to pass the time, he was colour-coding the way everyone laughed, approaching the exercise like a proper scientific study, recording the results on a clipboard.

"You," he said, pointing at Mbabazi. "Laugh, now. Let me hear it."

Mbabazi threw her head back and guffawed on command. Like Papa's, Mbabazi's laughter was big, originating from her belly.

"Ahhh, yes," Papa said, pleased. He delivered his verdict: "Your laughter is red like a flower for the birds."

Mbabazi said, "I love drunk Papa."

"Who says I'm drunk?" Papa protested.

"That empty bottle of waragi," Mama said, pointing to it on the windowsill.

He nuzzled Mama's earlobe. "Yours is silver," he said when Mama giggled. "The world's shiniest, most beautiful song."

"You are so drunk," Mama said and reminded him not to speak when the carollers arrived. "Not one word out of you."

When Papa asked Aine to laugh, she opened her mouth, but no sound came out. "What's wrong with her?" he asked Mbabazi.

"I don't know," Mbabazi said and commanded Aine to laugh, goddammit.

All three of them were looking at Aine with such disappointment in their eyes. She tried once more, feeling for her voice, but her laughter became a moth stuck inside her throat. It hurt just to breathe. A goitre-like swelling bulged under her chin.

She woke up to a boy, black headphones covering his ears, yelling, "Can you move over?"

She lifted her hand to her neck to feel for the goitre.

"Eh, eh," the boy said, pushing her with his knee. "Others also want to sit."

"Jesus," she muttered. What a nasty person. This boy was a joke. The waistband of his blue jeans hung really low, sitting almost under his ass, his white briefs in full view. She leaned closer to the window, turned her face to the glass. The bus was parked on a street in a town that was definitely not Kamwenge. The sun was rising over a row of buildings, most still closed. She panicked. Could they have possibly reached Mbarara already? She scrutinized a Vote For poster stuck to the whitewashed front board of a restaurant. Someone had drawn a funny moustache and horns on the photo of the candidate. "Member of Parliament for Ibanda Municipality." Whew! Ibanda Town. Already, she was the farthest from home she'd ever travelled on her own.

WHEN THE BUS REACHED MBARARA, the conductor pointed her to the Kampala terminal all the way across the bustling motor park. But getting to it was no minor feat. The park was a chaotic jumble of minibus taxis, several genres of music competing from various dukas. Stall-holders ululated their wares and prices, carolling over each other. Aine walked carefully. There were puddles of sludgy water everywhere, even though it didn't look as if it had rained recently. Boda bodas and bicycles squeezed through the narrowest of spaces, threatening to run her over.

A hawker stepped in front of her, rapping the prices of the fanny packs and crossbody bags he wore around his waist and across his chest. She tried to side-step him, but he was quick, blocking her path.

"A beautiful kyana like you should not carry a tattered backpack," he said, blocking her again when she tried to go around him. He was enjoying himself while Aine burned with rage and frustration. She ducked behind a guy pushing a wheelbarrow loaded with pineapples and watermelons. But now she found herself carrying her dirty old backpack with a degree of embarrassment, holding it in one hand like maybe it belonged to someone else.

Everywhere she turned there were men and women vying to sell her something: watches, jewellery, belts, chewing gum. The men were especially aggressive.

She made it to the Kampala terminal, and three different conductors swarmed her, each one trying to get her onto their bus. Four buses were parked in a row, all of them destined for Kampala, all of them apparently leaving "now-now," if the conductors were to be believed. She hurried to the orange-painted bus with Global Coaches silkscreened over the strip of yellow along the side. The conductor on the Kamwenge-Mbarara bus had advised her their service was supposedly unmatched.

The ticket cost her another twenty-five thousand shillings. Running away from home was proving to be costly.

"How long before departure?" she inquired, paying the ticket issuer, a man whose reddish-purple lips attested to years of heavy smoking.

He rose from his chair and went to peek inside the bus. "Fifteen minutes," he said uncertainly. "Give or take."

"I just need to make a quick phone call," she explained.

He pointed her to a yellow public payphone kiosk. "We will not leave you behind," he assured her and resumed his seat.

The woman inside the kiosk turned the landline around to face Aine. She dialed Mbabazi's number, but the phone rang and rang, and then the metallic voice said to try again later. She hung up and tried Achen, though she was unsure if she and Mbabazi were still together.

"Hello, this is Achen." Aine was happy to hear her standard greeting.

"It's me," she said. "Aine."

"You're not already here, are you?"

"Mbarara," she said. "Mbabazi said to call her when I got here, but she's not picking up."

"She's probably in with a patient," Achen said. "I'll text her and let her know you called. You'll be what, another four or five hours?"

"I don't know, maybe," she said. "The conductor said the bus would leave in fifteen minutes or so."

"It will be good to see you again, kidio," Achen said. "How are you keeping?"

"Sometimes I think I'm not perceptive enough." She felt tears threaten and cleared her throat. There was something about talking to Achen that brought all her sorrows and doubts to the surface. "What I do have is a good memory. I see things very clearly, but only after they've happened, never in the moment."

"What are you talking about?"

Aine could see now the held-back tears in her mother's eyes as she had turned to walk away after the slap. As if by hurting Aine, Mama had hurt herself as well.

"I didn't even leave Mama a note," Aine said, wondering how her mother felt when she'd woken up this morning to discover that Aine's room was empty, that her other daughter was gone. "She does this thing where she quarrels with you, and then in the morning, she acts as if nothing happened. As if the night is some reset button, you know? She'll never, ever apologize for anything. I swear to God, I've never heard my mother say the words *I'm sorry.*"

"You know, I wouldn't feel too sorry for her," Achen said.

"I know, I know." Aine just wished that the world wasn't driven by rules at once arbitrary and inflexible. Rules you weren't allowed to question or downright refute without risking a smack to the face. "What about you and Mbabazi? How are things?"

"Oh, I don't know," Achen said.

"Don't do that," Aine said. "Everyone does it to me, even Mbabazi. She never tells me what's really going on. And not telling? That's how we got to this breaking point, isn't it?"

"Well, there hasn't been a breaking point here," Achen said. "Not yet. But you know what? You get yourself on that bus, and we shall talk face to face, yeah?"

"Okay," Aine acquiesced. "See you soon."

She took the last available seat right at the front of the bus, a metal bar between her and the little stairwell. There was no room in the overhead storage. She sat with her bulging backpack on her lap before forcing it under the seat, behind her legs. The woman to her right was working an aluminium hook dizzyingly fast, crocheting the start of something. For now, her project had an intestinal quality, but Aine knew it would soon give way to a panel for a sweater or perhaps a tablecloth. Mama was a passionate crocheter. It's how she passed the hours sitting behind the counter at the duka. She crocheted and listened to Eschatos Brides, a gospel choir that still sold their a cappella music on CDs. Mama knew every song, and she sang along while she worked on blankets, shawls, and tiny baby things—socks, hats, and mittens—which she gave to new mothers. Sometimes she got commissions, and those people painstakingly chose what colour patterns they wanted her to use. Some brought pictures of designs they wanted sewn into their baby shawls. Farm animals, flowers, Bible verses. There was no design too intricate for Mama.

"It's a baby blanket," the woman said when Aine inquired about her project. "My daughter is due in two weeks. My first grandson."

"Ah. Congratulations!"

"Yes, I've already made the socks." She reached down into the sisal bag full of skeins of yarn and showed Aine three different pairs of the tiniest booties in white, blue, and green. The decorative laces at the front were tied together in a figure eight, the symbol of infinity.

"They're so teeny," Aine said, balancing the green pair on the palm of her hand. The booties reminded her of when Kemi's son, Sweezin, was a newborn, unbelievably tiny and fragile. He liked to ball his hands into fists inside the mittens Mama had made. His feet were always in the air, kicking at assailants visible only to him.

"I'm Mable, by the way," she said, shaking Aine's hand.

"Ainembabazi." Aine surprised herself by saying her first name in full. She'd stopped doing that after primary school. She'd wanted to reinvent herself in secondary school, and Ainembabazi was a mouthful. To the tourists who couldn't pronounce Aine, she said, "Like Ayn Rand, but with a 'nay' at the end. *Aynay*."

"I'm named for my sister, Mbabazi. She's older than me by more than a decade. I'm on my way to visit her."

The bus pulled into a petrol station in the town centre. Mable and a handful of other passengers went out to the attached supermarket. Many came back with paper cups of hot beverages and bagged snacks. The smell of chapati and fried onions made Aine hungry. Then the door hissed closed, and the bus seemed to kneel before it lurched forward. But Mable hadn't returned. Aine's heart leaped as the bus joined the main road, where it gained speed.

"Conductor!" she shouted. "You've left a woman behind."

He looked up from his smartphone.

"My neighbour!" Aine gestured at the bag of yarn in the seat beside her. "She went to the supermarket."

The conductor shouted at the driver to pull over.

"I see her," said someone from the back of the bus. "She's running."

"Are you stupid?" Mable demanded in angry Runyankole as she climbed into the bus. She was furious and out of breath. "Bloody fool," she said and sucked her teeth at the conductor. "Is it your first day on the job?"

Aine stepped into the aisle, letting Mable in to her middle seat.

The conductor made half-hearted excuses in Luganda. "I thought everyone came back."

"Are you blind?" Mable reprimanded, sitting down in a huff.

"Naye banaye," said a nearby male voice. "Would it have killed the driver to sound the horn before leaving?"

Everyone chimed in. The driver didn't acknowledge the salty affronts being thrown at him. But the conductor was defensive, equivocating, when he could end this angry discourse with an apology. What was wrong with people? And Mable, it turned out, could hurl endless insults. Aine leaned back into her seat to stay out of the crossfire. She fished a book out of her bag to distract herself.

In Masaka, the conductor announced a toilet break. Even before the coach pulled over, roadside vendors swarmed it, holding up skewered meats for passengers to buy through the windows. They crowded the entrance, too, some even squeezing inside as the passengers were trying to exit.

Aine followed two women toward a small brick building with Washroom written on its side in blue chalk. A man was standing under a sycamore tree with a basket in his hands. The women gave him coins, and he, in turn, handed them each a wad of toilet paper from his colourful basket. Aine had never paid to pee before. *Abagyenda bareba*, she thought. Travelling was an eye-opening experience. She took the coins from her shirt-dress pocket and counted. Eight hundred shillings.

"It's all I have," she said, the coins spread out on the palm of her hand.

"It's okay."

She couldn't help feeling, as he gave her the flimsy wad of toilet paper, that she'd probably overpaid. If she ever travelled by bus again, she'd pack her own roll of toilet paper.

She did her business quickly and hurried back to the bus; it was possible to be left behind. She navigated the rowdy vendors at the entrance: a woman trying to sell her bottled water, a man wanting her to buy blister packs of chewing gum. As the bus resumed its journey, she was glad for the calmness. Now the only noise came from the music blasting from the bus's stereo. Overly synthesized pop an impenetrable wall of sound.

Occasionally she zoned out, looking at the passing fields, at placid cows and short grass. An arid landscape gave way to wetlands. A strong wind swept through the papyruses, bending them as if testing the strength of their roots. Maybe the birds in this marsh were the same species as in Magombe. Maybe there was a crowned eagle hunting for its lunch right now, a great blue turaco with a beak so impressive the children here called it the "lipstick bird."

If Aine had to pick a favourite bird, she'd have to go with the great blue turaco. When she was little, Mbabazi told her that kamushungushungu was a great diviner. Since then, whenever they spotted it, they took turns consulting the showy turaco about their love prospects.

"Kamushungushungu oku noku ndyashwerwahe?" they sang at it and waited as the bird, almost cartoonish in its colouring, deliberated. It turned its gorgeous crested head this way and that. Whichever compass direction it pointed to last, that's where the singer's beloved would eventually come from. But each time Aine consulted the bird, it pointed to a different direction. How many loves did it see in her future?

She thought about Paulo, his mouth parting to meet hers, the heat she'd felt when he'd touched her breasts. Why did she slap his hand away when all she'd wanted was for him to lay her down and touch her everywhere? Maybe it was just as well. Doing that would have made their parting more unbearable. She'd tell him that. When she called him tonight, she'd say, *Do you know, Paulo? You got me through a tough night.*

Aine brought herself back to the copy of the *Daily Monitor* she'd bought in Masaka, the bus jolting as it went over speedbumps. Soldiers had brutalized Makerere University students protesting a dramatic hike in their tuition fees. The students had been on strike for two weeks, waving placards outside the university gate and refusing to go to their classes. A student leader told the reporter that soldiers had, the night before, switched off the lights across campus and burst into several residence halls. They had beaten the strike's ringleaders senseless. "They broke everything. My TV, my bed. My plates and cups. I have nothing left," the student leader said. In the small photograph, his left eye was swollen shut, one big purple bruise.

Was Elia harmed? she wondered, a nervous clutch in her belly. He struck her as the sort of boy to join a strike, to be at the front of it, in fact. He'd sent her a card wishing her success a week before finals, a week before her world toppled under Papa's death. A beautiful card with a drawing of a hummingbird, the end of its sword-like beak buried inside a hollyhock. He'd signed it "Yours sincerely, E." *Sincerely*, not *affectionately*. She wished she didn't fancy him so much. He'd probably sent the card out of loyalty to Mbabazi, who'd sent one of her own with a fifty-thousand-shilling note tucked inside. Chances were Mbabazi had bought both cards and had him sign one. To Elia, she was always going to be Mbabazi's little sister, nothing more. If love were a potato, she'd chuck hers for Elia out the window of this moving bus and be done with it.

THE SKYLINE OVER KAMPALA was floury, as if a million bakers working in roofless kitchens had just clapped their hands. There was an air of industry, packed-together block buildings rising jagged and disorderly. A storied brick structure, unfinished yet somehow already dilapidated, looked like it had been chewed by rats. A rusty array of iron bars protruded from where the roof should be. Beyond, a smiling woman taunted Aine from a towering billboard, the tagline reading "She's Keeping Herself for Marriage. What About You?"

The bus was stalling in heavy traffic. It let up a little, and now they turned right on another busy street. There were so many pedestrians that altogether they looked like a single superorganism pulsing and twitching to a secret rhythm. It was menacing, a beast that swallowed a red-jacketed man and spat him out seconds later on an adjacent street.

Finally, the bus entered the terminal, which was full of other Global Coaches destined for perhaps every district in the country. She was quick to alight, her backpack heavy in her right hand. The late afternoon air was humid, rank with a mix of dust, burnt rubber, and gasoline. She coughed. It was as if her lungs were rejecting the filthy air. She imagined her blood turning into black sludge. It was immediately clear to her: she was not cut out for city life.

Boda boda cyclists swarmed her and other disembarking passengers. Clamouring for business, they addressed everyone as sister or brother.

"Sista nkutwaleko wa?" One cyclist was bold enough to grab her by the hand, asking where he could take her. She yanked it away from him. The audacity! Special-hire drivers competed for her attention, too, talking about their air-conditioned cars. She ignored them, scanning the crowds for her sister. Beyond the metal bars of the terminal's fence, a stream of cars clogged the road. Aine began to cross to a telephone kiosk to call Mbabazi, and someone tapped her on the shoulder.

"For the love of God!" she shouted, ready to fight off yet another boda boda man trying to hustle her.

"Whoa, kidio!" Achen's arms shot up into the air, a surrender.

"Achen!" Aine laughed, her voice shaky with relief. She hugged Achen with ferocious energy.

"You're literally shaking," Achen observed. "I'm so sorry I gave you such a fright. I kept calling and waving, and you kept not seeing me. And then you started walking away!"

"This city," Aine said, looking up at her. "Everything is so sharp and loud. It's frightening."

"It's a shock to the senses at first," Achen said, pushing her large sunglasses back over her voluminous afro. "But you get used to it. You become part of the brightness and loudness of it all. I love it."

"Thanks for rescuing me anyway," Aine said.

Achen smelled delightful. She wore a blue T-shirt tucked into loose-fitting copper-coloured linen trousers, the same ones she always seemed to be wearing whenever Aine saw her. The hems were a little gauzy, as if they had endured a thousand washes.

"Mbabazi's day got unexpectedly busy," Achen said, taking Aine by the hand. "We shall head over to the clinic now, and by the time we get there, she'll be wrapping up. And then we'll all go home and have tea. How's that sound?"

"Sounds good." Aine kept a firm hold of Achen's hand as Achen guided her across the terminal.

She was reminded of when she was little and Mama walked her to school. Mama's love had been so intense, and she'd leaned into it. At the edge of the school playground, she'd release Aine's hand and hold her face between her palms. She'd smile as she kissed Aine's forehead, making her feel holy, a sacred being in her mother's eyes.

Achen released her hand as they neared her brown Toyota. "So," Aine said, sitting down in the car, the still air so hot she didn't want to buckle her seatbelt, "tell me about you and Mbabazi. You said we'd talk face to face."

"She says she's forgiven me," Achen said. "She says what's done is done."

"But you don't believe her?"

"The thing you must know about Mbabazi is this," she said, easing the vehicle one inch at a time into the line of slow-moving cars, "she makes all her big decisions when running. She says, 'I'll run on it, see what I think.' But she hasn't run since the marathon. Since everything. And it's been what, over two weeks now? What I worry about most of all is that when she does resume running, she'll come back and say, 'Hey, you know what? Fuck you. I'm leaving you.'"

"Seems to me like you're overthinking this," Aine said.

"I almost want her to go running," Achen said. "Not knowing what's coming—it's killing me."

"What if she never runs again?"

"That would be tragic."

"This is quite the conundrum you're in."

"You're telling me?"

The traffic progressed so slowly, walking would have been faster. They'd drive a short distance and then come to another standstill, the vehicles bumper to bumper in both lanes. And although the cars were gridlocked, drivers sounded their horns angrily and shouted salty insults if a car didn't move to fill the inch of space that had opened up in front of it.

"I was sorry to hear about your mum," Achen said. "That she hit you."

"It's not even that," Aine said. "It's that I was looking at her, at my mother, and a whole different woman had taken her place."

"It never occurred to me that she was capable of this," Achen said. "This violence. The disinheritance. And it's all my fault, really, isn't it?"

Aine almost laughed. "Please tell me how my mother's actions are your fault."

"I overstepped my boundaries, that's all there is to it," she said. "All I needed to do was pretend I didn't know M. But I don't know what came over me. Suddenly I wanted so desperately for your mum to love me. In fact, I was sure she already did."

"You were?"

"I was utterly intoxicated by her attention," she said. "All day long she had made me feel special. Like everything I did—fetching benches from the church, water from the pump—made her grief a little bearable, you know? Every time she smiled at me or squeezed my hand, I felt like, *Yes, I am where I need to be today*. But the moment I let it slip that I knew Mbabazi. Oh, how quickly the woman changed! It's like she already suspected something, and my saying M's name just confirmed it for her. There was nothing I could do or say after that."

"That's the thing with Mama," Aine said. "She knows what she knows, and you can't change her mind. Only God can. Or perhaps the reverend, and we know what *he* would say about you and Mbabazi."

Achen shook her head slowly, regretfully, and Aine felt the urge to slide across the seat and hug her. "You know that story you did?" she said. "The one where you'd been in bed for days, crippled by your depression, and your friend came over and showed you a documentary about that researcher and her African grey parrot?"

"Alex and Dr. Pepperberg."

"That's the one," Aine said. "Just how the parrot, the night before he died, told the researcher, 'You be good. I love you.' You said that it gave you permission to live. That you got out of bed, and you went outside, and you saw that the world was so incredibly beautiful it made you cry. And you went into a supermarket and bought yourself a carton of milk and chugged it, almost the whole thing, right there in the supermarket aisle, because it was the first time in days that you'd felt hunger and thirst despite eating and drinking nothing."

Achen nodded and then looked with concern at Aine.

There was that insistent pressure at the base of Aine's throat, combined with the feeling she'd been getting lately that she was sinking slowly into a bog, being swallowed by it. Everywhere she looked, within herself and outside, there was nothing giving her permission to be happy. Nothing that made her want to chug a jug of milk. Would she ever experience such joy again?

Traffic was in gridlock yet again, and little children wearing tattered clothes were dashing between the vehicles, holding out their dirty little hands for spare change. Child beggars, their shaved heads grey with ringworms and scabs. One girl, a preteen, carried on her hip a chubby baby girl, completely naked, a grotesque rash covering her skin. Aine turned away.

"You're going through a storm right now," Achen said, squeezing her shoulder. "But it'll pass. You'll see."

14

RAZOR WIRE COILED THREATENINGLY along the top of the brick wall, Medius Fertility Centre written on the dusty-rose signpost. Achen pulled up to the black-and-white-striped bar that blocked the entrance.

"Vipi!" she greeted the askari in genial Kiswahili, smiling at him with familiarity.

"Safi!" He raised the mechanical bar without leaving his station behind the window, but Achen remained there chatting with the man in rapid Kiswahili. Aine made out every few words, enough to pick up on the conversation via context.

Eventually, Achen drove through to the parking lot. The fertility centre had a look of luxury about it, more like a resort than a medical facility. They walked up a cobblestone footpath leading to a building labelled Consultation Block. Spirea stands hedged the narrow path. The groomed bushes were springy, little pink flowers detaching when Aine brushed her hands against them. Inside the air-conditioned waiting room, she lingered behind while Achen talked to the receptionist, asking her to let Dr. Kamara know they were here.

"Please have a seat," said the receptionist. Her smile was a bit off, like someone who'd been posing for a photograph for too long. "I'll inform the doctor."

They sat down on a brown leather sofa with a view of the glossy overblown photographs adorning the walls. Aine studied the pictures of pregnant women smiling adoringly at their convex bellies, a father and his toddler jumping happily among a pile of yellow leaves, a toothless infant gumming its own chubby toe. Aine was conscious of the fact that there were couples for whom infertility interventions didn't work. How did they feel when they saw these success stories?

"I read an article in *Science* magazine this morning," Achen said, looking at her phone.

"Yeah?" Aine said encouragingly.

Achen put the phone away and crossed her left leg over her right so that she was almost entirely facing Aine. "Get this," she said. "Astronomers using the Hubble Space Telescope have been observing the same star blowing itself up over and over again in a supernova explosion that happened nine billion years ago."

"A supernova explosion that happened nine billion years ago?" Aine repeated. It was as if Achen were speaking Kiswahili again. "How are they seeing it now if it happened nine billion years ago?"

"The light resulting from the explosion," Achen explained. "Light brighter than a thousand suns. It's still bouncing and ricocheting across different corners of the universe. That image of it exploding, that's what the astronomers have been observing time after time, not knowing what the hell they were seeing. Now scientists can pinpoint exactly when and where in the sky to aim their telescopes and observe again this death that occurred nine billion years ago."

Nine billion. It was a figure Aine just couldn't wrap her mind around. How was she supposed to understand the immensity of time that comprised nine billion years? She opened her mouth to speak, but whatever words were about to come out withdrew themselves.

A moment passed before Achen said, "So, I was supposed to drive out to Jinja for an interview this afternoon, but it fell through."

"It fell through, or you had to cancel your plans because of me?"

"Anyway," Achen said, "I'm thinking that for next week's podcast, I'll re-air a favourite episode of mine from a couple of years ago. It's about whether or not there's intelligent life elsewhere in the universe."

"What, like aliens?"

"My thinking is, and I'm not alone here, that if intelligent life is something that evolves given time, then we're almost certainly not alone," Achen said.

"Well, if these civilizations exist now, or did at some point," Aine said, "why hasn't that Hubble thing spotted those civilizations or anything suggesting their existence?"

"That, in a nutshell, is the Fermi paradox," Achen said. "It's what the whole episode is about. You'll have a listen, won't you?"

"All I've got is time."

"Actually," Achen said, "one of the scientists I interviewed on that show, a theoretical physics professor, he's got a new poetry collection out. I'm helping launch it tomorrow. He's reading, signing books, the works."

"He's a theoretical physicist and a published poet, this man?"

"Benya is brilliant as hell," she said. "You must come to the launch and meet him. It's good for you to meet other writers."

"I'm not a writer."

"Do you not write?" Achen asked.

Aine knew it should be a compliment being called a writer, but instead it stressed her out. This place with its lavender walls and grinning babies stressed her out. And where was Mbabazi anyway? Just thinking about her made the air collect in Aine's lungs and refuse to come out.

"I need the loo," she said, already on her feet.

"Down the hall to the left," Achen said.

The hallway floor glistened wetly as if recently waxed. As she passed the closed doors, she could hear activity and chatter that seemed to originate from within the walls themselves. The bathroom was top-to-bottom white. Was this the same toilet Papa had fawned over? She wanted her father; her father was dead.

She heard footsteps outside the door and ducked into the largest stall farthest from the entrance. The toilet was the sit-down kind, not like the one she'd paid to use in Masaka. She peered at the bluish still water inside the white hollow of the bowl. Then she put the lid down and sat on it, crying into her sweaty palms.

When she had the bathroom to herself again, she went to splash water on her face. Her reflection in the mirror startled her. The overhead light was too bright, reflecting her face so starkly she could almost see through the pores to the turbulence in her soul. Her hair was messy, like a haystack. She wet her hands and raked her fingers through her hair, pulling the coiling strays back into the scrunchie at her nape. She washed her face, patted it dry on a brown paper towel, and went out.

Mbabazi came striding toward her from the waiting room, nearly breaking into a sprint as she neared her. She embraced Aine tightly and began to sob uncontrollably in full view of another doctor and a couple talking to the receptionist. Mbabazi's chest heaved with each sob, making Aine fear that her sister was unravelling. She tightened her arms around Mbabazi as if to keep the parts of her together. They remained entwined for some time, wetting each other's clothes with their tears, neither of them speaking.

"Tachypsychia," Mbabazi said, finally extricating herself from Aine's arms. Her eyes were raw and red, her face wet. She sniffled. "Do you know what that means?"

"Is it a mental disease?"

"During a life-threatening event," her sister explained, "our minds stretch time. Papa's death happened quickly, but he'd have had plenty of time to realize he ran a good race. Lived a full life. It's possible he crossed the finish line a happy man."

Their father dying happy in a car crash. Aine wanted it to be true. Perhaps the best thing about time passing was the privilege of running out of it. Maybe Papa accepted that fact as he reached his finish. That time and the people he loved would march on without him, and that was fine.

"When was the last time you talked to him?" Aine asked.

"Just before my flight to Cape Town," Mbabazi said. "He told me that Eliud Kipchoge—you know, the record-holding marathoner—that when he's running and it starts to really hurt, he smiles. He grins through the pain, and it tricks his brain into thinking he's not in pain."

"Is that true?"

"I haven't fact-checked it. He said he heard it on a science program."

"Let me guess, on the BBC?" Aine laughed and immediately felt guilty, until Mbabazi chuckled, too, making her feel that it was okay to laugh at their father's near-religious devotion to boring radio programs. They went out and joined Achen on the veranda, but as they all walked out to the car, Mbabazi started crying again, a whimpering sound.

"I'm sorry," she apologized, reaching for Aine's hand. "I told myself that when I saw you, I wouldn't cry. I'm supposed to be strong for you."

"No need!" Aine was grateful to be holding her sister's hand.

They sat together in the back, Achen driving like a chauffeur. The evening sky was low and cloudy, but the rain held off. There were many people on the street, men and women walking determinedly, hawking their wares. They reminded Aine of worker bees.

"You know," Mbabazi said, "after you called me last night, I couldn't go back to sleep. I kept thinking about when I was little. Before you were born. Mama was always nauseous from pregnancy. There were weeks when everything made her sick. Nothing she ate stayed down. And then one day I'd come home from school and find her in bed. One look at her pale face and I'd know it had happened again. That she'd lost the pregnancy. I'd make bush tea for us. Lemongrass or mint. She'd let me climb in bed with her and snuggle. I'd rub amla oil in her hair and brush out the tangles. We were never closer than when we were grieving a miscarriage.

"But as the cycle repeated itself," Mbabazi continued, "I wanted it to stop. I couldn't understand how she could keep putting herself through it again and again. But eventually it happened. She got pregnant, the vomiting lasted weeks, and then it stopped. She'd never carried beyond the first trimester. I watched her get big, enormous. She waddled around like a giant duck. And the delivery was medical, very complicated and scary, but then you were born. Another daughter. I swear to God there are times even now when I think she loves you more than God himself."

"Even now?" Aine scoffed.

"Yes, even now," Mbabazi said, suddenly serious. "It will kill her that you've run away from her."

"What choice did I have?"

"No, I get it," Mbabazi said. "I'm just saying. If there was ever anything to break our mother's spirit? This is it. You abandoning her. I just want to make sure you know it too."

"That's unfair," Aine said.

"Unfair, Aine?" Mbabazi said, fire in her eyes. "You want to talk about unfair?"

"No," Aine said quietly, thoroughly chastised. "I'm sorry."

Mbabazi turned to face the window. The space inside the car felt taut, as if all three of them were holding their breath.

Soon, Achen turned left into a treed neighbourhood, assertive mansions with satellite dishes like large mechanical ears projecting from the slanting tiled roofs. She sounded the horn at some kids playing football in the middle of the road. They moved to the side and waved at her.

"What did I tell you?" She shook her finger at them. "Stay out of the road."

"Wapi!" one of the kids said, and all the others laughed.

She pulled up in front of a wide gate, scarlet bougain-villea spilling over the brick wall surrounding the estate. She pressed a button on a pad clipped to the visor, and the gate slid open to reveal a large bungalow with a facade the colour of baked clay.

"Whoa!" Aine said cheerily, attempting to alter Mbabazi's sour mood. "When you introduced Achen as your roommate, I assumed you were renting someone's boys' quarters annex, not some mansion. You should have introduced her as your mansion mate."

"Sounds like the title of a raunchy reality TV show," Achen remarked, parking the car under an avocado tree. "Next season on *Mansion Mates*," she said with the pizzazz of a radio announcer.

But Mbabazi didn't smile or respond as they disembarked from the car. Still, Aine couldn't contain her amazement; this place was thoroughly enchanting. There were flowers blossoming profusely everywhere while at the same time maintaining a look of discipline. It was as if someone had decided that while in this compound, you had no choice but to be happy. There were garden boxes all along the fence. Tomatoes, carrots, onions, cabbages, and some plants that looked like sukuma wiki, only larger-leafed. There was an orderliness to it all, a kind of aesthetic sensibility Aine had never associated with vegetable gardens.

"Achen's the gardener, of course," Mbabazi said, her eyes sweeping over the yard.

"Of course." Aine chuckled. Mbabazi was so averse

to dirt that she had often paid Aine to load the charcoal onto the sigiri and peel the matooke, as if the sap were poisonous to her skin. She also had Aine pick out jackfruit pods for her from the rind on account, again, of the sap. "You can't even cook. You'd probably starve if it weren't for Achen."

"I have my strengths," Mbabazi said, crossing to the front porch bordered with roses and peonies.

"A great many strengths," Achen confirmed, opening the door into the house.

Aine took in the spacious porch. Six cushioned wicker chairs were gathered around a table with a potted plant for a centrepiece. It was a plump succulent, the fleshy sort that thrived in deserts.

When Achen opened the door, an ugly feline creature emerged onto the porch.

"What is this?" Aine jumped, hiding behind Mbabazi.

"Sir Dobby," Mbabazi said, scooping the creature up into her arms. It was hairless, a cross between a cat and a naked mole rat. Mbabazi nuzzled it behind its perky ears. "I brought him back from Canada."

"Poor thing," Aine said. "Was it in a fire?"

"He's a Sphynx," Mbabazi said. "Born with no hair. It's hard for them to regulate their body temperature."

"So, you brought him to Uganda as a punishment?"

"He knows to stay out of the sun. Don't you, Sir Dobby?" Mbabazi said, modulating her voice as though she were talking to a baby.

"What kind of a name is that, anyway?"

"D-O-B-B-Y, as in the elf from the Harry Potter series," Achen said. "Did you not read Harry Potter?"

Aine shook her head. "Our entertainment prefect brought the DVDs to school, but the savedees made a fuss."

"Because?" Achen said.

"Something about demons," Aine said. "The chaplain said it was about witches and wizards."

"Jesus Christ on a wooden bicycle!" Achen exclaimed. "Ayi ayi ayi."

In the foyer, they all removed their shoes. Aine followed Mbabazi into the open sitting room separated from the kitchen by a tall island flanked by white stools.

"Juice or water?" asked Achen, marching toward the fridge.

"Juice please," Aine said.

Like a moth to light, she was drawn to the floor-to-ceiling bookshelves spanning the length of the sitting room wall. She touched the spines of the ones she could reach, scanning the titles. "There are at least as many books in here as in a bookshop," she observed as Achen brought her a glass of passionfruit juice.

"This isn't even all of them," Achen said. "There's more in my office. In my bedroom as well. Do you want a tour?"

"Why don't you wash up first?" Mbabazi picked up Aine's backpack from the floor by the kitchen island. "The books aren't going anywhere."

Aine followed her sister down the hall, the tiled floor an off-white eggshell colour. Mbabazi opened a door at the end. The four-poster bed in the centre was big and plush, a mosquito net suspended above it in a chunky blue ball. The drapes were heavy and ornate, which Aine accepted as extremely luxurious. "How can you afford all this?" she said, setting her half-empty glass of juice on the desk by the window.

"By having jobs," Mbabazi said with knives in her voice. But when Aine looked at her, she smiled tiredly, almost apologetically.

"Achen moved in here first," she said, setting the backpack on top of the long leather trunk at the foot of the bed. "She was house-sitting for a Ugandan she knew from her Oxford days. A computer engineer. But then he got offered a high-paying job in Silicon Valley and never came back. At least not yet. We rent it from him, take care of the maintenance and whatnot. When he comes to visit, this is his room. He's a guest in his own house."

"Does he come back often?"

"At Christmas sometimes." Mbabazi opened the sliding doors of the closet to show Aine the spare blankets and pillows, a stack of white towels. There were T-shirts and sweaters on hangers, a folded ironing board leaning against the wall. "I haven't seen him since before I went to Canada.

"And this is the bathroom," Mbabazi continued, indicating the door that was slightly ajar. "I'll go set the table now. When you're finished washing up, come eat."

"Thank you," Aine said. "For letting me come here. After everything I did."

"You're welcome." She began to cross to the door but stopped, looking at Aine's wrist. "Is that Papa's watch?"

"Survived the crash." Aine took it off and gave it to her.

"Wow," Mbabazi said, turning the silver watch gently in her hands. "If only our bodies were as tough, you know? Thousands of years from now, this is all that's going to be left of us. Trinkets and scraps of metal we wore. Archaeologists will dig them up and try to piece together how we lived. How we died."

Tears were sliding down her cheeks again.

"Keep it," Aine said when Mbabazi went to give her back the watch. "I want you to have it."

"I don't need it." She laid it in the palm of Aine's hand and closed her fingers over it like a gift she was giving her.

AINE STEPPED INTO THE white tub and tried to figure out the shower. Giving up, she plugged the drain and sat in the clean tub like an infant in a basin. The water rose warmly around her like a loved one's hug. She lathered herself from the bar soap, which, though unattractively black, smelled like roses. She leaned back as if lying on a lounger. Closing her eyes, she concentrated only on how relaxed she felt with her body warm and fragrant. She wished she could live here forever, with Mbabazi and Achen. The road back to Bigodi, back to Mama, seemed in her mind like a closed-off tunnel, no way through. Yet she would have to go back at some point. She'd have to complete her tour guiding fieldwork and then work hard at the sanctuary. She'd put every shilling she earned toward her university fees. Every corner of the house and the compound, and perhaps the whole village now bore the marks of Papa's absence. Her heart caved inside her chest at the thought of living with only Mama, no prospect of Mbabazi coming home, not even for Christmas or Easter. She mopped a wet hand across her face as if to erase these thoughts. She forced a quietness into her mind and body. For now, she was under the same roof as Mbabazi. Her sister was, at this very moment, setting the table so that they'd dine together. Such goodness. Such mercy.

She changed into a wrinkled T-shirt and pyjama shorts and joined Mbabazi and Achen. She hoisted herself onto the tall stool next to Mbabazi. The elaborate light fixture above the marble island hung low, illuminating a large bowl of yellow soup prettied with herbs. There was a wooden bowl with shredded leafy greens dressed in a white sauce. Aine preferred her greens steamed or boiled and sprinkled with a little salt. But the chunky biscuits were appetizing.

"None for me." She covered the top of her glass with her hand when Achen made to pour her some wine. "I don't drink wine. I learned that last night."

"Someone gave you wine to drink last night?" Mbabazi said. When she raised her eyebrows like that, she was the spitting image of Mama. "Was it the game ranger?"

Aine told them about the town clerk's wedding anniversary. "Wine tastes like rotten, expired banana juice. How can you stand it?"

"You probably had some cheap brand," said Achen, urging Aine to venture a taste of her white wine, which, in the long-stemmed glass, was tinged with amber.

"No, thank you," Aine said. "Can I borrow your phone though? I want to send a quick text message."

"Who are you texting?" Mbabazi demanded.

"Mama."

"And you want to use Achen's phone for that?"

"I've texted her from Achen's phone before," Aine said. "When Achen gave me a lift to school."

Achen slid the phone across the table to her.

"Agandi Mama," Aine wrote. "I have arrived at Mbabazi and Achen's in Kampala. It's so nice here. Achen has so many books, I'm spoiled for choice. I could spend my entire vacation here and still not get through them all. Anyway, please don't worry about me. I remain yours truly, Aine."

She sent the message and turned the phone face down on the table. "The soup smells exquisite," she said. "What's in it?"

"Lentils," Achen said. "All the ingredients, except the lentils, of course, are from my garden. The tomatoes, onions, the garden eggs. I grew them myself."

Having a vegetable garden was hardly anything special, Aine thought. But perhaps here in the city it was?

"Tastes so good too," Aine said after a spoonful. The soup was creamy and buttery, the garden eggs giving it a hint of delicious bitterness. "Is there anything you aren't good at?"

"The trick is to blend the lentils," Achen said. "Easy recipe. I'll show you if you like."

"Yes, please."

They ate in silence until Aine noticed that Mbabazi was picking at her salad, distractedly pushing the greens around with her fork. Looking at her, Aine felt a familiar knot taking shape in her stomach. Lately she'd been catching herself gritting her teeth at the strangest of times. How was Mbabazi coping? Years ago, Papa had coined the phrase *Mbabazi emanzi*—Mbabazi the brave— after Mbabazi completed a marathon that raised money for cancer patients. Just before the race started, practically minutes before she arrived at the starting line, Mbabazi's period had hijacked her. The cramps were like a fist, she said, squeezing her ovaries with every stride she took.

"And you didn't stop?" Papa had marvelled.

"If I had," Mbabazi said, "I wouldn't have been able to start again."

"Ori emanzi," Aine said now, repeating Papa's words to Mbabazi. *You're so brave.*

Mbabazi said, "The thing with Papa was that it didn't take much to make him happy."

"No," Aine agreed. "Didn't take much at all."

She helped with the dishes after supper and then retired to her room. She lay in bed, toying with the silky bedcover, poking her fingertips into the many tiny divots. An array of them in perfect symmetry, as if a flotilla of tiny spaceships had landed on the bed and left very precise impressions. She heard a soft knock on the door and sat up.

"It's open," she said.

"You're still awake?" Mbabazi entered and closed the door behind her. She'd changed into a lilac pyjama set, a matching bonnet over her hair. In shorts she looked even taller, as if her body was two-thirds legs. Thin but strong, not an ounce of fat. "Mind if I sleep with you tonight?"

"Not at all." But Aine was curious. "Won't Achen miss you?"

"We have separate bedrooms." Mbabazi climbed in and covered herself, tucking the duvet under her arms. "It doesn't work out for us sharing a room. She works really late, like three a.m. late, and sleeps in. I get up early for work."

"Huh." So much about Achen and Mbabazi's life together challenged the notions Aine held about romantic relationships. There was an inventiveness, a kind of freedom, as if the rules that bound heterosexual relationships didn't apply. The very idea of them living together like this was unhinged from any frame or time Aine could think of.

Years ago, she'd read an account of Kabaka Mwanga, who had ascended the throne of the Buganda Kingdom just as European colonialists were partitioning Africa among themselves, fracturing Buganda along religious lines. Members of the Church Missionary Society were converting his subjects to Protestantism, the French White Fathers to Catholicism, the Arabs to Islam. Kabaka Mwanga, at eighteen years old, was erratic and sometimes irresponsible. Suspicious of the missionaries, he issued a decree forbidding his subjects from converting or even working for the colonialists. Those who did, he burned at the stake. The burnings inspired Muslim, Catholic, and Protestant missionaries to form a coalition, which succeeded in deposing the Kabaka. The coalition was helped along by disgruntled members of the king's court who alleged that he practised homosexuality, and that it was his devotion to that "abominable vice" that put him in conflict with the missionaries.

Yet present-day politicians argued that homosexuality was a Western import. Did they not know this bit of history? Was it lost on them that homophobia, not homosexuality, was the import?

The sisters lay side by side, the balled-up mosquito net floating above them like an unlit chandelier, the digital clock on the nightstand casting dim light. In Aine's darkest moments she wished it was Mama who'd died, but that wasn't something she could ever say out loud. "When did you first realize that if you had to pick one parent over the other, you'd choose Papa?"

"I've never considered such a thing," Mbabazi said, as if the very idea were insane.

"Me neither," Aine said. "Until there was just the one, and she banished you."

Mbabazi pulled up her knees, tenting the bedding. "This one time in Primary Six," she said, turning on her side to face Aine, "my first cross-country race. All the primary schools in the region had sent two of their best long-distance runners. A boy and a girl. Only six of us would proceed to the district finals in Fort Portal. And Papa came. Took the day off and drove me to Kamwenge. He liked to pretend he was my coach or something. Giving me tips and all that."

"He never came to a single one of my debates," Aine complained. "No one ever did, except for you that one time, and it was a fluke. You just happened to be in Kamwenge after running away from home the evening before."

"You don't need supplies in a debate," Mbabazi said. "You don't need someone to give you glucose-infused water at the halfway mile, so you don't pass out."

"The moral support would have been nice."

But Mbabazi carried on with her story. She had been making good time in the race, but as she neared the half-way point where Papa was waiting for her, she started to lag. It was the tracksuit her sports teacher had insisted she wear and the sneakers that were too heavy on her feet. She had trained barefoot until two weeks before race day when the sports teacher had sprung the sneakers on her. A donation from the local council chief. And now other runners were passing her. Mbabazi slowed to accept the glucose water from Papa and complained about the shoes and the tracksuit, how they were holding her back.

"And he said to get rid of them," Mbabazi said.

"The sneakers?" Aine asked.

"Everything." Mbabazi chuckled. "All I had remaining was my little tank top and my pink undies printed all over with butterflies."

Aine was aghast. "No way!"

"I'd just turned thirteen and had the flat chest of a little boy," she said. "But man did I fly after that. I was passing a runner every few minutes. I'd never felt so nimble, almost aerodynamic."

"Did you win?"

"I qualified for the district finals!" she said.

"Papa allowed you to run almost naked through Kamwenge Town in broad daylight? That's bonkers!"

"Mama was livid when she heard." Mbabazi laughed. "All evening long Papa followed her around the compound, placating her. He was telling her, 'Owangye, many people didn't even notice she was a girl. All the boys also ditched their tracksuits; it was only fair.'"

Aine laughed until she was teary-eyed and her abdominal muscles ached. "I haven't laughed this much in so long," she said.

"Me neither," Mbabazi said.

They lay quietly in the darkness, the soft night expanding around them.

"You know," Mbabazi said, "if it was Mama who'd died, we'd be lying here digging up memories of her. It's what death does to people we love. It snatches them away and makes them perfect."

"Past perfect," Aine said.

"Exactly."

After a while, Aine was acutely aware that the moments she shared with Papa, Mbabazi, and Mama were sacred, were less and also more than they seemed.

Mbabazi had turned her back to Aine, so she wasn't really sure if she was still awake. "Don't be mad at me anymore," Aine said.

A long while later, when Aine was fairly certain her plea had fallen on the hard parabola of her sister's back, she heard, "Okay. I forgive you."

Aine passed from forgiveness to sleep.

15

A N ISLAMIC CALL TO prayer roused Aine from sleep. She opened her eyes to see Mbabazi pushing away the covers, swinging her legs out of the bed.

"Are you getting up?" Aine asked sleepily.

"The muezzin's my alarm," Mbabazi said, giving herself a back-bending stretch. "I have to get ready for work."

"So early?"

"I have to beat the morning traffic, or I'll be late," she said. "I'll be home no later than six."

"Okay. Have a good day."

Aine stumbled into the bathroom. What a luxury to have the loo so near, inside the house. She came back to bed and nodded off when the muezzin concluded his melodious song.

When she woke up again, shards of light were shooting into the room through the perforations in the ventilation bricks above the window. She got up and opened the window. There was, in the corner and right up against the brick fence, a passionfruit trellis. The hanging fruits, green and purple, shone in the bright morning sun.

She padded down the hall and found Sir Dobby with his face inside a shiny metal bowl. Unbothered by the intrusion, he carried on crunching his food noisily. Sometimes Rafiki brought dead birds and laid them at Aine's feet like a taunt. Other times she hid rodent carcasses in a corner of the gazebo and forgot them there, stinking up the whole place. She could be such an asshole, that cat.

Aine could make out, through the large picture window, Achen sitting on the veranda. She was reading from an tablet propped up on the table, a steaming mug in her hands.

She looked up as Aine emerged onto the veranda. "How'd you sleep, kidio?" She was wearing floral dungarees roomy enough to accommodate two of her.

"Like a baby," Aine said, pulling up a chair. "You?"

"I slept all right, thanks," she said. "Fancy a latte?"

"A latte being?"

"Let's fix you one, and you'll know what it is."

In the kitchen, Aine hoisted herself up to sit in the patch of sunlight on the counter. She watched Achen work, compacting coffee grounds into a small metal cup that she screwed onto the Breville machine. Coffee the blackest black dripped down into two mugs.

"I worked as a barista all through my undergrad," Achen shouted. Pressure was hissing through a nozzle she'd dipped into a metal cup with milk in it. "It still surprises me the amount of money people are willing to pay for a beverage they can make at home."

"Didn't you have a full scholarship?" Aine said.

"It's not cheap living in Oxford." She topped up the coffee mugs with the frothed milk, concentrating as she created a floral design resembling a lotus.

"It's too pretty to drink," Aine said, not wanting to ruin the design, which up close looked more like a Wi-Fi symbol than a lotus.

"Take it as a lesson in impermanence," Achen said, urging Aine to take a sip. "Everything we create soon ceases to exist."

Aine appreciated the heavy dose of philosophy. Unfortunately, while the latte was beautiful in appearance, it was made from coffee, and coffee was bitter. "Isn't it weird that a beverage this bitter comes from a bean that's sweet?"

"Add some sugar." Achen took the bowl from an overhead cabinet.

They took their breakfast out on the veranda. Slices of toasted Hot Loaf bread smeared with jam. They talked and read. Aine from a novella she'd plucked from the bookshelf. Achen browsed newspapers on her tablet.

"Hey, if a small novel is a novella," Achen said, "why isn't a nap a sleepella?"

"Or a small storm a stormella?" Aine said.

"A jog would be a runella."

"An infatuation a lovella?" Aine chuckled. "English

would be so easy to learn. Everyone would speak it well."

"It would be boring though." Achen rose from her seat. "I better go in, get started on the day's work."

Aine stayed outside on the veranda, engrossed in the novella. Time always flew by when she read fiction. Her senses sharpened, connecting her to a world where people were dealing with problems much like her own, making her feel less alone. By the time Achen came outside to ask if she was hungry for lunch, Aine was barrelling toward the denouement.

"Just a minute," she said, her eyes glued to the page.

"Don't forget we've got that poetry book launch at four," Achen said, hovering. "Did you pack something nice to wear?"

Aine bookmarked the page with a whorl of sage she had plucked from a nearby planter. "When I packed my bag, I didn't think I'd be going to a poetry reading. Not that I'd know what to wear to such a thing."

"We'll find something nice for you in my closet," Achen said.

"Okay, thanks." She hoped the outfit Achen had in mind for her was nothing like those unflattering dungarees she had on.

Achen's bedroom had a neutral, under-inhabited feeling, the spare furnishings giving it a vastness. It looked as though she were in the process of moving out, many of her belongings already packed away. A few shirts, T-shirts, and dresses dangled in the spacious wardrobe.

"Are these all the clothes you own?" Aine asked and

then reproached herself for the intrusive questioning.

"I haven't worn this one in so long." Achen was opening a garment bag she'd pulled from the farthest corner of the wardrobe. "I wore it to an awards gala in Nairobi last year."

"A business suit?" Aine was looking at a black blazer with a crisp white shirt inside, the black trousers pinched onto the wooden hanger.

"A tuxedo," Achen said. "Do you want to try it on?"

"Why not?"

Aine had her doubts about wearing what she considered men's clothes, but the tuxedo surprised her. The trousers were a little loose in the waist but not noticeably so once she tucked the white shirt inside them.

"Full Windsor or half?" Achen asked, helping Aine with the necktie.

"Definitely full." Aine had always loved the chunkiness of a full Windsor knot.

"You look dashing," Achen said even before Aine pulled on the blazer with its shiny lapels.

"I really, really do, don't I?" Aine said, appraising herself in the full-length mirror. "I don't ever want to take it off."

"Then it's yours!"

"For real?"

Achen laughed. "Look around you. I don't hold onto things that have outlived their usefulness to me."

"But you'll win another award," Aine said with certainty.

"I'm not one to count my chickens before they hatch."

Aine hugged her and thanked her many times over. "By the way," she said, "did my mother reply to my message?"

Achen shook her head apologetically. "Sorry, love."

THEY WALKED THE HALF hour or so to the art gallery, a two-storey red brick building off Prince Charles Drive. The receptionist—the name plate pinned to her chest read Shamim—wore a tight-fitting white dress with big puffy sleeves. Her red-lacquered lips put blood to shame.

"Yes, of course," she smiled brightly when Achen told her she was here to host the launch of Benjamin Olam's poetry collection. "Do I know you from somewhere?" Shamim said. "Your voice."

"I host a podcast."

"Yes!" Shamim's entire being seemed to light up inside her olive skin. "Achen Roy. Let me tell you, I'm the biggest fan of your podcast. I don't miss an episode. I don't even care if it's a rerun, I can listen to the same story a bunch of times."

As she guided them through a cavernous room with large abstracts hanging on the white walls, Shamim gushed unrelentingly while Achen made self-deprecating noises.

"You know," Shamim said, "after listening to your podcast last week, I think I see Stella Nyanzi a little clearer now. Her activism. It's her language I'm still struggling with. For me, it's like if you want to insult the president,

I'm behind you a hundred percent. But why abuse his mother, eh? She could not have known that her son would turn into a greedy, murderous autocrat!"

They were going through another room, and Aine saw two men studying a colourful tryptic. One of the men's hands was in the back pocket of his companion's tight jeans.

"As it happens," Achen said, "she's got a book of poems out too. Stella, that is. Not the president's mother."

"Are they any good?" Shamim said.

"I'll let you be the judge of that," Achen said.

"This is you," said Shamim, showing them into a long and narrow rectangular room, rows of chairs facing the table at the front set up with two microphones and a stack of books.

Achen thanked the receptionist. "So lovely to have met you," she said as the woman turned to leave.

A few people conversed in scattered pairs and small groupings. The narrowness of the room seemed to amplify every noise: a cough, a chair being dragged against the concrete floor.

A tall fellow in a colourful dashiki and jeans strode toward them and kissed Achen twice, once on each cheek.

"You have brought a catalogue model as your date?" he said and shook Aine's hand. "I'm Benjamin."

"Aine." She smiled shyly; she was definitely over-dressed in this tuxedo. Everyone else in the room was casual, some of the men even wore shorts and tennis visors. How ironic. Two nights before she'd been hands-down the worst-dressed person at the bureaucrat's wedding anniversary.

"Aine is Mbabazi's sister," Achen said, touching her lightly on her shoulder. "She's visiting from Bigodi."

"How do you do, Aine?"

"All right, thanks," Aine said, taken aback by his formality, as though he were an adult greeting a child. "Congratulations on your book."

"Thank you," he said. "I appreciate you."

"Have you given some thought to how you want this to go?" Achen asked him.

"Was I supposed to?" he said.

They strode toward the front of the room, talking logistics, and Aine wandered off, drifting toward the display in an adjoining, much larger room. Grim-looking sculptures rested on top of cubic plinths. Backless torsos with incomplete heads, contorted faces intriguingly morose. An exhibit statement was written against the white wall. It said that the sculptor had used discarded plastic bottles, sand, charcoal, and other waste materials to mould the figures, which celebrated insecurities and body flaws, disabusing the viewer of their notions of perfection and imperfection. "Imperfect moments and experiences," the statement said, "are where authenticity dwells."

Aine went closer to a head that had as its neck a wooden support. The face was round, cut off just before the ears. Its muddy eyes were melancholy, poking at Aine's grief, a mental pain that had taken permanent residence at the bottom of her skull. She supressed a tentacle-like urge to reach out and touch the face, feel the rough texture of its cheeks.

"I went to school with the artist," said a man with a sculpted jaw, his dreadlocked hair in a big topknot. He wore navy blue shorts and a white polo shirt buttoned up to his throat.

"What's he like?" Aine asked the man now coming to stand next to her.

"Very quiet," he said. "Didn't come to class much. He was always off doing his own thing. Collecting plastic bottles from rubbish dumps. It was like the rest of us needed the validation of our professors, permission to become artists, but he never cared about all that. And look at him now. Exhibitions here, in South Africa, even in Berlin. And it's still very anti-art, don't you think?"

"Maybe it's all those classes he bunked off," Aine said, not exactly understanding what he meant by *anti-art*.

The guy chortled. "I mean, look at this." He gestured widely to encompass the whole room. "These are portraits of his family members and his friends. It is art that imitates people. The people in his life, they don't just inspire his art, he physically builds it on them. On their faces and their bodies. I can't think of anything more beautiful."

The sweetness of it all wanted to break Aine's heart. "Are you an artist too?"

"I'm more carpenter than artist these days," he said.

"Furniture?"

"Coffins mostly," he said. "But I paint, too, yes. On wood."

"Do you paint on the coffins as well?"

"Now there's an idea!"

In the next room the microphone crackled, Achen testing it.

"Are you coming to the poetry reading?" Aine said.

"You go on ahead," he said. "I'll be along in a minute."

Aine left him alone with the sculptures. Somehow, every last seat was now taken, so Aine stood at the back of the room, hands inside the pockets of her lavish trousers.

Achen read her introduction of Benjamin Olam, then invited him to talk about the poems in his book before reading one. As he read, the tenor of his voice, the music in it, made everything grow still. Ideas from physics infused his poems. He read that light, before you looked at it, was both a wave and a particle. That the observer, simply by looking, created.

Aine pictured Benjamin at his writing desk, allowing himself to go off on tangents, giving himself the permission to excavate far away from the central idea, and then circling back. It made her want to run back home, grab her notebook, and write down all the thoughts clanking about in her head.

She joined in the applause when he finished reading a longer prose poem. Then Achen was asking him questions about how his work as a theoretical physicist inspired his poetry. He said scientists in Europe had used a machine called the Large Hadron Collider to smash heavy ions together and create the plasma thought to have existed shortly after the Big Bang. "When you hear something like that," he said, "the poem begins to write itself."

Then he said, "Hey, do you want to hear a joke?"

"Is it one of your quantum physics jokes where you have to explain the punchline?" Achen replied. "I hate to tell you this, Benya, but if you have to explain a joke—"

"So, Higgs boson walks into the cathedral, right?" Benya cut her off, inciting scattered laughter from the audience. "Priest says, 'Go away, Higgs boson, nobody wants you here.' Higgs boson laughs its head off, says to the priest, 'Father, you can't have mass without me.'"

The laughter was significantly spottier than before.

"What'd I tell you?" Achen said. "These esoteric jokes of yours make those of us who dropped physics in Senior Two feel stupid."

But a bunch of people in the audience were talking all at once. Aine heard "God particle" more than a few times. Someone shouted over the din that Higgs boson was the manifestation that gave all particles mass.

"Ohhhh," the whole room seemed to say as finally everyone got the joke. In the ensuing laughter, Aine saw, out of the corner of her eye, Mbabazi entering the room, trying to minimize the clicking of her heels against the floor. Her trousers were loose and grey blue, a colour like wet cement.

"Why are you dressed like you're about to walk on a red carpet?" she said, standing close to Aine.

"What, this old thing?" Aine said casually.

"I've got something to tell you," Mbabazi said.

Aine's heartbeat drilled straight through her. "What's happened?"

"Not here."

Aine knew, as they snuck out into the larger room with the perfect-imperfect sculptures, that her sorrow was about to multiply.

"You'll never guess who just called," Mbabazi said as they exited the art gallery and crossed toward the parking lot.

"Mama?" Aine just knew.

"It was the weirdest phone call I've ever received," Mbabazi said. "I keep saying, 'Hello, hello, Mama, are you there?' No response. So, I hang up. But right away, the phone rings again. And it's her number. And I know she's there. I can hear her breathing. Hear her heart beating, her stomach rumbling. I swear I can hear the wheels of her brain spinning. I can smell her."

"Oh my god, Mbabazi, get to the point."

"I said, 'I know you're there, Mama, I can hear you breathing,'" Mbabazi said in Rukiga. "I figured she was looking for you. Wanted to know that her *precious child* was okay."

"All right," Aine said, feeling a little attacked.

"So I told her that you're here, you're fine, you'll go back home when you're good and ready."

"And?"

"And still she said nothing," Mbabazi said. "That's when I got really mad. This burning rage in my chest. Oh,

I laid into her, Kanyonyi. I called her selfish and bigoted. I told her everything I've ever wanted to say but never had the stomach. And you know what, I feel lighter for it. I feel fantastic. It's like this great big weight has been lifted from my chest."

But Aine wondered why, if Mbabazi felt light and fantastic, she was gesturing wildly, pacing back and forth like a cat on the prowl. "Then I thanked her for severing our ties. For setting me free."

That word, *severing*. The wounding finality of it. It conjured in Aine's mind the sound sharp scissors make when cutting through something organic. *Snip*. "But you don't mean that," she said. "You're not happy she cut you off. You're upset."

"Upset?" Mbabazi glowered. "Upset's what I've been all my life. Today I got a chance to disown her too. Now it's a fucking mutual disownment."

"She really didn't say a single word?"

"Nothing," she said, sweeping the palms of her hands together. *Swish*. "When you're queer," Mbabazi continued, "learning to let go of people is an important survival skill. It's not easy, but I've managed it today. You should be proud of me."

"If she'd said something," Aine said, "if Mama had talked to you, what would you have wanted her to say?"

Mbabazi folded her arms against her frilly blouse, greenish blue like seafoam. She tilted her head up pensively, as if to consult the homing geese that were traversing the jewel-blue sky in an arrow pattern.

"Muhara wangye," she said, finally, arcs of tears trembling on her eyelashes. "Just those two words." *My daughter.*

Aine went to hug her, but Mbabazi turned to face the car. She covered her face with her hands and sobbed unreservedly. Aine could see that her sister wasn't feeling light, not at all; she was feeling crushed under the weight of this severing. Helpless, she cried too.

ABOUT AN HOUR AFTER they got back home, a man delivered pizzas on the back of a motorcycle: a two-for-one deal.

"My favourite," Mbabazi said as she opened a box for Aine to see. "Margherita."

Aine put a long wobbly slice onto her plate. She'd never had pizza before, but she'd encountered the meal in a couple of dirty Mills & Boon romances set in Italy. She hadn't expected to see tomato slices trapped inside melted cheese, and greens that looked like, but weren't, spinach.

"Basil," Mbabazi said when Aine picked out the limp herb.

Earlier, on the drive home, Mbabazi had told Achen about the one-sided phone conversation, and Achen had said that Mama's epic silence was godlike and that what Mbabazi had done, baring her soul to Mama like that, was akin to praying. "Mothers are by definition a higher power," she'd argued when Mbabazi protested. "It's just how it is. There's nothing to be done about it."

Now Mbabazi seemed in weirdly high spirits, more talkative than ever. She teased Achen mercilessly for using a fork and a knife to eat her pizza instead of her hands, "like a normal, non-bougie person."

"I lived in Naples for three months," Achen said, wiping her mouth on a white paper serviette.

"Lived? Please," Mbabazi said snidely. "I hate to break it to you, my love, but less than six months in a city, that's hardly living there. You visited Naples."

"Okay, sheesh," Achen said. "And not once in those three months did I see a native Italian eat pizza with their fingers. It is not finger food."

"So, you're saying Aine and I are bush?" Mbabazi said.

"Oh my god!" Achen said, exasperated. "She treats me so poorly, your sister," she complained to Aine. "I'm so deprived!"

Aine chuckled, though she wasn't sure if Achen's hurt—her pouting—was for real or pretend.

"Well," Mbabazi said, "currently my head is filled with knives and about a few hundred people to throw them at."

AFTER DINNER, AINE TRIED to watch television with her hosts, but Achen kept narrating and explaining, ruining the viewing experience altogether. The show followed two charmingly whimsical British men who used hand-held metal detectors to search for buried treasure in the pastoral fields of a fictional English town. Soon after turning on the show, Achen had paused it to explain about the Anglo-Saxons and how a treasure hoard from that long ego era, the Middle Ages, could prove lucrative for the men. They could sell it to wealthy collectors or even a museum. Hence the men's commitment to the search. Their treasure detectors beeped if there was something promising in the ground, and then the men had to dig for it using shovels. Unfortunately, their digging kept turning up old bottle caps and useless buttons, but they were not discouraged. Tomorrow was another day to continue their hunt. For now, the shorter of the detectorists, with big eyes like a bug, was also fixated on winning back the love of his ex-wife. He was composing a song called "New Age Girl" that he wanted to teach his buddy, the other detectorist, so the two of them could sing it at the pub's karaoke night with the ex-wife in the audience.

"I've been there," Achen said when the camera showed the exterior view of the pub. "I drove out there once, in pouring rain, for a date with a woman I met online."

"The weird artist, right?" Mbabazi said. Her feet were in Achen's lap; she was massaging them vigorously with lotion. The cat was also sitting on the couch, his eyes barely open.

"Did we decide she was weird?" Achen said somewhat defensively.

"She took you to her studio and taped cling film over your crotch," Mbabazi said. "If that's not weird I don't know what is."

"She did what?" Aine said, alarmed.

"I modelled for her," Achen explained. "A plaster body cast." The cling film protected Achen's pubic area from

the liquid plaster the sculptor—her name was Siobhan—
applied in strips from just below Achen's nostrils to just
above her knees.

"Another time she convinced Achen to model for a full
body cast, and she almost died," Mbabazi said.

"I panicked." Achen laughed. "My eyes were sealed in
total darkness. I struggled to breathe through the teeny
straws she'd put in my nostrils. I thought I was going to
pass out. I screamed like a bloody demon. 'Take this shit
off me right now!'"

"Dear God." Aine was impressed, but now she was
also tired. Supressing a yawn, she rose to her feet. As she
left the sitting room, the cat leaped down from his perch
and pranced alongside her, accompanying her down the
hall to her room. He remained outside the door when
Aine entered. A perfect gentleman, this Canadian cat.

She bathed quickly, before changing into her pyjamas.
She was about to climb into bed when she heard a knock
on the door.

"Come in," she said, wondering if Mbabazi wanted to
share a bed again tonight.

"Someone on the phone for you," Mbabazi said,
entering. The phone was pressed to her chest.

"Who is it?" Aine said, her heart suddenly beating like
a loud drum in her ears. She did not have the presence of
mind to talk to Mama.

"Elia," Mbabazi said. "He called earlier today, and I
mentioned you're visiting. I promised I'd have you call
him, but I forgot. Want to talk to him?"

First, Aine remembered with sinking regret how she'd forgotten all about calling Paulo. But if there was the remotest chance that Elia was interested in her, well, then Paulo would have to wait. "Yes," she said, accepting the phone from Mbabazi, whom she then waved out the door before closing it.

"Aine!"

The sound of his voice set her heart aflutter. "Hi!" she said.

"I can't believe you're in town," he said. "When do I get to see you?"

"You know where to find me."

"I have a show tomorrow evening," he said.

"*Jesus Christ Superstar* is still going?"

"It was meant to finish end of October, but now it's on every Friday and Saturday until Christmas," he said. "There's talk of a tour across East Africa next year."

"Congratulations!" Aine said. "That sounds exciting."

"Would you like to see it?" he said. "I can reserve a ticket for you."

"Yes, please!" she said. "I'll get Mbabazi to drive me. Has she been to see it already? Maybe she'll want to come too!"

"Achen and Mbabazi have seen it twice already," he said. "Three times is overkill."

"I can't believe I get to see you play Jesus," Aine said. "But doesn't it get monotonous putting on the same performance night after night?" In her mind, reprising the same role again and again felt akin to chewing a piece of gum long after it had lost its sweetness.

"I'll admit a bit of the magic does wear off after some time," he said. "But not tomorrow. Tomorrow will be full-on magic because you'll be there."

"Well, I can't wait!"

"I also wanted to say how sorry I am about your dad."

"Thank you." Because she knew that his dad had died when Elia was a child, she found it easy to be vulnerable with him, to lay bare her grief. "Sometimes it feels as though I'm in a film. Like someone has written a script and I'm just acting my part in it."

"And then for your mum to be so savage!"

So Mbabazi had told him then. "It never rains, does it?" she said.

"I know that Doc appreciates you standing with her," he said. "She told me today it's a gift like no other she has ever been given. I wish it didn't come at such a high cost. That you didn't have to choose between a sister and a mother."

"It's just not feeling real yet," she said. "Today, when we were walking to the gallery, Achen said she was craving firinda and I told her that Mama had a recipe for the creamiest firinda. And that I would call her up and get it. Of course, Achen reminded me that if I were to call Mama, we probably wouldn't be talking bean soup recipes."

"Right."

"I can't even call her, you know?" she said. "I send her these messages like a coward. Anyway, can we talk about something else?"

"So, Achen took you to an art gallery today?"

"A poet was launching a collection," she said. "Benjamin Olam. Do you know him?"

"That guy's writing is too cerebral," he said. "The images go straight over my head. I always feel like I only understand maybe ten percent of what he's trying to say."

"That's not entirely a bad thing," Aine said. "The poems are short. I like when I can take something new away each time I reread a poem."

"But poetry is supposed to be fun, edifying," Elia argued. "How am I going to be interested in rereading a poem I didn't get the first time around?"

"You don't like to be challenged?"

"Not that much," he said. "By the way, do you know Benya and Achen used to be an item?"

"An item?"

"A couple," he said. "They almost moved in together."

"What? Is she not a lesbian?"

"Well, yes and no." Elia said that when Achen first came out to Benya back when they were still dating, that when she told him she was into both men and women, he got disproportionately excited. "He tried to convince her to hook up with other women and bring those women home so that he could be included in the action."

Aine gasped, her face flushing. "Should we be gossiping about Achen like this?"

Elia sucked his teeth. "Are you kidding? Most kuchu folks are like closed houses. Doors and windows shut. But not her. Not Achen. She holds nothing back."

Aine agreed. Talking to Achen always left her wide-eyed and grateful for her generosity. "Is that why they broke up, do you think?"

"Achen said the idea of being in a threesome stressed her out," he said. "But I'm not sure that's why she left him. Maybe you should ask her."

"Hell no. Where would I start?"

"Hey, listen," he said. "Would you like to grab dinner with me tomorrow? After the show."

"Absolutely, as long as it's not pizza," she said. "I had way too much of that today."

"Got it," he said. "No pizza."

IN THE MORNING, AFTER breakfast, Mbabazi took Aine shopping. A girl in very short shorts was taking a selfie by the water feature that took up much of the entrance to Acacia Mall. There were green and purple lights built into the bottom of the fountain, arcs of water shooting up before splashing back into the round concrete pool.

"You toss in a coin and make a wish," Mbabazi said when Aine went to stare into the water, coins gold and silver littering the bottom.

"What if I'm wishing for money?" she said. "Can I scoop up these coins and take them?"

"I actually don't think anyone could stop you," Mbabazi said. "Like, what would they charge you with? Stealing from the gods of the wishing well?"

"I'm dead serious," Aine said. "Can I get in and take some or not?"

"No, obviously." Disgruntled, Mbabazi grabbed her by the hand and marched her through the door. "Tinkwenda ebyokunshwaza nyowe." She didn't wish to be embarrassed today.

Inside, the mall was enormous and luminous, people criss-crossing it with their shopping bags, pushing babies in prams. It was its own world just as busy but separate from the one outside. Strings of colourful lights blinked along the metal railings, reflecting against the linoleum flooring. The brightly lit shops gave a feeling of wellness and abundance. A Bollywood ghazal floated from out-of-view speakers somewhere above.

"Let's get you some ice cream, yeah?" Mbabazi said as they walked up to a café named Cafesserie. She ordered the ice cream briskly and efficiently and looked around the busy café, her sweeping gaze sharp as if she were critical of the noise of the place, or of the people working at their laptops while nibbling on pastries, others engrossed in their smartphones.

"Six thousand," the clerk said when they went to the till.

"For two scoops?" Aine whispered in Mbabazi's ear so as not to embarrass her. "It's extortion."

"Don't you worry about that," Mbabazi said, paying with her debit card.

They ate their delicious ice cream using the tiny plastic spoons, which they licked while window-shopping on the ground floor. Outside Woolworths, the security guard asked them to throw their cups in the trash before entering the enormous shop. Here, like in every shop they'd been, there were price tags attached to the items so that no one could really haggle. But where was the fun in that? Aine's favourite bargaining tactic was to find a small blemish—a loose button, a sticky zipper—to get the seller to knock off five hundred shillings or more. If that didn't work, she'd set the item down and start to walk away. Almost always, the seller called her back and said, "Okay, all right, but you're robbing me blind!" Or "Don't you want my children to eat?" But then again, all the clothes and shoes in these shops were new, not second-hand, which was perhaps why the prices were non-negotiable.

"How about this one?" Mbabazi held up a cotton dress printed with a linked design that reminded Aine of the double helix shape of DNA.

"They all look the same." Aine didn't like how, on the rack, there were at least a dozen other dresses exactly like it, except in different sizes. "I've worn uniforms all my life."

"Okay, we'll go to my favourite boutique," Mbabazi said, adding that she'd hoped to avoid going there today. "It's hard to leave empty-handed. I can't help myself."

"You have way too many clothes," Aine said. She'd been in Mbabazi's bedroom earlier and noticed how her closet, a separate room unto itself, was full of enough clothes, shoes, and handbags to stock a small duka.

"Achen lectures me constantly. I don't need it from you too. She goes on about how the fashion industry is eroding 'Mother Earth.'" Mbabazi drew air quotes as if personifying the planet were bonkers. "She's got this aristocratic disdain for shopping. And it's charming, I have to admit. She's not at all self-conscious about the ugly, frayed clothes she wears out in public. But I swear to God, she acts like every time I buy a new blouse or a pair of shoes, a butterfly drops dead."

"Is that true about the fashion industry?"

"Yeah, but she acts like the fate of the Earth is in our hands, just mine and hers," Mbabazi said. "Do you know we have a washing machine that I'm not allowed to use without being subjected to a long article or some documentary narrated by Richard Attenborough? I told her I can't work from Monday to Friday and then spend my weekends washing and pressing clothes. No way. So, then she hires these people. I don't know where she finds them. She pays these women to come and clean the house and wash our clothes. They iron my clothes that don't need ironing, and they ruin my shoes. I don't like these strangers coming into our house, entering my room. But I also really don't want to handwash my clothes."

"You can't really fault her for caring about the fate of the Earth."

"Sometimes I hide my shopping in the car and sneak it into the house when she's working," Mbabazi said.

"Wow! So, you don't give a damn about the butterflies?"

"And when I wear something new and she's like, 'Oh, is that new?' I'm forced to lie and be like, 'What, this old thing? I brought it back from Canada.' But then I start feeling so guilty, I end up returning half my purchases."

Aine laughed. She wondered what it was like to love someone so deeply their beliefs shifted your own and even changed you.

They entered the boutique and an attendant welcomed them cheerily, asking if they were looking for anything in particular and if she could be helpful in finding it.

"Just browsing," Mbabazi said.

"You ladies let me know if you need anything, 'kay?" she said, smiling amiably. Both she and the clerk behind the counter were tall and skinny, but not like Mbabazi. They looked emaciated and a little fragile, their clothes hanging loosely from their bony shoulders. Maybe they were fashion models? The sculpted cheekbones, the buzzed-off hair that accentuated said cheekbones.

"They are fashion models," Mbabazi confirmed on the way to the changing rooms when Aine asked her about the scrawny girls. "The woman who owns this boutique is a designer, and she manages a modelling agency."

"That looks so good on you," one of them told Mbabazi when she was appraising herself in the larger mirror outside the changing stalls.

"Yeah, I love that for you," the same attendant said when Aine emerged in the short blue dress Mbabazi had picked out for her. "May I suggest a strapless bra? What's your size?"

"No clue," Aine said.

The model produced a measuring tape from her fanny pack and went about measuring Aine's bust.

"It's too tight," Aine told Mbabazi when the model hurried off. "It makes my hips look too big."

"Enjoy your teenage chub," Mbabazi said. "You'll miss it when its gone."

"No, I won't."

Aine tried to convince herself, once she was wearing the strapless bra under it, that the dress made her look older than eighteen, and sophisticated too. It was sure to make Elia see her not as Mbabazi's baby sister, but as a mature woman, perhaps one he'd even want to kiss.

But later, at home, once she'd showered and had Mbabazi do her hair in a thick cornrow that wrapped like a crown around her head, she put the new dress on, and it suddenly seemed too much. Like she was trying too hard. She changed into the tuxedo and felt more comfortable.

"So tell me why I wasted good money on that dress?" Mbabazi complained when she saw Aine.

"I will wear it another day," Aine promised. She turned to Achen. "Can I cut a few stems of your red roses?"

Mbabazi arched her brow. "You're bringing him flowers?"

"Isn't that what you do when your friend is in a play?" Aine replied.

"I didn't bring him any flowers."

"But I want to," Aine said. "Can I, please?"

If Achen and Mbabazi thought she was trying too hard, they hid it well. Not even once did she catch them exchanging a complicit glance. Achen went into the storage room off the veranda and came out wearing thick gloves, a pair of garden shears in her hands. Aine followed her to a rosebush, the one with flowers so red they almost looked fake.

"This is my fantastic Mister Lincoln," she said, taking the shears to a sturdy, healthy stem.

"Like Abraham Lincoln?" Aine asked.

"Possibly," Achen said. "All I know is that I grew them from seed, and it said Mister Lincoln on the packaging."

"I always thought roses only grew from cuttings," Aine said.

"You know what the hardest thing was about living in London all those years?" Achen said. "Not having this. Space to plant a seed and watch it grow. No spot of dirt to dig my hands into. It does something to a person, you know? Tall buildings blocking out the sun so you go days without seeing it."

"Without seeing the sun?"

"The English sky is grey, kidio," she said. "Especially in the winter. Clouds and rain for weeks on end."

"Is it very cold?"

"Like you wouldn't believe."

In the kitchen, Achen masterfully tied the six rose stems together with a pink ribbon she ripped from a shopping bag. In the meantime, Mbabazi was programming her iPod with Aine's email address, making it into something of a messaging device. Aine would take it along with a small MiFi modem to ensure the iPod always had an internet connection.

"You can text or FaceTime," Mbabazi said, showing

Aine the applications for both. She put the devices in a leather clutch with a chain strap Aine was to wear around her wrist at all times.

"This is Kampala," she said. "Someone will snatch it off you in the blink of an eye."

"In the theatre?" Aine said.

"Our receptionist lost her phone in church," Mbabazi said. "She got robbed in a place of worship."

"Wow," Aine said. "That thief probably prayed for forgiveness right away."

NILE AVENUE WAS WITHOUT a doubt the loveliest of any street Aine had been on so far, more beautiful even than Mbabazi and Achen's affluent neighbourhood. The trees lining the road were dressed in a lavender-pink inflorescence so stunning that aliens could likely spot it from beyond the Milky Way. Aine smiled. All day today with Mbabazi she'd felt a little joyful; the world was slowly regaining its colour. It was the most hopeful she'd been since they locked Papa in a wooden box and stuck him in the earth. Rolling down her window, she noticed how beautiful everything was: other trees in full leaf, the birds flitting among the branches.

In a moment of bravery, she turned to Mbabazi. "What's the plan?" she said. "You said that I should come to Kampala and that we'd make a plan. What are we going to do about Mama?"

"What is there to be done about her?" Mbabazi said. "Now I worry only for you. Whatever you want to do, that will be the plan. Of course I'd love for you to stay. Both Achen and I want that very much. But if you want to go back home, there's absolutely nothing wrong with that."

Aine let that sink in. Now, home was a place where Mbabazi would never set foot again. If only there were someone to whom Aine could report this injustice, someone who could force Mama to see the error of her ways and keep the family from breaking apart. "I'll come back and visit," she said, tears threatening to spill. "It's just that birding is the only job I've trained for, and I think I'm quite good at it. Plus, I need to save up for uni."

"I'll chip in for that," Mbabazi said.

"You will?"

"Of course," Mbabazi said. "But yes, you should go. Be a tour guide. You'll be splendid at it. I can just see you wowing every tourist lucky enough to get you for a guide."

"And I'll come visit every chance I get," she said again. "We both know Mama can't stop me."

"I know." Mbabazi smiled. "Did I tell you Uncle Nshuti called today?"

"What?" A glimmer of hope. "When?"

"Early morning," she said. "Before we went to the mall."

"What did he say?"

"I didn't pick up," she said. "I'm not talking to any of them."

"He's a sweet guy, Uncle," Aine said. "He's not like Mama."

Mbabazi scoffed. "Hope's a dangerous thing, Kanyonyi. I'm done trying."

16

PROTESTERS CROWDED THE ENTRANCE to the Uganda National Cultural Centre. They wore matching purple T-shirts, wwjd emblazoned across the front. *What Would Jesus Do*. And they waved handwritten signs: Saviour Not Rockstar. Judas Was a Liar. The Coming of the Lord Is Nigh.

"For it is written that the devil entered Judas when he was leaving the Last Supper," a sweaty man preached loudly through a megaphone at the cars that slowed as they pulled up to the entrance. "Brethren, this play that you are going to see, it is a mockery of our Lord and saviour Jesus Christ. It is the work of Satan himself."

"I thought savedees were pacifists," Aine said, craning her neck to look back at the group of protesters. "These ones are all fired up."

"There were even more of them on the night of the premiere," Mbabazi said. "I can't believe they're still at it."

"I just hope Satan writes a good musical," Aine joked.

"Well, you know what they say." Mbabazi chuckled. "The devil gets all the best tunes."

"I've never heard that one before."

"I must have read it somewhere."

"Do you want me to walk you in?" Mbabazi said, pulling up near a towering monument, a sculpture of three people beating at the same drum. "I can find parking and hang out for a bit."

"No, thank you." Aine felt tall, mature, and capable. She was no longer a secondary school student; she required no chaperone. She gathered her fragrant rose bouquet, and with her borrowed clutch hanging from her wrist, she stepped out into the evening. "I'll message if I need a lift home."

"Have fun," Mbabazi said.

Aine waved. A drop of rain splattered on her nose as she crossed to the entrance. Built in the late 1950s in the shape of a grand piano, the Uganda National Cultural Centre looked much older than the black-and-white photos in Aine's history textbook, the facade of concrete rings coated with dust.

She told the woman behind the wicket that Elia, one of the actors, had reserved her a ticket. "What's your name, dear?" the woman asked, and Aine told her.

The woman found Aine's name on a list and handed her a program with information about the musical and the ensemble performing it. "Enjoy the show."

Aine smiled at a photograph of Elia. His biography said

that he was a student of dramatic theatre and that he also taught children how to play guitar and piano. This was his first foray into musical theatre.

She emerged into the large auditorium, the rows of tiered seats climbing all the way to an upper level of more seats. The red velvet of the thin cushions shone in the dim light. There was the noise of people laughing and shuffling in their seats. She went down to the lower level in search of a seat as close to the stage as possible and settled for one on the edge of the middle third row. She'd just sat down when a grey-haired man wearing a black blazer over a white kanzu came toward her and asked, "Is this one taken?" indicating the seat to her right, where she'd rested her bouquet.

"No," she said, retrieving the roses and setting them in her lap. The old man's short-cropped hair was uniformly grey, the dirty colour of ash.

"You know one of the actors?" he asked, pointing to the roses with his lips.

"Jesus," she said and then corrected herself. "My friend plays Jesus."

"Judas is my grandson," the mzee smiled. "I have been coming here every Saturday for the past two months. I'm an old man. Not much else to do."

"I'm sure he appreciates your support," Aine said, admiring the mzee's English, which reminded her of the recently deceased newscaster Bbale Francis, the kind of English Papa had called proper.

"But I have not brought him flowers," he said. "Not once."

"Seeing his play so many times," Aine said. "That has got to be better than flowers."

"Thank you for saying so."

The lights dimmed, and a bearded man in a kikoy shirt and tan slacks emerged from behind the great red curtains to stand at the proscenium. "Banyabo nebassebo," he said and welcomed them all to the performance in Luganda and then again in English.

Aine slid forward in her seat, holding her breath. The director finished the announcements, and the curtains parted to reveal the orchestra already in place, winds and pipes and strings, the choir joining them on stage, a rumbunctious group of young men and women whispering and laughing and high-fiving, dancing to the orchestral music.

Elia's emergence onto the stage had a physical effect on her; she exhaled deeply and settled back in her seat. As Jesus, he was skinny in his white kaftan, a sash cinching his waist, leather sandals on his feet. The chorus dancers were swarming him, singing questions at him while he ministered to them, looking handsome and wise.

Then Judas appeared as if out of nowhere, shrieking his lyrics in a bracing rockstar voice. He was accusing Jesus of believing the things people said about him, of thinking he mattered more than the gospel he preached.

And Jesus responded. His voice was quietly confident, a voice that stretched time, decorated it, and then dissolved it.

As the show progressed, approaching the betrayal,

Aine felt a marvellous pain, a physical ache deep down in her marrow. Onstage, Mary was comforting Jesus, rubbing his shoulders, stroking his hair. "Everything is all right, yes, everything's fine."

There was something about it, the way Jesus rested his head in Mary's lap. A dark wave of unbearable sweetness and sorrow swept across the theatre. What Mary didn't know was that the next time she ministered to Jesus, he'd be dead. She'd wash the blood off his body and wrap him up in white linen, weeping over every moment they'd shared and those she wished they had. It killed Aine to think that Jesus knew what was coming. The cross was right there, a looming shadow projected against the wall behind the stage. The son of God knew all this, and he allowed Mary to console him. "Relax, think of nothing tonight…"

The tears were unexpected, flowing faster than she could dry them on the sleeve of her jacket. From then on, her thoughts kept flying away, and she kept willing them back, only for them to get away from her again.

Once, when she was eight or nine years old, she'd accidentally set the kitchen roof on fire. Their kitchen at the time was a shack: a mud and wattle thing with a thatch roof. She'd been playing with a long stick of firewood, twirling it like a baton, the flyaway embers decorating the night like fireflies. Before she knew it, a small fire was burning on top of the kitchen's domed roof. She looked from her fiery baton to the thatch and couldn't believe what she had done. She threw jugfuls of water at the fire, but the flames grew vicious, hungrily consuming the dried grass.

"Mama!" she yelled. "Akayungu nakosya!" *I've set the kitchen on fire!*

Her parents were already running into the compound. The shock on their faces as they saw the flames! Certain that severe punishment awaited her, Aine ran. She cut across the banana plantation, leaped over the mounds of Mama's just-planted sweet potato garden, not slowing until she'd made it to the other side of Magombe Swamp. There, in the clearing, she sat shivering under a tulip tree, her back pressed against the trunk. She considered her options. Going back home was not one of them. She was going to have to learn how to survive in the jungle. The Batwa did it. They ate roots and climbed trees for fruit and slept in grass tents. She'd have to build one of those for herself. But then she heard hyenas laughing, and fear locked her in place. She sobbed quietly, her forehead pressed to her pulled-up knees, which she hugged tightly to contain her fear. She sat shaking for what felt like an eternity. Then she heard Papa calling her name, and she opened her eyes. The light of his big torch illuminated her hiding place.

"Aha!" Papa exclaimed as she shot to her feet, her legs suddenly strong. She ran and threw herself into his waiting arms.

"You found me," she said, her voice shaking.

"I found you."

He carried her home on his back, assuring her there

would be no punishment if she promised never to play with fire again.

At home, Mama hugged her, shedding tears of joy. She'd been all over the village knocking on doors, looking for her, gathering a search party. Aine's night of terror quickly turned into one of the most memorable nights of her life, a night when she felt loved, treasured even. She'd burned the kitchen to the ground, but "Akayungu nakosya" became a story every adult in the village teased her about but never reproached her for. And the new kitchen, which Papa built with the help of Uncle Ambrose, was a log cabin with an iron-sheet roof.

But she saw no silver lining in her latest run away from home. Papa was gone; there was no one coming to find her and bring her back. She didn't want to go back home to Mama, yet she had to. It seemed to her that Mama, too, though she didn't know it, was lost.

"Here you go." The mzee, her neighbour, was offering Aine a handkerchief, white with blue trim, neatly folded into a perfect square. "Take it," he insisted when she hesitated. She'd always teased Papa for being the only human who still carried around this relic.

"Thank you." She dabbed at her eyes with the soft cloth.

"You may keep it," the old man insisted when Aine returned the handkerchief.

"Are you sure?"

"As certain as the fate of the son of God."

By the end of the production Aine's body ached from the near-constant pressure in her chest. Only after the curtain call did she relax, a sensation like she'd finally been released from a powerful magic spell.

IT HAD RAINED WHILE she was inside the theatre, as if the sky, too, had been moved to tears. The wet street lamps glowed orange and looked, from a certain angle, like quotation marks. She crossed to stand under the statue of the three drummers, where she'd have a good view of everyone exiting the theatre.

She spotted Elia emerging through the doors and raised her hand to catch his attention. She watched him say goodbye to Mary and Judas and a couple of girls Aine recognized from the choir. He half jogged toward her, a great big smile opening his face.

"I almost didn't recognize you," he said, adjusting the strap of his crossbody bag.

"Oh, the tux?" she said. "Achen gave it to me. I had nothing of my own to wear."

"You look smashing," he said. "Are those for me?"

Now Aine remembered the rose bouquet. "Yes," she said, handing it to him. "You were unbelievable. How do you do that? How do you disappear so completely into the role? You were not Elia in there; you were Jesus!"

"That's very kind of you," he said, raising the roses to his nose. He closed his eyes very briefly as he smelled them. "I don't think anyone has ever given me flowers before."

"Well, I just thought..." Aine's voice trailed off. He'd closed the small distance between them and was standing so near, his face mere inches from her own. "Are you going to kiss me now?" she wondered out loud.

"Would that be all right?" he said.

She nodded her head vigorously.

HE FELT HER UP in the back of the Uber as it took them back to his hall of residence, dinner plans abandoned. They took a break from snogging, and she asked about the student strike and he said it was still ongoing, but now the university administration had threatened that students who refused to sit the end-of-year finals would have to retake those classes the following year.

"I can't repeat second year," he said. "Mama would kill me. You know her."

"Yes, I do," Aine said.

At intervals he kissed her hand, and each time he did, a current spread through her body, relaxing entire muscle groups. Would they have sex? she wondered. What would it feel like, his full weight bearing down on her, his tongue probing the soft reaches of her mouth?

The Uber dropped them off outside an old building with a low privacy wall around it. The signpost read Makerere University, and below it, Nkrumah Hall. As they walked up to the entrance, Elia explained that all the students who resided in this particular hall were Pan-Africanists like the former Ghanian leader, whose statue graced the front entrance.

"Is there an interview process?" Aine said. "Which hall takes the students who don't believe in a united Africa?"

"Oh, you don't want to *not* live here," he said. "Our sports teams always win, and our cafeteria serves the best food on campus."

"Are girls allowed?" she asked, noticing a whole lot of boys and not a single girl.

"The halls are not mixed," he said. "But there are some hostels off-campus that are coed."

The hall looked even older on the inside, the white and green paint peeling from the walls. As soon as Elia opened the door to his room and switched on the lights, they resumed kissing, as if it was all that had been on both theirs minds the whole time. They untucked, unbuttoned, unbuckled. Aine felt feverish, like a thirsty person who suddenly had too much water pouring down her throat. She was equally excited and nervous. Their naked bodies pressing together, they moved awkwardly toward the unmade bed that was pushed right up against the wall.

As Elia lay on top of her, Aine braced herself for the initial thrusts that Kemi had warned her would hurt terribly—the loss of her virginity. But no amount of clenching helped ease the insistent pain of him moving in and out of her. A scream formed in her belly and rose into her throat, but she swallowed it down. She tightened her muscles as hard as she could.

"That feels so good," Elia moaned. "Keep doing that."

As he pushed in deeper and faster, she resisted the urge to push him off or to tell him to stop. She focused all her energy on clenching her muscles against the pain. Then he was gasping and grunting, and he collapsed, sated, on top of her.

"Did you climax?" he asked after his breathing had returned to normal.

She grimaced. She didn't want to lie to him and say she'd enjoyed any of whatever that was, in case he got any ideas about an encore. She didn't want to tell the truth either and make him feel bad.

"So hot in here," she said, fanning herself with her hand. "Can I have some water?"

"Of course." He rolled away from her and sat on the edge of the bed, his back to her. The condom made a rude smacking sound when he dropped it onto the floor. She watched him as he crossed to the small fridge in the corner. He poured water out of a gallon jug into a tumbler and crossed back to her. Naked, he looked stronger, his shoulders broad; clothed, he always seemed skinny, almost vulnerable. She wondered how he saw her, and if she, too, was bigger naked. She was suddenly self-conscious. Sitting up to accept the water, she covered her breasts with her left arm.

"Thank you," she said after guzzling half the water.

He drank the rest of it and set the empty cup down on the floor. Lying beside her, he lifted her hand away from her chest and traced circles around the wide base of her breasts. His ice-cold fingers felt around the hollows above her collarbones, his expression serious, as though he were performing a thorough anatomical examination, committing her body's geography to memory. He was smiling boyishly as he moved toward the foot of the bed, drawing, as he went, a line from her cleavage down to her navel, opening her in two. He parted her legs, and his face disappeared between them.

Oh god. Oh my god!

"Tell me you love me," she said afterwards when he came to lie down beside her. "Even if it's not true. Just say it."

"I do like you so very much."

That would have to do, she decided and fell asleep.

Elia woke her up not long after. "Doc is pissed," he said, pulling on his trousers. "So many angry texts."

"What time is it?"

"Almost two a.m." He pointed to her clothes folded over the headboard. "I'm calling an Uber."

ON THE DRIVE HOME they agreed that how they'd spent their time after the theatre was none of Mbabazi or Achen's business. When they pulled up in front of the gate, the Uber driver sounded the horn and the gate opened. Mbabazi was pacing the length of the veranda.

"It was my idea to go back to his place," Aine immediately confessed, the words pouring out as if of their own volition. "I initiated the kiss. He didn't force me to do anything I didn't want to do."

"Whoa!" Elia said. "You, like, forgot everything we discussed."

"I am going to kill you," Mbabazi told Elia, and she looked like she meant it.

"I didn't—she didn't—we are—" Elia stammered.

"Zip it," Mbabazi said. "Go home. I'll call you."

She grabbed Aine by the hand and pulled her into the house, then down the hall toward the guest room.

"I'm not a child." Aine yanked her hand out of Mbabazi's grip.

"Then tell me: Why do you keep behaving like one?" Mbabazi closed the door.

"Listen," Aine said calmly as she removed her tuxedo jacket and put it on a hanger. "I'm sorry I didn't call or text or respond to your many messages. I'm sure you were worried. But I'm not going to apologize for anything else besides that."

"Did you two have sex?"

"I don't want to talk about it."

Mbabazi sat down on the bed. "Come," she said, inviting Aine to join her. "Sit."

"I don't want to talk about it," Aine repeated and stayed where she was standing in front of the closet door.

"I was just reading this article," Mbabazi said.

"Oh, here we go."

"It's about how you shouldn't make serious, potentially life-changing decisions while mourning someone very important to you."

"What life-changing decisions?"

"Did you use a condom, at least?"

"Oh my god, Mbabazi, leave it alone."

"The point is grief makes you vulnerable," her sister said. "It makes you impulsive. People can take advantage of that."

"That's bonkers," Aine said. "He did not take advantage of me. I gave him the advantage."

"So, you did sleep with him!"

"No comment."

Mbabazi dropped her head to her chest and pressed the bridge of her nose between her thumb and index finger, her eyes shut. Another gesture she had in common with Mama. "Was it your first time?" she asked after a moment, her expression a mix of curiosity and concern.

"Can we not talk about this right now, please?" Aine just wanted to be left alone to lie down and go over the whole evening in her mind, to play the events over until it all started to feel real. Only then could she decide what parts of it she wanted to share and in what detail.

"Then just answer me this," Mbabazi said. "Did he wear a condom? Because if he didn't, Aine, we have to go to the pharmacy now-now. Can you imagine how your life would change if you were to become pregnant by a university student?"

"But I'm not."

"You're absolutely sure?"

"Hundred percent."

"Good." Mbabazi sprang to her feet and crossed to the door, but turned back again. "Would you rather talk to Achen instead of me? She's awake."

"No," Aine said. "I just want to sleep."

Aine fell back onto the bed. But she didn't hear the door close. She sat up abruptly to see her sister still lurking in the frame. She watched as a solitary tear, big and pearly, made a glistening track down the side of Mbabazi's face.

"Jesus Christ, Mbabazi," she said, going to her. "What do you want me to say? I'm sorry I had sex with a guy I really, really like?"

Mbabazi hugged her, a surprise. "Promise me you're okay."

"I'm more than fine," Aine said. "I'm ecstatic. I'm not an eighteen-year-old virgin anymore."

17

ELIA WAS BUSY WITH exams, but they texted throughout the day and FaceTimed every night. On Wednesday evening he came over. They walked to Kisementi, the bustling neighbourhood near Acacia Mall, and ate fried tilapia at a café hidden from view by ancient birches with thick droopy branches. Elia's friend Tinka worked there. He was Deaf, so they scribbled their orders directly into his small notebook. He gave them a thumbs-up and brought them their spicy chai—with the perfect amount of cardamom—while the tilapia was on the grill. When it arrived, they savoured it slowly, including the tail, which was the perfect amount of crunchy.

Satiated, they walked around the neighbourhood leisurely, enjoying each other's company. Some of the street names, like Elizabeth Avenue—a vestige of colonialism—pissed Aine off, but she was too giddy to complain. Elia kept his arm around her neck, and she kept one arm around his waist as they stumbled down the lovely streets like a couple of drunks.

"I could get used to this," he said, and she felt the all-encompassing heat of his love. Any day soon, she thought, he'd declare it.

When they got home, they tiptoed through the eerily quiet house and locked themselves in her room. She'd succeeded in convincing both Mbabazi and Achen to call it Aine's room.

He watched her undress, his face fiercely tender, contorted as though with mute cherishing.

"Your turn," she whispered. The house might be quiet, but it wasn't empty; the light had been on in Achen's office. "Take off your clothes."

"I like that," he said. "Say it again."

"Take off your clothes."

"That's so hot," he said, obedient. She lay across the bed and he bent over her, nosed her belly. Kneeling, he spread her legs.

ON SATURDAY, ELIA CAME over in the morning to take Aine to what he called his favourite spot in the whole city. They shared a boda boda, a big one, Aine sandwiched between the cyclist at the front and Elia behind her, his hands clasped around her waist. After about half an hour weaving in and out of traffic, they arrived at the bottom of a hill. At its peak was an imposing building, circular in shape. A spire projected from the conical dome high on the roof.

"A church?" she questioned him as they walked up to the gate. The words Bahai House of Worship were written in blue paint against a patch of whitewashed wall near the entrance. "Your favourite spot in the city is a church?"

"Patience, my darling," he said, grinning boyishly.

As they walked up the dirt lane leading to the magnificent building, Aine looked around at the expansive gardens—an abundance of trees and flowers, the grass intensely green. Pied crows swooped between jacarandas, surprising the Abyssinian citrils, who took to the air. Starlings hopped about, the purple of their heads and necks iridescent in the sun. So many birds. Was that why he'd brought her here? She counted more than five species in under a minute. It made her homesick for Magombe.

He led her around to the back of the building, which looked like an enormous traditional hut but clad in fancy mosaic tiles and coloured glass, as opposed to mud and wattle. As they stood on a knoll unobstructed by trees, Kampala City emerged before them. A wide vista of concrete jungle set against a hazy horizon. Millions of houses filled valleys and climbed hills before falling away to where earth seemed to meet heaven.

Aine touched her hand to her chest, the view clobbering her right in the heart. "Wow."

"When I first came here, I was on a spiritual quest," he said. "I was searching for a faith community where the rules weren't too rigid, but what I discovered instead was this view."

Aine was only half listening. She gave a prolonged whistle of amazement, a perfect replica of Papa's when something surprised him. Taking in the seemingly endless expanse that was Kampala City, she sat down on the grass and a wash of tiny grasshoppers flew up in her face, some almost entering her nose. She was starting to lose track of where she stopped and other life began. She imagined the millions of people that were right now going about their daily lives in all those houses. Office workers hastening to make end-of-day deadlines. Mothers planning supper. Lovers quarrelling or making up. Babies being born, drawing their first breaths. People breathing their last, their existence extinguished.

"It's something, is it not?" Elia said, crouching. He sat behind her on the hillock and stretched his legs out on either side of her hips.

"Is this one of your moves?" she asked, allowing herself to lean back and soften against his hard chest. "You bring girls here and blow their minds with the view? Then feel them up?"

"When you go back home," he said, "can I come visit? You can also blow my mind with your favourite view. You can also feel me up every which way you like."

"Mbabazi told you I was going back?"

"She wanted to know my intentions," he said. "But the woman can utter threats! She doesn't hold actors in high regard. She thinks we're all—what's the word? Players."

"Yeah, she's warned me about you a lot."

"She has?"

Changing the subject, Aine told him about the even higher elevation in Rwetera, where she and Mbabazi always hiked on New Year's Day. "Top of the World viewpoint."

"Top of the World? Why have I never heard of this place?"

"When you reach the top, you have a bird's-eye view of the forest and the surrounding crater lakes," she said. "Mbabazi says it's like looking into the eyes of God."

"What about you?" he said. "What does it look like to you from the top of the world?"

"Like the forest is a living, breathing organism." Not unlike the wide vista that was Kampala City, but purer somehow and not at all overwhelming. "It's like visiting a garden where the light is magical."

"You must take me there," he said and snuggled in closer.

THE NEXT DAY, MBABAZI and Achen's friends started arriving at noon so that by the time the CECAFA football finals kicked off at three, Lule—the buff ultramarathoner and gym owner—was already drunk on the six-pack of Hunter's Dry he'd brought in a paper bag. Aliamin—the radio show host on Hot100 FM—glided between the kitchen and the sitting room, pressing fresh juice and making popcorn in the microwave as if he was in his own home. He'd arrived wearing a leather trench coat, which he immediately removed to show off a white tank top and tight maroon shorts. An emerald jewel sparkled in his belly button piercing. His fluffy hair was bigger than Achen's and dyed a fiery orange. His lilting speech switched fluidly between English and Swahili.

"Je, mchezo unakaribia kuanza?" he called, crossing from the kitchen, swaying his hips like a fashion model on the catwalk. "I want it to start now."

He, Elia, and Chemutai—the hair stylist—poked fun at the extreme football fanatics on TV, young fans with their faces painted red and yellow. The colours of the national flag were also the colours of the national team: the Uganda Cranes.

Benya, the poet-physicist, was the last to come, arriving on his motorcycle just before kickoff. He swooped into the sitting room and parked himself in front of where Achen and Mbabazi sat on the leather sectional, sitting with his legs crossed on the carpet like an excited little boy. Without asking, Aliamin went to the fridge and brought Benya a bottle of Nile Special. There were so many bottles of beer on the coffee table Aine wondered how everyone kept track of which bottle was theirs.

"We go, we go," chanted the supporters in the stadium, which was packed to the rafters.

Elia brought a stool from the kitchen island and sat next to Aine behind Mbabazi and Achen. He told her the names of the Uganda Cranes as they emerged, to raucous applause, onto the field. Charles Lukwago. Mustafa. Allan Okello. Madondo. He explained what positions they played. "Fahad Bayo is the one who got us to the finals," he said. "He scored the winning goal against Tanzania in the semis."

She was happy just to sit with him and experience the game through his eyes, but as it gained momentum she grew invested in the boys' efforts, becoming so tense she was sitting on the edge of her stool. She screamed when Anukani, the Crane's midfielder, edged out his Eritrean opponent to face off with the goalkeeper before scoring with a low finish.

"Yes!" Elia drummed his chest like a male chimpanzee, zipping from one end of the room to the other. "We go, we go!"

But almost immediately, an Eritrean midfielder broke through on an equalizing goal. Thankfully the Cranes goalkeeper caught it.

"Whew," Aine exhaled, relieved.

"If we win today," Elia told her during halftime, "this will be our fifteenth CECAFA Cup."

"That's a lot of cups."

"We want all the cups," he said.

And the boys worked hard for it too. Not long into the second half, Mustafa scored the second goal, and then Madondo kicked a third to bone-jarring shrieks from the sitting room, as well as in the stadium.

When the final whistle blew, an impromptu dance party erupted in the sitting room. There was much howling and fist-pumping and high-fiving. Lule was lifting people, squeezing them hard, and then setting them back down.

"Put me down," Aine squealed when he swept her off the floor and raised her up in the air like Rafiki holding Simba over the cliff.

Even Achen was jumping up and down, whooping maniacally.

Taking in the joyous racket, Aine realized that home, strictly speaking, did not mean one's place of birth, the houses where mothers lived, where fathers were buried. Mbabazi had this eclectic mix of people in her life, including a radio deejay whose gender was difficult to pin down. She observed how openly happy Mbabazi looked. She was zooming around like a firefly, wagging her little behind in tiny precise jerks. Aine wanted to remember this moment in great detail. Maybe she'd have a chance to describe it all to Mama. Tell her how full Mbabazi's life was.

"I feel like running," Mbabazi said, while everyone was still dancing and celebrating.

"But you've been drinking, M!" Achen was visibly panicky.

"Two bottles of Tusker Lite?" Mbabazi scoffed. "You call that drinking?"

"Should I come with you?" Achen said.

"Since when do you run?" Mbabazi almost skipped to her bedroom, presumably to change into her running clothes.

Aine went to sit beside Achen where she had slumped back into the sofa. "She's not going to run away from you," she said quietly.

"At least she's running again," Achen said, springing to her feet. "That's progress."

She crossed toward the kitchen, where she wet a tea towel and began wiping the marble countertop, scrubbing it with vigour, working her way toward the corner, where the coffee maker and the kettle sat. Aine rose to go reassure Achen, but Benya was already by Achen's side, talking to her while she scrubbed the sink. She'd moved the dish rack out of the way and the water was running.

Mbabazi emerged into the sitting room in her running tights and a loose T-shirt. Lule went to her. "I'm taking off soon," he said, hugging Mbabazi. "I will not be here when you get back."

"I'm going soon too," Benya said from the kitchen. "Have a good jog!"

Soon there was only Aine and Elia in the sitting room while Achen and Benya bagged empty bottles.

"Let's go to my place," Elia said, explaining he needed to study tonight for the theatre exam he was writing first thing tomorrow.

"Won't I distract you?" she asked.

"No way," he said. "I just need to refamiliarize myself with some concepts."

"Go," Achen said when Aine turned to her for permission. "Frankly, it might be better if I'm here alone when M gets back."

AINE AND ELIA SHARED the back seat of Benya's oversized motorcycle. Wind swept the clouds away, exposing a sky that was ink-blue. The evening cooled dramatically, and she was glad for Elia's arms around her. His presence near her was by turns comforting and intoxicating. But now that she'd made the decision to return to Bigodi, the days were shorter somehow, their length halved by her desire to enter his warmth, to live inside it. All day yesterday and today, whenever he'd left her line of sight for longer than a minute, she'd feared forgetting what he looked like, the contours of his face. She leaned back into his chest, his breath tickling her neck.

In Wandegeya, there was a four-way stop controlled by an afande in white uniform. A whistle in his mouth, he kept one hand slightly in the air and with the other waved the southbound traffic through, always alert, Aine thought, not to get run over by the moving vehicles, bicycles, and motorcycles. The methodical way he moved his body reminded her of a choir conductor, music in his joints.

As soon as he turned to face the westbound traffic, before he signalled movement, Benya and all other traffic barrelled forward as though in a race.

"Asante, bwana," Elia thanked Benya when he dropped them off in front of Nkrumah Hall. They hurried, almost jogged, to Elia's room. They didn't even wait to take off all their clothes. They made love frantically, clumsily—but noiselessly—conscious of the voices and laughter from the neighbouring rooms and in the hallway.

"Read to me," she asked him afterwards, fetching the textbook that was open on his desk.

"You want me to read to you about the evolution of theatre?"

"I know nothing about it," she said, bringing him the book.

He read to her about how Konstantin Stanislavski, the

Russian theatre practitioner, built a recognizable world for the play through a profusion of details taken from everyday life. "With the Stanislavski method," he explained, "actors take on more of the responsibility in developing the characters they are playing. Rehearsals are a process of discovery, a partnership between the actor and the director. Between the actors themselves. It introduced this playful experimentation and spontaneity that not only makes acting immersive and fun but makes everyone who is involved feel as though they are an important part of the whole ecosystem. Doesn't it make you want to be an actor?"

"No, it calls on all my insecurities," she said. "It makes me want to crawl into my shell."

"But you are a competitive debater," he said. "Isn't that a kind of performance?"

"I've sweated my way through each and every single debate," she said. "Stress sweat. The stinkiest of all sweats. It's absolute torture. I don't know why I've put myself through it for so many years. I think I'm ready now to leave it all behind."

"So why did you keep doing it?"

"There was this one time at St. Leo's when I was in Senior Two," she said. "The motion was about conservation or reforestation or some such, I don't remember exactly. At some point, early in the debate, I had an out-of-body experience. It was like someone infinitely smarter than me, someone more eloquent, was typing the words on the screen of my mind, and I was just reciting them, just hearing myself advance these brilliant ideas about trees and their intelligent underground network of roots, how they share nutrients, can recognize their offspring. Stuff I didn't know I knew. It was so effortless, the most relaxed I've ever been doing something difficult. Man, it was a high. Not a single drop of sweat. People came up to me afterwards, even teachers. They were like, 'Whoa, Kamara, you were on fire up there.'"

"And that's why you kept debating? The high?"

"It never happened again," she said. "Not like that first time anyway. I don't know what that was."

"Maybe you will experience it again," he said, "but as a writer."

"Is acting like that at all?" she asked, uncomfortable with the topic of her writing.

"If the script is good," he said, "if I can feel the story with all my senses, all I have to do is follow it through to the end.

"Let's go eat a rolex," he said, pushing the textbook to the side. "I know this vendor, if you pay him a bit more, he adds obutuzi. Do you like mushrooms?"

"Not particularly." Two days before, she and Achen had split a rolex in a downtown café. The snack didn't sit well in Aine's stomach. Omelettes had never appealed to her, even ones, it turned out, with cabbage and eggs rolled up inside chapati. "But I do think I should go, so you can study properly. Plus, if Mbabazi does end up dumping Achen, she might need someone to comfort her. It would be awkward though. Who would I sympathize with? My sister, who did the dumping, or my friend, the dumped?" It was suddenly all very stressful to consider such an outcome.

"I can't imagine them not being a couple," Elia said, as they walked out the door. "Their whole vibe is my relationship goals."

"How's that?"

"You know how there's a certain type of couple who are always making mean jokes about each other?" he said. "They'll say little things like, 'Abeli is allergic to fun, ha ha ha,' or 'We're having rice and chicken stew again because it is the only meal my wife knows how to cook, ha ha ha.' And it's like, okay, fine, I get it, this is their relationship dynamic, but god, does it make me want to vomit."

"I don't know any couples like that, but I think I know what you mean."

"You will never catch Doc and Achen diminishing each other like that," he said. As they were passing a deserted swimming pool, he told her about the first time he hung out with Achen and Mbabazi. It was a week or so after Mbabazi came back from Canada. They'd had lunch at home, and they were sitting on the veranda, drinking beer. Achen, noticing that the leaves of her cabbage and tomato plants were starting to droop in the blazing sun, excused herself to water them.

"And Doc, she gets up too," he said. "She goes inside and fetches a tube of sunscreen."

"She's obsessed with sunscreen!" Aine said.

"And she follows Achen to the garden boxes. And

she's sweeping her braids up from her face and neck and piling them on top of her head in a massive bun. And she's rubbing the lotion on her face and her neck and her arms. And it's the most intimate, most beautiful thing I've ever witnessed between a couple outside of movies. Just how tenderly she does all this, and Achen's almost childlike submission, how she offers her arms with this big grin on her face. I'm thinking the whole time, *Please God, I want that too. Everything in this scene, I want it.*"

"Maybe they have to be extra caring," Aine said, "because the world is hostile to what they have."

"It's true," he said. "I just want love like that. Sensual and nurturing. And deeply honest."

"I want that too," Aine admitted.

"Aine." He halted just outside the main campus gate, making her stop too. "Could we be like that, do you think? Me and you."

"What, care about each other so much it's almost nauseating?" she said.

"Yeah, totally gross."

It was not a confession of love, but she'd take it. "I think I can manage that."

He kissed her then, and the cyclists sitting idly on their boda bodas whooped and whistled, encouraging Elia, in Luganda, to use his tongue. Aine considered how if it were Achen and Mbabazi kissing in public, those same men would most likely beat the women with tire irons.

Just the month before, a civilian mob had invaded the offices of a human rights group that worked with LGBTQ youth in Kampala. Newspaper reports said that when police arrived on the scene, they searched the office and confiscated condoms and lubricant. They rounded up the activists and took them to the police station, where they were stripped and violated, subjected to shameful body searches.

"Call me when you reach," Elia said, putting her on the back of a boda boda. He gave the cyclist clear directions to the house in Kololo. "I'll text Achen and let her know you're on the way."

Aine let herself in; Achen had insisted she take one of the key fobs that opened the gate.

"I'm home," she called. The house was quiet. The lights were on, but only Sir Dobby was about, staring at Aine like a concerned parent.

"Mbabazi?" Aine called, knocking gently on her sister's bedroom door.

"Coming." Mbabazi opened the door a smidge, squeezed through, and closed it behind her. "What's up?" she said, raking her fingers through her messy short hair and pulling her bathrobe closed.

"Were you sleeping already?" Aine tried to open the door, but Mbabazi blocked it.

"Kind of."

"Where's Achen?"

"In my room," Mbabazi said. "She's helping me fold the laundry."

"What laundry?" Aine had handwashed a mountain of clothes yesterday, and after it had dried on the clothesline, she had folded and sorted it into three piles: hers, Mbabazi's, and Achen's.

The door opened behind Mbabazi, and Achen, also in a bathrobe, stood behind her.

"Oh god," Aine said, suddenly embarrassed, yet relieved at the same time. "Is folding laundry your euphemism for sex? Because, guys, I think you can do better."

"I don't *not* like it." Achen laughed, resting her chin on Mbabazi's shoulder.

"Pretend I'm not here," Aine said, hurrying toward her room. She was anxious to call Elia to let him know that disaster had been averted. All would be well in the Mbabazi-Achen household.

18

T HE MUEZZIN WAS STILL singing his morning call to prayer when Achen came to Aine's room and told her that she was going to drop Mbabazi off at work. Achen needed the car to drive the two hours to Jinja Town to interview a woman whose baby had died at a non-profit organization run by an American missionary. Did Aine want to come with?

"I don't think so," Aine said sleepily, crossing to the bathroom.

"This American woman," Achen said behind the closed door, "she walked around in a white lab coat, a stethoscope around her neck, and so everyone thought she was a doctor. They called her the White Doctor."

"I take it she wasn't?"

"She's a homeschooled high school graduate from Virginia."

"Homeschooled?"

"Her mum educated her at home instead of sending her to school." Achen explained that the woman had, after a summer of volunteering at an orphanage in Jinja when she was nineteen years old, presumably heard the Lord calling her to serve his Ugandan children. And so, she had gone back home to the US and raised funds from her church and community, and upon returning to Uganda, she set up a treatment centre for malnourished children. But because she wasn't in fact a doctor, some of the severely malnourished kids, upward of a hundred, had died under her care. And now a pro bono legal initiative was suing the so-called White Doctor on behalf of the grieving mothers. "Are you sure you don't want to come with me?"

Aine climbed back into bed. This story, Achen's interview, had grief written all over it, and Aine was carrying enough of her own. "Do you mind if I stay?"

"Not at all," Achen said. "I'll be back by lunch. Or shortly after, depending on the traffic."

Alone all morning, Aine tried to write, but she had a hard time getting started. As soon as she touched pencil to paper, everything she wanted to write about collided together and formed a glut in her head so that she was immediately stuck, not knowing where to start. Her thoughts were like a skein of yarn a cat had found. She put the pencil down and went to water Achen's vegetable garden. She had noticed that whenever two or three days passed without rain, Achen used the hose that was attached to the enormous rain barrel to soak the soil around the vegetables. A few days ago, she had kept her company while she did this, and Achen had told her the names of the plants. Poetic names. What Aine knew as dodo—amaranth—Achen called love-lies-bleeding. A stand of them had gone to seed, tall plants with velvet tassels that drooped all melancholy-like. The carpet of scorpion grasses covering the ground between the raised garden boxes were forget-me-nots. Preferable because, unlike paspalum, they required zero maintenance, Achen explained. "I don't have to water or cut them. They never get too tall." The biringanya with mottled white stripes were graffiti aubergines. The carrots were Hercules, named for their ability to thrive in even the poorest soil.

As she watered, Aine considered starting a vege-table garden of her own at home in Bigodi. Mama grew the main staples: bananas, cassava, beans, groundnuts, potatoes both sweet and Irish, maize. But everything else—tomatoes, onions, garden eggs—she bought from the market. She steam-cooked dodo and eshwiga that grew wild in the banana plantation. Every so often, obutuzi sprouted in random places in the bushes. One day there was nothing there, and then in the morning there were little mushrooms everywhere. Mama filled baskets. She spread the oyster mushrooms on a mat to dry under the sun and cooked them in groundnut sauce. That, and sweet potatoes, were Papa's favourite dish. A proper Bakiga meal, he called it, saying it reminded him of his own mother's cooking.

Lately, Aine was having variations of the same dream

where she was at school and Papa came to pick her up, and he was dapper in his grey Kaunda suit and she was dapper in her black tuxedo and he said, "Ha! You thought I wouldn't come pick you up, didn't you?" and she said, "Can you believe it, Papa? Everyone thinks you're dead."

"What? I'm gone a couple of weeks, and everyone assumes I died?"

In the dream there's the sense that he's alive, that he'd taken some European tourists on safari to Kenya or Tanzania, and she's the only one in the family who knows the truth. She tries hard to hold onto this faith on the drive home, but always she arrives in the kamunye and walks straight to his grave.

After finishing in the garden, she returned to the house and Sir Dobby followed her around, mewling like a neglected baby. As Aine poured his food into the metal bowl, one hard pellet skittered across the floor and he chased after it before pawing it into his mouth. It gave Aine an idea. Sitting cross-legged on the kitchen floor, she lifted the bowl into her lap and tossed the brown pellets in random directions. The cat chased after them, a hunt.

She heard a loud knock at the gate and set down the bowl. When she opened the door in the gate, a man dressed sharply in a black suit and tie entered. His forehead and nose were ringed with beads of sweat.

"Who are you?" she asked as the man adjusted the strap of the bag he wore over his right shoulder.

The man responded with a question of his own. "Are your parents home?"

"Yes," she lied, a little scared. "What do you want with them?"

The man's short hair had a smattering of grey, but his face, shaved clean, was almost youthful. From his bag he retrieved a clipboard with a stack of colourful papers, brochures maybe, clipped to it.

"Are you conducting a survey?" she asked uncertainly.

"Do you know why there's so much suffering in the world?" he said. "Psalm 83:18 says that men may know that thou, whose name alone is Jehovah, art the Most High—"

"Whoa, whoa, whoa." Aine had heard enough already. "Please leave before I call my dad." She pulled the small gate door open for him.

"Can I have some water to drink first?" He produced an empty water bottle from his bag and handed it to her. "Please. The sun is becoming very hot."

"Okay, but you wait here." She ran into the house to fill his bottle with cold water from the fridge. The man reminded her of Mr. Kabamba back home in Bigodi. He and his extended family belonged to the Faith of Unity Movement. At the end of every month, the Kabambas donned their white robes and began their long trek, on foot, to worship with their cult leader, a man named Dosteo Bisaka, in faraway Kagadi. The journey probably took them three days. She wondered if the cult prohibited public transport or if the Kabambas just couldn't afford it.

When she brought the man his water, rather than thank her, he gave her a flimsy magazine titled *Awake!*

"I urge you please to read it," he said, mopping his forehead with the back of his hand. "All this suffering in the world, it is a sign of the end. God is bringing Armageddon to destroy Satan and all evil for good."

"Goodbye," Aine said, closing the gate behind him, a man willing to accept Armageddon as necessary and perhaps even merciful. She would allow him his unquestioning belief, his escapism, but she wasn't going to open that door to anyone like him again.

WHEN ACHEN GOT HOME she parked the car and checked her phone. Her eyes grew wide. "It's—" she said, walking up to Aine on the veranda. "Your uncle is here."

"Uncle Ambrose?"

"Nshuti!"

Achen showed her the text messages, which were from Mbabazi: "He just showed up at work. Are you back from Jinja?" "I'm bringing him home, okay? He wants to talk to both of us." "Hello???"

"Say okay," Aine pleaded. "Please say he can come."

"Why is he here?" Achen looked distressed.

"He wouldn't come all this way if it wasn't in peace," Aine said calmly, wishing desperately for her words to be true. She loved her uncle, but she had no idea what he knew about the situation, what Mama would have told him about Mbabazi and Achen. Two days before, Mbabazi had said that Uncle Nshuti was still calling; he wasn't taking the hint that her not picking up the phone meant she didn't want to talk to him.

"I've got a bad feeling about this," Achen said, entering the house. "I'm already emotionally exhausted from this bloody interview."

She put her phone and her bags on the kitchen island and went to wash her face at the sink. The phone pinged and Aine jumped to take a look.

"It's Mbabazi again," she said, bringing the phone to Achen. A bunch of question marks comprised the entire message.

"I'm going take my computer and work from the country club for the rest of the day," Achen said definitively. "Give you all a chance to talk. A family meeting."

"But Mbabazi wants you here," Aine said. "You met Uncle Nshuti at the funeral. He's a real sweetheart of a guy."

Achen, water dripping from her chin, texted back, "Is he fuming or calm?"

"Friendly," Mbabazi responded immediately.

"C u in a bit," Achen texted.

"Already on the way," Mbabazi wrote.

"I'm going to my office to sit," Achen said, leaving her phone by the sink. By now, Aine understood that by *sit*, Achen meant meditate.

Aine filled a pan with water and set it to boil on the stove. She scoured the overhead cupboards for tea ingredients. At home, she'd normally cut fresh lemongrass from the ever-expanding clump behind the kitchen, and there were always thumbs of tangawuzi lying around. But the herbs Achen grew in little pots lining the kitchen window were unfamiliar to Aine. She added a palmful of Mukwano tea to the pan, threw in some shredded mdalasini she found in a large glass jar.

On the veranda, she wiped the table clean, figuring it was best to keep Uncle Nshuti outside the house until he'd made his intentions clear. She dusted the earthen pot that held the table's centrepiece, a menacing cactus with a fuzzy but prickly coat. Back in the kitchen she set a tray with mugs, a sugar bowl, a bag of bread, though there were only four slices left, and margarine. She strained the chai into a jumbo thermos to keep it piping hot; nobody she knew liked their tea cold. She placed a jug of water and a piece of soap in a basin on the veranda so that her uncle could wash his hands without having to go inside. Everything set, she grabbed the extra key fob from the red basket and stood ready, waiting for Mbabazi and Uncle. As soon as she heard the beep of a car horn, she opened the gate.

A green pickup truck rolled in, Uncle Nshuti driving, Mbabazi his sole passenger. Aine immediately recognized the single cabin truck as Apuli's—the manager at the sanctuary. On the truck's side, the words "Bigodi Wetlands Sanctuary" arched over a picture of a great blue turaco.

She smiled nervously as Uncle stepped out of the truck. Perhaps Mama had sent him to bring Aine home right away, by force if necessary. Or Uncle, taking Mama's side, had come with even more threats for Mbabazi and Achen. And just when Mbabazi seemed to be recovering from everything!

"Webare kwija, Uncle," she welcomed him.

"I can see why you don't want to leave this place," he said, gathering her in a hug. "Look at this big house. The tiled roof. The rain cannot even wake you up in the night!"

Aine noticed that he was wearing Papa's shiny black shoes instead of his usual cheap rugabire sandals made from old tires. She didn't know how she felt about him wearing her father's shoes, but she supposed Mama would have given them to him.

"Welcome." Achen was crossing the veranda toward them. "Please, come and sit."

"You left Bigodi quickly without saying goodbye," Uncle said, after shaking Achen's hand. "I was hurt."

"I'm terribly sorry for the way I left," Achen said.

"I did not get the chance to thank you for everything you did for us."

"It was my pleasure," she said. "Please. Come sit. Aine has made tea."

"Aine," Mbabazi hissed, beckoning her over to where she lingered by the truck. With a jerk of her head, she indicated the truck's cargo bed. Aine went over to see. The truck was loaded with enough fresh produce to stock a market stall. Two big bunches of matooke, ripe pineapples and pawpaws, sweet potatoes, a bulbous jackfruit, and bwaise yams. A joyful overture surged through Aine. No one who came to provoke brought sustenance. She reached in to grab the jerry can of Uncle Nshuti's honey, but Mbabazi stopped her.

"Later," she whispered.

They joined Uncle and Achen on the veranda. As Achen helped Nshuti wash, pouring water over his hands while he rubbed them with soap, Aine filled the mugs with chai. Achen sat assertively next to Mbabazi, their chair arms touching. Uncle was still raving about how lovely everything in their home was when Sir Dobby appeared behind the window glass, pressing his curious face right up against it.

"Yesu Kristo!" Uncle nearly fell backward from his chair. "What animal is that?"

"Just a cat, Uncle," Mbabazi said almost coldly, as if to discourage further questions. She could be extremely protective of Sir Dobby.

"But why is it like that?" Uncle insisted, a little chastened.

Mbabazi rolled her eyes. She often acted, Aine thought, as though she and that cat knew something about life nobody else did and she was loath to explain.

"He comes from a line of cats born without fur," Achen explained, probably uncomfortable with Mbabazi's non-response. "A friend of Mbabazi's in Canada, she was going through a difficult time and was going to be without a place of her own."

"A bald cat!" Uncle smacked his hands together. "Now I have seen everything." And then he busied himself smoothing a thick layer of margarine onto two pieces of bread, which he pressed together like a sandwich. "Is there some milk for the tea?"

Aine pushed her chair back. "I'll get it."

When she came back with a cup of milk she'd warmed in the microwave, Uncle was speaking, his gaze shifting between Mbabazi and Achen.

"She told me that she has been fasting and asking God to show her what to do about everything, but that so far, she is hearing nothing," he said. "Actually, she said that she's hearing her own thoughts reflected back to her." He shrugged. "Those are her words exactly."

Aine knew he was talking about Mama.

"Did she tell you what those thoughts were?" Mbabazi asked.

"I'm not sure you want to hear them, my dear." Uncle closed his eyes and shook his head. Then he opened them and poured a dollop of milk into his chai, dipped a corner of his bread sandwich in it, and slurped it noisily.

"But she did not oppose me when I said I was coming to see you," he said, his mouth still full. "Of course, I was hoping for her to say, 'I will come with you, Brother, I will make things right.' But what I have learned in this life is that if a person is living in denial, you cannot make them see the reality. You can talk and talk until the cows come home, but it will not change anything."

Aine watched Mbabazi, watched her grip Achen's hand, and place their clasped palms, almost defiantly, on the table.

"I'm a man of few words, you understand?" Uncle continued. "I'm not educated, and I try to keep my uneducated opinions to myself. But when I heard what happened, I could not keep quiet. The problem with savedees such as my sister is that when things become hard, they don't stand up tall. They fall on their knees and cry to a god the white people made up and brought to us to replace our own gods, whom they hated as much as they hated us. Do you see what I'm saying?"

Achen was hanging on to Uncle's every word, nodding her head like someone who knows the song.

"For me, when I'm in need of guidance, I talk to my mother," he said. "Your grandmother is a wise woman. She always points me in the right direction. When I told her that you were refusing to answer my phone calls, she told me to come here."

Uncle leaned forward slightly. "Your Kaaka told me to tell you this: Ahu amaguru gaza hacweka omuhanda."

"Where many people walk, a new path will be cleared," Mbabazi interpreted the Rukiga proverb for Achen's benefit.

"Yes," Uncle said, reaching across the table to cover Mbabazi and Achen's joined hands with his own. "Of course, you understand this path cannot be cleared overnight."

Tears pricked Aine's eyes. She was transported back to June, back to Mbabazi saying, "Write about this, Kanyonyi. Write that you're embracing the woman I love and that I'm bawling my eyes out."

I will write about this, she decided, the narrative filling itself out almost effortlessly in her head, from her first meeting of Achen at school to this moment here. She'd give everyone, including herself, new names, but everything else would stay the same. Her life was suddenly filled with meaning and purpose, the powerful force that was creativity. Already, a cast of characters was assembling in her mind, the people in her life, the people she loved. She would not let them down. Her writing would free her. It would sustain her through what was sure to be a difficult living situation with Mama. She pictured herself in Papa's gazebo surrounded by piles of notebooks filled with her writing, and that image seduced her. She felt immense gratitude toward her uncle for coming. She would go home with him, no more putting off the inevitable.

Mbabazi and Achen, too, seemed transformed by Uncle's presence and by Kaaka Nyirasafari's message. They were sitting taller in their chairs as if lifted by his words, their hands still joined.

"Where many people walk, a new path will be cleared," Uncle repeated, almost to himself. He looked from one face to another, as if to make certain that everyone understood. But as the moment extended, a line appeared between his brows, giving his fading smile a worried edge.

"When you go back," Mbabazi said, smiling, "tell her we're fine, okay? Tell Mama that everything is fine here."

Acknowledgements

Many people helped make this book a reality. Alissa York, ninkusiima—I thank you—for showing me how to tend to and nurture this story way back when it was still a seed. Your mentorship allowed it to blossom. Amy Roher and Darla Tenold, my friends in life and in sentences. Mwebare munonga for reading and encouragement. Jedidiah Mugarura, who always knows the most beautiful way to express a thought in Runyankole/Rukiga. Madonna Hamel for welcoming me into your home and then leaving me there for a week to write and enjoy Grasslands National Park. My agent, Carolyn Forde, for your input and all your work on behalf of the book. And my wonderful editor, Shirarose Wilensky, for sharing my vision and for your care and guidance. For your sharp-eyed edits and observations, webare munonga.

To my family in Uganda, nimbakunda kandi nimbe-baza munonga. My dad, Ntwirenabo, and my siblings,

Pesh and Dorah: I couldn't have written this novel without your love and support. Words are not enough to express the depth of hope and love I have for my Ugandan queer sisters and brothers and all those whose identities fall off the grid of a translational vocabulary. Rukundo egumeho! May love (and peace) prevail.

Kandi ninsiima munonga my family here in Canada. Webare Robin, my heart and my pillar. Mwebare Precious and Jordan for the constant supply of hugs and humour. David for support and friendship. Wayne and Li, thank you for beating my drum.

Grants from SK Arts and the Canada Council for the Arts provided me the time to work on this novel. Thank you to the Saskatchewan Writers' Guild and the City of Regina Writing Award, which gave me an extra boost to finalize the work.

IRYN TUSHABE is a Ugandan-Canadian writer and journalist. Her creative nonfiction has appeared in *Briarpatch Magazine*, *Adda*, *Prairies North*, the *Walrus*, and on CBC Saskatchewan. Her short fiction has been published in *Grain Magazine*, the *Carter V. Cooper Short Fiction Anthology*, and the *Journey Prize Stories*. She won the City of Regina Writing Award in 2020 and 2024, was a finalist for the Caine Prize for African Writing in 2021, and won the 2023 Writers' Trust McClelland & Stewart Journey Prize. She lives in Regina.